Call Me Crazy

By USA TODAY Bestselling Author

Quinn Loftis

Call Me Crazy

Copyright © 2013 Quinn Loftis Books LLC

All rights reserved. No part of this publication may be reproduced, distributed, or transmitted in any form or by any means, including photocopying, recording, or other electronic or mechanical methods, without the prior written permission of the publisher

This eBook is licensed for your personal enjoyment only. This eBook may not be re-sold or given away to other people. If you would like to share this book with another person, please purchase an additional copy for each recipient. If you're reading this book and did not purchase it, or it was not purchased for your use only, then please return it , and purchase your own copy. Thank you for respecting the hard work of this author.

Dedication

I dedicate this book to Kathleen Campbell. You are missed dearly and I will never forget the love, grace, and wisdom you shared with me. Rest in God's hands and save a place at His table for me.

Acknowledgements

There are so many people who have become such important parts of my writing process. It would take nearly a whole book to thank them all but I will give it my best shot in one paragraph. Thank you to my family for their constant support and encouragement. Thank you to my beloved husband for taking care of the house, our son, the bills, laundry, and all other sorts of things that wouldn't get done while I'm away in my writing cave. Thank you to the ever amazing Wolf Pack, as usual your support is invaluable and I thank God so much that he brought each of you into my life. Thank you to Candace Selph for your relentless dedication to my books. You are a treasure to me and I am so glad that we are friends. Thank you Hell Cats, you girls keep me sane on even the toughest of days and all of your wisdom and guidance is so very appreciated. Thank you to every psychiatrist I have ever known for the knowledge and tools you gave me to make healthy choices and live an abundant life even while living with bipolar disorder. Thank you to one of my best friends, Megan, for being there when I needed to vent and for not giving up on me when I wasn't very pleasant to be around,.You are truly one of a kind. Thank you to the beautiful Jodi, another best friend and one of my most favorite people in the world for allowing me to use her face as Tally. There are so many more I need to thank and I hope that all of you know that I appreciate more than words all of your help and support. And any author worth their salt knows that none of this would be possible without you the readers. Thank you for taking your time to read my books. Thank you for your emails, Facebook messages, tweets, and Goodreads comments. Time and again people amaze me with their kindness and I can't ever say enough what a blessing it has been to get to share my crazy worlds with all of you!

Other titles by Quinn

The Grey Wolves Series:
Prince of Wolves, Book 1
Blood Rites, Book 2
Just One Drop, Book 3
Out of the Dark, Book 4
Beyond the Veil, Book 5
Fate and Fury, Book 6
Sacrifice of Love, Book 7
Luna of Mine, Book 8

The Gypsy Healer Series:
Into the Fae, Book 1
Wolf of Stone, Book 2

Elfin Series:
Elfin, Book 1
Rapture, Book 2

Prologue

"I'm looking out from inside the chaos. It must be a one-way mirror because no one seems to be able to see back inside to where I am. The looks on their faces, the judgment in their eyes, tells me everything I need to know. The most frustrating part about the whole messed up situation is that even though I'm the one that they stare at in shock, I am just as shocked as they are. I know no more than they do of why I lose control. What they don't know is that I am more scared of myself than they could ever be." ~ Tally Baker

    I walk into my second period history class. It takes every ounce of willpower that I have left to take my seat today. I need to be up moving around. I don't need to be sitting still—I can't sit still. I need to walk so that I can think. My mind darts from one thought to the next, never bothering to stop and complete any of them. Of course I didn't do the assigned reading last night. I can only hope that Mr. Dickinson will not call on me.

    I can hear the whispers from the other students. I can feel their stares on the back of my neck and I just want to turn and scream at them. My foot is tapping restlessly; my hands are shaking like an addict desperate for a fix. I'm not an addict. I'm not going through any form of withdrawal. I'm broken. Something inside of me is defective and refuses to operate properly, like a busted radio that won't tune into your favorite station.

    Looking down, I notice that I actually brought my

history book today. I utter a prayer of thanks as I pull it out of my backpack. I open it to a random page because I have no idea what unit we are on. I have no idea what the topic has been for the past couple of weeks actually. Would I like to know? Absolutely. I would love to do my homework like everyone else. I would love to pass a test once in a while. But broken people don't do homework and broken people can't pass tests. And as much as I would love to do those things, the shattered soul inside me brings me to a place where I don't care. Getting from one second to the next is all I care about, it's all I can think about. Just breathe Tally, in-out-in-out.

I don't even realize that class has started until I hear my name. My jaw clenches as Mr. Dickinson's nasally voice reaches my ears.

"Tally."

I look up, briefly meeting his stare before my eyes dart away. I wonder what he sees when he looks at me. Does he see the monster crawling under my skin, clawing to get out, to take over? If he does, he gives no indication of it.

"Would you care to summarize last night's reading?" He gives me a knowing smirk; or maybe I just perceive it that way.

"I can't," I admit, and my voice is dry and gravelly, sounding more like a smoker of twenty years than that of a seventeen year old.

He adjusts his glasses on his long beaklike nose. His condescending smile reveals two rows of coffee-stained teeth. "You can't, or you won't?" He asks me.

My pulse is racing and my hands are growing clammier by the second. I'm clenching them tightly, trying to clear my head and fight the rage that is building inside of me. I don't know why I'm so angry. Mr. Dickinson is a jerk and everyone knows it. Every student in his class has, at some point, been on the receiving end of his degradation. Somehow I know that it is not him that I am truly angry at, but that doesn't matter to me right now. All that matters right now is that I can't handle his smartass comments. I can't handle his belittling. I feel small enough right now.

"If my answer had been *I won't* then that is what I would have said. The word *won't* is a contraction of two words—WILL and NOT," I continue, placing an emphasis on the two words as my voice steadily rises. "This would imply that an individual has the ability to perform a task, but chooses not to for whatever reason. Since that was not what I said, then that is not what I meant. Any person of average intelligence with even a rudimentary comprehension of the English language would know that when I said that I *can't* summarize the reading, I meant that I don't have the ability to summarize the reading."

Some far away part of me knows that I need to shut up. It almost feels like I'm watching someone else say those things. Unfortunately, it's not someone else, it's me and no amount of telling myself to stop talking will work. "At this point, an appropriate follow up question you might ask would be something like, 'why *can't* you summarize the reading?' That would give me the opportunity to tell you that it is because I did not *do* the reading." I look down and realize that I'm standing. At some point in my tirade I have gotten to my feet. I look around at my classmates staring at me in horror. When I look back to Mr. Dickinson his face is bright red and I can tell that he is about to let me have it. I want to tell him that screaming at me at this moment would be the dumbest move of his life. Instead, I calmly walk to the classroom door. I ignore him calling my name, threatening to have me suspended, like I care. My movements feel mechanical as I walk to the girls' bathroom. There is only one thing that will pacify this pain, this rage that scares me to death.

After checking to make sure that I'm alone, I let out a slow breath and pull the blade from my pocket. I slowly sit down with my back against the wall and pull my sleeves up. I shake with the anticipation of the relief that I know is coming. The razor glides across my skin and the sting nearly sends me into a trance. But the trance is fleeting. So I cut again, and again, over and over, craving the single moment of physical pain. I don't notice the blood pooling around me and I don't even hear the screams. All I know is that there is relief for a tiny second in time and I don't care if I have to cut every inch of my body, because I need the pain like I need air to breathe.

~

"Mr. and Mrs. Baker, I'm glad that you could join us today," Dr. Stacey says with a genuine smile.

It's been a month since my melt down in history class. A month without a blade of any kind, not even a butter knife. A month of therapy, observation by Dr. Stacey and the other staff of Mercy Psychiatric Facility. A month of deciding the best course of action for treatment. One month, and my life is forever changed.

"Do you know anything about bipolar disorder?" she asks my parents.

Both shake their heads and I watch as my dad leans forward, adopting his *I'm listening* posture. I slump down in my chair and try to keep from drawing their attention. I dread the looks of worry and pity that I know will be on their faces after this conversation.

"Bipolar disorder is a mental health condition caused by certain chemicals in the brain becoming imbalanced. Some are depleted and some become overproduced. Patients suffering from bipolar disorder experience severe mood swings, hence the name. In severe cases it can be similar to schizophrenia. It can be difficult to diagnose because people often seek help only when they are depressed. Generally, the mood swings don't happen hourly or even daily like you might think. A person with bipolar disorder might be depressed for months, sometimes years, and then they will swing the other direction, to what we call mania. Again, just as the depression can last years, so can the manic phase." She takes a deep breath and glances over at me. I'm thankful that the look on her face is one of concern, but not of defeat. I avoid looking at my parents. I don't want to see the pain or fear in their eyes—the same pain I saw the night they brought me to Mercy. I don't ever want to see those looks on their faces ever again.

"The main thing you need to know is that bipolar is very treatable. While it can take a while to find an effective combination of medicines, Tally can lead a normal life if she remains on her medication and does therapy as needed. She will likely have to have her medicine adjusted periodically over time. But as long as she takes care of herself, she will be able to manage the disease rather than the disease managing her."

My parents are silent. Out of the corner of my eye

I see my mom shift nervously. My father is motionless. I can't tell what thoughts are running through their heads. I try not to shift in my own chair but the silence is beginning to make me uncomfortable. Finally, my mom speaks and her words rip wider the already bleeding hole inside of me.

"How long will she be this way?" She asks, as if I'm just an old carburetor that needs to be replaced.

I feel the familiar rush of anger that has been out of my control and grip the arms of my chair to keep from jumping up and telling them both to go to hell. I grind my teeth in an attempt to keep my mouth shut and try to take slow breaths like Dr. Stacey showed me.

Dr. Stacey sidesteps the questions and continues on with her explanation of my diagnosis. "We are beginning a combination of medicines that has proven to work well for other bipolar patients and we hope that it will help level her out. It takes several weeks for the medicine to get in her system so we won't know for about a month if the medicines are going to help. My suggestion is that she stays here through the summer. She needs to learn healthy ways to deal with the emotions that make her feel out of control." Her face grows serious. "I need you to understand that your daughter is not defective, she is not fragile or broken, though she may feel that way. What she needs most from you is for you to treat her normally. If you make her feel like there is something wrong with her, then you will hinder her therapy."

"I'm right here you know," I grumble.

Dr. Stacey gives me a brief smile. She is very good at dealing with my surly attitude and I have to admit that there are days that I purposely try to provoke her, though I don't understand why.

My mom turns to look at me. Her face is blank. Any emotion a mother might show for her daughter in such a difficult situation is absent and I feel it to the depths of my messed up soul.

"We love you," her words are clipped and sound about as full of love as a dried and wasted desert is full of water. "We expect you to do your best to fix this," she continues, "so that another embarrassing situation doesn't arise again."

I nod, but I don't speak. I know that if I do I will break down completely. I'm so angry and it's so easy for others to become the object of my wrath, deserved or not.

When the meeting is over my parents both give me awkward hugs but there are no promises of to call and check in and no lies of understanding of how hard this must be for me. Mom passes me a letter from Natalie, my best friend, and tells me that she'll be by later that week.

"Tally," Dr. Stacey's voice has me stopping before I can exit her office. I turn to look at her and I can instantly see that, as usual, she sees much more than I want her to.

"It's okay to be angry; it's what you do with that anger that matters."

My eyes are empty. I know they are empty because I am empty. I am empty and nothing seems to fill the void. "Whatever you say, doc."

Her lips purse as she gives me a solemn nod. "How about you take some time to yourself? You can spend time in your room or anywhere else you can find some peace."

I'm surprised by her suggestion because we aren't typically allowed much alone time during the day. Doc says it's because alone time fosters self-pity and depression. Personally, I think they just like watching the crazies interact with one another. It can be quite entertaining when a yelling match ensues over who was using the colored pencils first. Yes, I said colored pencils. Scary, I know.

I make it back to my room without incident. By the time I walk in my breathing is shallow and I'm biting my lip to keep back the tears. Tears make me angry because they are just one more reminder of how broken I feel. I shut the door behind me and slide to the cold, hard floor. I pull my long sleeves up and stare down at my arms. The cuts are almost all healed, but the scars left behind will always be a silent reminder that I am fragmented, unable to be solid and whole. I will never wear short sleeves again. I close my eyes and search for something inside me that I recognize, anything to remind me that I wasn't always this way and I wasn't always such a mess. I don't even recognize myself anymore and every day I seem to fade even more. The worst part, the absolute worst part, is that I don't understand why I feel this way. Why do I feel like the end of the world is one step away? Why does breathing hurt and why does despair seem to be my only friend? What has happened that could possibly make me feel so completely and utterly damaged. My parents haven't always been so cold and distant. They were never the most affectionate people, but they weren't so awful to cause me to have a complete and total meltdown of outrageous proportion.

I bang my head against the door as I begin to feel the constant rush of emotions, that I don't know how to restrain, boiling up inside. I don't want to be this person.

"WHY?!" I finally give in and scream. "WHAT IS WRONG WITH ME?!" I'm rocking now and I know that I should stop. I'm telling myself to stop but I can't. The flood gates are open and nothing will close them until I'm utterly exhausted. I thrust my hands into my hair and pull, feeling a slight measure of relief from the emotional agony as the physical pain briefly distracts my fragmented mind. I release my hair and begin to scratch my arms until blood is welling up and skin is gathering under my nails. I don't care; I just don't want to feel anymore; I don't want to hurt anymore. I hear myself screaming incoherently until all that's left is whimpers.

As I roll to my side and curl up in a ball, I begin to shake as if the temperature had suddenly dropped and a raging blizzard is swirling around me. It's then that I realize that I'm not broken. Broken implies that I might be able to be fixed. No, I'm not broken. I'm shattered beyond repair, beyond hope. I let myself sink into the darkness and welcome the familiar comfort of knowing that I won't live forever. Someday I will die and this torment will be over.

Chapter 1

Mental Illness: a psychological pattern or anomaly, potentially reflected in behavior, that is generally associated with distress or disability, and which is not considered part of normal development of a person's culture. ~Wikipedia.

Mental Illness: FUBAR. ~Tally Baker

"I'm not going!" A shrill, familiar voice pierces my ears as I walk by Candy's room. Candy runs through her usual morning routine, screaming the same thing over and over again as orderlies coerce her out the door and into the medicine line. Though the screaming can become quite painful to the ears, I find it strangely comforting. In a world where things seem to be unreliable, unpredictable, and chaotic, Candy's morning tantrums remained as constant as the sun rising. Therefore I treasured them—weird, I know.

As I walk past room after room, I hear patients, or clients as the good doctor likes to call us, begin to stir. Most are not in a hurry, after all where do they have to be? The med line, the cafeteria, group therapy; none of those things are going anywhere, so very few of them bothered to rush. No, those of us here at Mercy Psychiatric Facility are just trying to make it to the next minute, and sometimes even that feels like too much.

"Morning Ms. T.," Zeke, one of the orderlies, smiles at me. Zeke is another reliable part of my messed up life at Mercy. Every morning, without fail, he's waiting by the med window to say *"morning."* He stopped prefacing it with the word *good* after the first greeting when I sort of screamed at him. *"What the hell could be so good about another day that I have to get through?!"* I admit that it was rude, and any person in their right mind would not yell at a large man over six feet tall, with hands big enough to crush a human skull, but then, when I arrived at Mercy I wasn't in my right mind. Since then I have learned that though Zeke is massive, he is a big teddy bear. His skin is so dark that when he smiles his teeth nearly glow and his eyes are warm and soulful. He has a Mississippi accent that reminds me of blues and muddy water.

Despite my outburst, Zeke was unfazed. He just grinned at me with his kind eyes and nodded his head, as if he understands so much more of the world than I ever could. I haven't yelled at him since, even on the worst of days.

It's hard to believe that over two months have passed. Two and a half months ago I had been falling apart on the inside, and the brokenness had finally caught up with me, leaving me to explode onto anyone in my path.

"Morning Zeke," I actually felt like smiling this morning and, as instructed, tried to grab that tiny victory. Dr. Stacey was continually harping on me to claim the tiny victories. I'm still wearing long sleeves, but then Rome didn't fall in a day.

"The tiny victories are the ones that really matter," she says over and over again. And deep down I know she's right. Those victories over the everyday challenges that we face, things that a normal person wouldn't even bat an eye at, are vital to someone like me; someone just trying to keep breathing.

I walked up to the med window and stared down at the nurse sitting behind the glass. Her *out of the bottle* red hair is piled up on top of her head like a basketful of bird nests. One too many layers of makeup coats her face. Sheila has been the med nurse at Mercy for ten years, or so Candy tells me. Candy also tells me that Sheila has been known to help herself to a Xanax from an inattentive patient's pill cup. She smiles up at me as she hands me the little white paper cup that holds the key to my sanity. I take the cup and stare into it, counting the pills, not only to ensure myself that they are all present and accounted for, but also to ensure that the pills are indeed the ones that the doctor says that I am supposed to be taking. I have the colors of the pills memorized. If one of the colors is missing from the rainbow of drugs, Shelia and I will have a nice talk about how dumb it is to mess with a crazy person's meds.

Five pills, they're all there, staring silently back at me. I hold the cup to my lips and tip my head back, pouring all of them into my mouth. I chase the pills with a swig from the cup of water sitting on the counter and wash them down. I take one more sip before I open my mouth and allow Sheila to see that I had indeed swallowed the pills. She nods and waves me on, already gathering the next patient's medications. Out of the corner of my eye I see her hand quickly dart forward. I turn my head just in time to see her snag one of the little blue pills from one of the cups. I don't think. I rarely do, I'm kind of impulsive like that. I slam my hands down on the counter right in front of her and begin yelling, "STRANGER DANGER, STRANGER DANGER!" Why those particular words popped into my head, we may never know. Shelia jumps and the pill falls from her hand. Her eyes shoot up to mine and I give a subtle shake of my head. The commotion behind me is keeping Zeke busy. Just a side note, if you ever need a distraction in a mental hospital, just scream. For some reason it's like a howl to a pack of wolves and the crazies all feel the need to join in. I lean forward close to the opening of the window and I hold her gaze. "If I ever see you doing that again I'll cut off your thumbs so that you have no way to pluck one of those little pills from the cups." Her face pales and I try to feel bad that I've sort of come across as a little psycho, but then I remember that I'm in a mental hospital, so psycho is sort of expected.

After I fill my tray with my standard breakfast, peanut butter and butter toast, I take my usual seat in the far back corner of the cafeteria. I'm sitting for less than a minute when the chair across from me is pulled out from the table. Candy plops down across from me with a wicked grin on her wrinkled face. Her light blue eyes dance with humor and childlike delight.

"You got out of it again didn't you?" I ask with a smile of my own.

Candy nods at me victoriously. "I told them from the beginning I'm not doing group therapy. I have no need to pour out the ugly details of my messed up life so that they can all foam and slobber at the taste of my wretchedness."

"Gee, tell us how you really feel Candy," I tease.

She gives me a confused frown, "I just did. I would use more colorful language but I've been warned by the doc that if I don't tone down my potty mouth then I will be losing privileges." She lets out a humorless snort. "I pointed out that there are a few things wrong with their way of thinking. First off, who the hell uses the term *potty mouth* to refer to cussing and what privileges do they honestly think we have in this nut house?"

I have to laugh. Only Candy could get away with talking like that to the doctors and nurses and whoever else came into the line of fire. You see, she is a permanent fixture at MPF; she has been deemed by the courts as unfit for society. As such, she gets away with a lot more than the others do. It's not like they have a whole lot of options as to where they can send her, no other facility would likely take her.

"What was the good doctor's response to your inquiry?" I ask her.

She shrugs. "Who knows? I was already closing the door behind me when she started talking."

As I swallow down the last of my orange juice I see the familiar glint in Candy's eyes. That glint was the one that usually meant there was mischief brewing in her wacked out mind.

"So what's on the agenda for today?" She asks me as she rubs her hands together.

"Well, unlike some people, I have to go to group therapy and then I have a session with Dr. Stacey."

Candy groans. "Ahh, come on, ditch group today."

I shake my head at her. "Can't. I only have one month until school starts and I need to get my walking papers by then."

"But it's sooooo boring when you aren't around," she whines.

I can't help but laugh at her. Candy, a sixty year old woman, whining like a ten year old. Shouldn't be funny, but it is.

"So let me get this straight," I give her my best *are you freaking serious* face. "You want me to skip group therapy and risk having my sentence extended because you get bored without me?"

"Just when I think you might not be the sharpest tool in the shed, you go and surprise me with your shocking astuteness."

"Glad to know that I can still shock you, you crazy old bat," I tell her as I roll my eyes.

Candy lets out a loud cackle. "What's it going to be Pinky?"

I wish I could tell you that her nickname for me annoyed me, but truthfully, I found it endearing. She had started calling me Pinky the minute she met me because of the pink highlights in my hair. Candy was known for her nicknames. She said it was the only way for her to remember people. I think she just likes to annoy them.

I groan. "Fine, I'll play hooky with you, but this is the last time." I'm such a sucker for a crazy old lady with the inability to entertain herself.

Two hours later I find myself hiding out with Candy in one of the quiet rooms. Really, it's an isolation room for the patients who get a little violent, or a lot violent. The "administration" seems to think that if they call it the quiet room then it won't seem so sinister. It amazes me how often the staff mistake *crazy* for *stupid*. I can tell you for a fact that some of the most intelligent people I have ever met are off their rocker, bat mess crazy.

Candy had swiped some racquets and a racquet ball from the exercise room. We are playing, and I use the term playing very loosely, considering Candy has planted her butt on the floor and is sitting cross legged. Really I'm running around hitting the ball while she simply reaches out every now and then, when the ball is in her reach, and gives it a good whack.

"Did you hear we're getting a new inmate?" She asks me.

"Oh yeah? What are they in for?"

"Schizo."

"Nice."

"Apparently she tried to off herself and her son found her."

"Damn," I mutter. "That had to be tough. How old is the kid?"

"Well I wouldn't call him a kid. He's eighteen." Candy grunts as she reaches for the bounding ball. She smacks it hard and I have to dive out of the way to keep from getting hit in the head. Of course she finds this funny as all get out.

I give up chasing the stupid ball and take a seat on the floor across from her.

"Candy, how do you find out so much about other patients?"

"The walls have ears," she tells me in the creepy voice she likes to use on the more paranoid patients.

"That's just freaky; don't say crap like that."

She chuckles at me as she shakes her head. "You scare too easy."

"That or you just do demented, possessed old lady a little too well," I counter.

"Hello Clarice...," she growls in response, grinning all the while.

I lie back on the ground and look up at the stark white ceiling. The clinical florescent lights cause me to squint my eyes and the white walls and white floor don't help. I don't understand how they could expect a person to be calmed in a room so uninviting, where you felt more likely to be probed and dissected rather than be soothed. But then I'm just an inmate, as Candy likes to call us. What do I know?

"So when does said Schizo arrive?" I ask her.

Candy looks at her wrist. She doesn't wear a watch, yet she has an uncanny knack for knowing what time of day it is. Any minute now, want to go be nosy?" The familiar gleam is back again, dancing in her pale blue eyes, which are surrounded by aged skin and drooping eye lids.

"Nosy is your middle name, not mine," I remind her.

Candy clucks her tongue at me. "You're middle name is smartass, seems to me you have me beat."

I stand and hold my hand out to help pull her to her feet.

"That may be, my old friend, but your maiden name is Bush. I don't think it gets much worse than Candy Bush." I laugh just as hard as I did the first time she had told me her name.

She swats my backside as she walks past me and mutters. "Ungrateful brat."

"Oh, make no mistake, Ms. Bush, I am *very* grateful my name is not Ca...,"

"Not another word, Pinky," she cuts me off with a snap of her fingers.

I laugh again as I follow her out the door and down the hall towards the new–patient exam rooms.

Chapter 2

"Hold on to what is good, even if it's but a handful of earth. Hold on to what you believe, even if it's but a simple tree that stands alone. Hold on to what you must do, even if it's a long way from where you are. Hold on to your life, even if it's easier to let go. Hold on to my hand, even if someday I'll be gone away from you."
~Native American Prayer

~Trey~

I am White Mountain Apache, son of the former Tribe Chief. I did not ask for this role, but I play it willingly. Spirits have attacked my family and it falls to me to drive them away. I wish I had the wisdom of my grandmother or the patience of my grandfather. Lately, all I feel is restlessness.

"Trey, where is your mind?" My grandmother asks me. I blink twice to clear my head as I stand in front of the kitchen sink. I've turned the faucet on to wash my hands and didn't realized that I was simply standing there, lost in thought with my hands held under the warm rush of water.

I turn the water off and grab the hand towel hanging on the front of the dishwasher and turn to face her as I dry my hands. My grandmother is a small woman, especially compared to my six foot three frame. She barely reaches my chest, but she is as hard as bedrock, made from the earth itself. She smells of soil and leather. Her deeply lined face tells countless stories of our Native American heritage. Grandmother's name is traditional Apache, Bly Swift, meaning *Tall Child*. Her hair is dark, sprinkled with strands of gray falling in a single long braid down her back. Her high cheek bones and straight nose speak of the pride of our ancient people. Though more than a century has passed since the time of our ancestors, she still practices the old ways and lives according to tribe law.

"Sorry Shichu, I'm just thinking about her. She will have been transferred already and I know I need to go see her." I have been doing my best to keep it together. I know that I need to be strong for my grandmother, but each day seems to weigh on me a little more than the last.

Her eyes soften as she looks at me and I can see the worry hiding behind them.

"You bear so much on your shoulders for one so young."

I smile at her as she reaches up and tucks my long black hair behind my ear. While I usually keep it in the same traditional single braid down my back, I haven't bothered with it this morning. "I guess it's a good thing I was given such broad shoulders then," I tease.

"Even the strongest tree must learn to bend with the wind, for if they do not, eventually even their great trunks will crack and come crashing down. The branches, which had relied on the tree's great strength, come crashing down with it." My Shichu often speaks in metaphors and riddles as a way to impart wisdom. Most of the time I wish she would just speak plainly and tell me the direction that I should go. But I know how she would respond :'*Just as a mother bird cannot fly for her babies, neither could she walk my path for me.* She would say that '*As the baby birds must learn to use their wings for their own journey, so I would learn to use my mind to lead me on mine.*'

"I hear you Grandmother," I tell her. "I'm going to go and check on her now. Do you want to come?"

She shakes her head. "I will go later. You need to spend some time with her and remember she loves you. She is just not able to get her mouth to tell you what is hidden in her mind."

I give her a quick hug and then head out to my beat up old truck. Ugly it may be, but it gets me where I need to go and it beats walking any day.

As I pull into the parking spot, I look up at the foreboding building in front of me. The sign on the dry, dead grass of the front lawn declares it to be Mercy Psychiatric Facility. I wasn't sure exactly what kind of mercy they were hoping to impart with such a depressing first impression. Staring at it was actually making me depressed and I imagine that they might have had a few, if not more, patients who had admitted themselves just from driving by and feeling the despair of the place crash over them.

I try to shake off the gloom as I climb out of my truck and remind myself that things aren't always what they seem. For all I know the inside might be warm and inviting, not likely, but I was trying to be positive.

I walk into the entrance of the building and try not to cuss my own stupidity at wanting to believe that the inside would actually be better than the outside. Not surprisingly, the foyer was as drab as I had imagined. The stale air holds a hint of disinfectant and the lingering aroma of what must have been a terribly greasy breakfast. As I look up I see the word *Information* above a desk directly across from the front doors. I move towards the chubby woman who occupies the seat beneath it. Her name badge unceremoniously declares her to be Mildred, Front Desk Staff. Her white hair is twisted in a tight bun and she wears thick glasses with pointed ends, vintage 1950, I'm betting. The bright pink lipstick painted across her narrow mouth is slightly smudged and the blush on her cheeks makes the rest of her aged face appear pale with a greyish hue. She looks up at me and smiles. It's a sweet smile, even if the teeth she reveals are crooked and yellow with age. There is a gentleness in her eyes that reveals the kind spirit encased inside.

"Hello," she says in a sweet, grandmotherly tone. "How can I help you, son?"

I catch a whiff of her perfume as she shifts in her chair and try not to cough as the musky scent assails my nose and burns my eyes.

"I'm here to see my mother," I croak. "She should have been transferred here earlier today."

"What is her name dear?" Mildred asks as she begins poking the keyboard in front of her with one hand. Her eyes stay on the computer screen as she waits for my answer.

"Lolotea Swift."

Her fingers move with surprising speed across the keys and the clicking of them seems to echo in the quiet, stark area.

"Mm hmm, yes, yes, I see." She mutters to herself. Finally, after several closing taps, she looks up at me with the same sweet smile.

"She did arrive and has been all settled in her room. According to her schedule, right now she should be in the recreation hall. Just sign in here," she points to a clip board. I sign my name and hand her back her pen. Mildred swivels in her seat and points down a hallway to the right. "If you will follow that hallway and then take the first right you will run straight into the rec hall."

I give her my thanks and head off in the direction that she indicated. I begin to hear the soft hum of murmuring as I draw closer to the end of the hallway. Just before I turn to go down the next corridor, I take a steadying breath and steel myself for what I might see.

The last time I had seen my mother had been two days ago. She had been so thin that her bones protruded from her face. Her eyes were sunken in their sockets and her hair was dull and limp. She was slowly wasting away as the disease that plagued her mind began to eat away at her body as well. She had been diagnosed with schizophrenia three years ago, after my grandmother and I had begun to realize that she was seeing things and talking to people that weren't really there. At first she had refused to see a doctor. But after the first suicide attempt, she finally relented. Since then it had been an ongoing battle for her to keep her mind clear and rational. There were good days and bad. She had been on many different medications but the doctor she had been seeing couldn't find a combination that seemed to work well for her.

I had asked him why the meds weren't working and he had told me that the disease affected each person differently, just as any other disease might. Though there were similarities, each mind was as unique as the body that held it. So after three years of unsuccessful treatment, he had finally told us to put her in a psychiatric hospital where they could monitor her behavior and, hopefully, in the controlled environment, find a combination of drugs that would work. That is how I found myself driving across state lines from Arizona to Oklahoma, final destination—Broken Arrow.

The ultimate decision had come when I had found her in her bathroom floor cutting her legs. Blood had pooled around her on the white tile floor as she mumbled incoherently. I had asked her why she was doing it and she had told me that a kind man had told her she needed to get the bad blood out of her body. That had been a week ago. Now here I stand in the mental hospital that I hope can save her life.

I finally turn the corner and see just a few feet down, the open double doors that lead into the rec room. As I slowly push past the doors, I stop and scan the room, searching for my mother. The large room is just as white as the entryway that I had previously occupied only moments before. The harsh florescent lighting does nothing to alleviate the starkness. I see a unique mixture of people. Some are dressed in what appear to be common hospital gowns or pants, but others are wearing normal casual clothing. Several of the patients are pacing restlessly, muttering under their breaths and occasionally pointing at nothing in particular. A few are sitting around tables and coloring in children's books. Still others are staring out the barred windows.

I blow out a breath as I finally locate my mother in the furthest left–hand corner of the room. She is sitting in a rocking chair, back against the wall, facing the room. Her unusually light brown eyes are glazed over. She stares down at her hands which twitch nervously. She isn't a small woman, standing five foot six inches, though the disease that ensnares her mind seems to have withered her body as well. Her long dark hair, peppered with silver, is done in a braid and lies over her shoulder, the wisps that have escaped frame her troubled face. As I start in her direction, my attention is caught briefly by movement out of the corner of my eye. I turn my head, only to catch a glimpse of short pink–streaked blond hair dropping below the table as the owner of the hair kneels down. My mind gets the brief impression of a scared ground hog ducking for cover. I am intrigued by the behavior, not to mention the hair, but my attention is needed elsewhere so I turn back towards my mother.

When I reach her, I kneel down so that I can be eye level and wait for her to look at me. When she doesn't acknowledge me I speak up. "Hey mom," I say gently not wanting to startle her if she hasn't realized that I am there. "How are you doing?"

At the sound of my voice she finally looks up. Her eyes meet mine and I internally shutter at the hopelessness that has taken root inside of her. She reaches up with a boney hand and pats my cheek. "You're a good boy." Her voice is hoarse and weak and as she drops her hand she lets out a sigh that testifies as to just how much strength it takes for her to complete the simple action.

"Can I get anything for you?"

She shakes her head slowly. "You should just go, Trey."

My chest tightens at the use of my name. It feels like forever since she has spoken it.

"There is nothing for you here," she continues, "but death."

"Don't say that Lo," I use the shortened version of her name that my grandmother used to use when she was being stern with her daughter. "You are here and you are going to get better and I'm going to be here for you."

I see her eyes begin to fill with tears and for the

millionth time since her life had begun to unravel, I wish I could take it all from her. I wish that I could bear her burden so that she would smile again.

"It is I who should be there for you. What sort of mother leaves her son to fend for himself? Your grandfather would be ashamed that I have let the spirits take over."

"It isn't the spirits mother. It's an illness; that is all. You haven't done anything wrong." It is a common argument between us. My mother believes, like most in my tribe, that we are in control of our own bodies and it is up to us to keep the evil and dark spirits from meddling with us. Too many of the members of our tribe believe that my mother's condition is of her own making because of weakness. They love her, don't mistake that, but they still believe in the old ways. It was hard to leave our tribe but it was necessary.

"You're a good boy," she tells me again, though she doesn't pat my face this time. I see her eyes glaze back over and know that my time with her for the day is over. She has retreated back inside to the world that only she knows, one where I cannot go.

Chapter 3

"Do you ever have a moment in time where you wish you could hit the pause button and just observe the scene? Like in a particularly busy part of a movie where you can't seem to take in all that muddles the screen so you pause the film to allow your eyes to roam over the action and take in the details. That is what I wish I could do in this moment. I wish I could pause it and take in the person before me because the sheer presence of him muddles my brain and I can't seem to take him all in."
~ Tally

I'm hunched down beneath the table like a frightened rabbit as I watch the tall figure kneel before the new patient across the room. I'm not sure how I came to be hunched down. All I know is that the moment he walked in the room, I felt the uncomfortable rush of something pouring through me. I'm not sure if I liked it or not.

He is Native American; there is no doubt in my mind about that based on his extremely apparent features. His long, black, amazingly shiny hair would have any woman envious of the obvious health in the locks. It flows down his back like a cascading waterfall. His naturally tan skin appears as smooth as silk and his piercing dark eyes don't seem to miss a thing. He had even caught my movement and had glanced in my direction when I had so brilliantly decided to hide from a person I didn't even know. I watch as he slowly stands and continues to look down at the woman before him. By the hesitancy in his movements she is obviously very important to him and I'm awed by the tenderness that such a large, imposing guy can show. After several minutes he turns to leave and my eyes never leave his retreating form until I can no longer see him. I feel a kick to my ribs and scramble up with a grunt.

"Crap Candy," I growl at my snickering companion as I rub my side and glare at her. "What was that for?"

"A better question would be why were you hunkered down under the table drooling over Kemosabe?"

I frown at her. "That's tacky don't you think?"

"I'm sixty years old and crazy; I can do tacky if I want," she snorts at me.

I can't really argue with her there. Like pregnant women, old, crazy ladies pretty much get a free pass on crassness and eccentricity.

"So come on," she pats the chair that I had so quickly vacated, "tell Candy all about it."

I roll my eyes. "He just took me off guard, that's all," I lie smoothly.

Candy isn't buying it. "He was hot, just admit it. Hot and he got you bothered."

I cringe. "Candy, you calling a guy young enough to be your grandson hot is just not right."

"Psht," she flips her hand at me. "I'm old, not blind or dead. Besides, I didn't say I wanted to jump his exotic bones."

I groan as I bang my head against the table. "Where do you learn these terms? I mean it's not normal for someone your age to blurt out crap like that."

"Did you just use the term normal in a sentence describing me?" She raises her brow surprisingly at me.

I laugh. "Good point."

"So, are you going to tell me why Pocahontas' brother had you running for the hills?"

"There is something wrong with you, you know that, right?"

She smiles at me. "That's what the voices in my head keep telling me. Now spill it."

I know she isn't going to relent until I tell her something, so I decide to surrender. "I don't really know, just that when he walked into the room, I immediately knew something was different about him. I've never been drawn to a guy before, but I was definitely drawn to him."

Candy tapped her chin with one of her long fingers. "Hmm, so it was lust at first sight?"

I grin at her. "I will admit he was pretty hot."

She scoffs. "That's like saying the Grand Canyon is kind of deep."

"Once again, you basically saying a teenage guys is eye candy is really creeping me out."

"If that's the creepiest thing you ever hear from me then consider yourself lucky," she winks wickedly.

"I mean, yes, I noticed that he was good looking, but that wasn't it," I try to explain. "It's like he was one pole of a magnet and I'm the opposite and I'm drawn to him. It sort of freaked me out and I went into fight or flight mode."

"Ahh," she says with a single brow raised. "So you are a runner?"

"Well did you want me to walk up to him and smack him in the face?" I ask her.

"With your lips?" she laughs.

I shake my head at her with a chuckle. Just the picture of me going up to him and kissing a perfect stranger, albeit a mega–hot stranger, and seeing the shocked look on his face was rather hilarious.

"Well I'm sure he'll be back for another visit soon. Are you going to run and hide every time you see our new little fascination?"

I blow air out of my mouth and my cheeks puff up. "It's a distinct possibility."

"Not on my watch. Candy stands up and grabs my hand pulling me to my feet. "Knowledge is power, my little protégé. Maybe if you know a little something about our new toy then you won't feel the need to hide."

"Did you seriously just call him a toy?" I ask incredulously.

"No," she says as she tugs me towards the entrance of the rec room. "I called him our new toy."

"Have you ever considered that maybe you need therapy," I tease.

"That's what *they* tell me, and by *they*, I mean the entire medical community and a Judge." Candy cackles as we walk down the hall—well she walks while she drags me behind her.

"Hey, Mildew," Candy slaps her hand down on the counter of the front desk but Mildred is so used to her antics that she doesn't even flinch at the movement or the deliberate slip of her name.

"What can I do for you Candace?" Mildred's voice is dry and though she usually smiles sweetly at everyone, she is looking at Candy with obvious annoyance.

"Well I promise to leave peacefully if you will let

me have a looksee at the sign–in clip board." Candy bats her eyelashes flirtatiously.

"Why?" Mildred draws the word out as she looks up over her glasses at Candy.

"It's a secret, but don't worry, I'm not planning anyone's demise, not just yet. Pinky and I just want to know what that tall drink of water's name was."

I roll my eyes as I look around Candy's shoulder. "Don't mind her, Mildred; she's in rare form today." Mildred glances back at Candy and then to me.

"No Tally, I'm afraid this is her usual form. His name is Trey and that is all I'm going to tell you. Now off with you. Tally, you have a meeting with Dr. Stacey in a few minutes I suggest you not miss it."

I smile at her and grab Candy's hand, pulling her quickly away from the front desk before she can smart off to Mildred and get herself in trouble. Candy loved to aggravate Mildred and for some reason I had the sneaky suspicion that Mildred was one of those people you could only push so far before she reared back and stabbed you with a pencil.

"Trey?" Candy says his name as if he is a strange new fungus. "He doesn't look like a Trey."

"What were you expecting?"

"I don't know, maybe Running Eagle, or something more Native American-ish."

I shake my head at her. "Stereotype much? This isn't a movie you know?"

Candy snaps her fingers. "Damn and here I thought I was Wynona Ryder and you were Angelina Jolie in *Girl Interrupted*."

"Phuulease, if anyone is Angelina's character, it is your crazy old ass." I keep walking as she stops.

"Where are you going?" She asks me.

"In case you missed it, I have a therapy session," I tell her as I turn around but continue to walk backwards.

"What about planning your next encounter with tall, dark and...,"

"If you say lickable, I'm going to puke," I warn her.

She winks at me. "You're the one who said it Pinky."

I throw my hands in the air and turn around, ignoring her hollering about my future children needing names that reflect their mixed heritage. I swear that woman is going to scare me sane.

~

"Hi Tally," Dr. Stacey waves me in as she continues to stack files that are scattered across her desk. I take my usual spot on the plaid love seat across from the two mahogany chairs that circled around a matching mahogany coffee table. I watch as she calmly finishes what she is doing and I'm struck again by how collected she always appears. I've never seen her frazzled or out of sorts. I wonder what that must be like because I always feel frazzled and out of sorts. I wonder what I must look like to her. She must think I'm such a mess, which, duh, I kind of am, hence my current residence at a psychiatric hospital. I shrug inwardly and take comfort in knowing that I am far from the worst patient in this place.

I turn to look out the window and notice that the sky has clouded over and rain is beginning to sporadically pelt the ground. My mind wanders as I listen to the pitter patter of the rain drops on the glass. I wonder where the guy from the rec room has gone, what he's doing, and how nice it must be to have the freedom to leave this place. The thought suddenly makes me feel smothered and I try to take a slow breath to keep from hyperventilating right there in the middle of the doc's office.

"Tally?"

I turn at the sound of my name and based on the look on Dr. Stacey's face, she must have called my name several times before I finally looked at her. Back when I had first begun sessions with Dr. Stacey, I had put up a wall as tall as the Great Wall of China, hiding behind my usual sarcasm and smartass-ness. She had taken it with much grace and patience and I had grown to respect the fact that she didn't reach across the table and smack me, which I totally deserved. I was finally worn down by her persistent kindness and had begun to be cooperative.

"Where'd you go?" She asks me with a gentle smile.

I learned early on that lying to her wasn't an option. Dr. Stacey had a way of reading me. I always felt as if she could see the truth in my mind, even when I wasn't telling it. I think that somewhere along the line, she had majored in deciphering psychiatric patient bovine scatology.

"I was just thinking about how nice it would be to be able to come and go from here instead of being stuck in this building all the time," I admitted.

She nodded and I see the compassion in her soft hazel eyes.

"I know that it must be hard to be here, especially

at your age, when everything inside you is telling you to run free and enjoy your youth. I want that for you, Tally, but we need to make sure that you are ready to function in situations that you can't control. We both know that you don't want to have another incident like you had before you were brought here."

I nod, agreeing with her but not wanting to discuss what had happened. Once again I wonder if she can read my mind.

"I know you don't like to talk about it, but you have a month until your senior year starts and we need to talk about healthy ways to handle stress and moments when you begin to feel out of control. The medicine will help, but medicine is only 10 percent of the solution. The rest is learning to manage the disease, not letting the disease manage you."

"Okay," I let out a deep breath, readying myself to delve into the memories that I try to keep locked up.

"What was the final straw?" She asks.

"My history teacher being a condescending ass."

To my surprise, Dr. Stacey blurts out a laugh. "I'm sorry, that really isn't very professional but it's just that I remember having a teacher like that when I was in college and I wanted to punch him on a good day, so I can only imagine what you must have felt like on one of your bad days."

I nodded. "For days I had begun to feel agitated over nothing. I just felt like at any moment I was going to explode, a ticking time bomb. Little things would cause me to react so irrationally. That morning I hadn't been able to find my keys and I had yelled at my mom and thrown my book bag at the front door. In my mind I was asking myself what the hell is wrong with me, but I couldn't stop."

My breathing increases as I talk about that day and I begin to remember exactly how it felt to be so out of control. "I remember thinking that I must seem so crazy to my parents and they kept asking me to calm down, but I couldn't."

"It's hard to believe because you can't see your brain, but that reaction is entirely chemical," Dr. Stacey responds. "Our emotions and moods are affected by different levels of certain chemicals in the brain. Let's look at someone with diabetes, for example. They have a lack of insulin in their body that helps control their sugar levels. When the insulin is depleted, their body reacts negatively, becoming 'out of whack' if you will. If they don't know what is happening, there is nothing they can do about it. The same is true of bipolar disorder. You have low levels of chemicals, and sometimes excessive amounts of chemicals, in your brain that make you 'all out of whack,' for lack of a better term. Up until now you didn't know it. So of course you didn't know what was going on, but now we know, and knowledge is half the battle."

"So I've been told, G.I. Joe," I mutter as I think back to Candy's words. Dr. Stacey smiles at me. She's become accustomed to my little quips and to my surprise she just rolls with them.

"My point is, now that we know what is going on, we can work to help you deal with the times that you begin to feel out of control."

I nod. "Okay, I can do that." I glance away as I try to form the words that I want to say, the fears that I want to express but have been too scared to give them names.

"What if I can't get better? What if I have to stay here forever?" I know she sees the panic inside of me and though I try to stop it, I feel a tear slip down my cheek.

Dr. Stacey hands me a tissue from the box sitting on the coffee table.

"That's a perfectly normal fear, Tally. You don't have to be ashamed to voice it."

I let out a snort as I wipe my eyes. "I swear you can read minds."

She chuckles. "No, but I'm very adept at reading facial expressions and body language. In fact, they usually reveal much more than a person's words."

She doesn't say anything else, just lets me collect myself. It's one of the things I really like about her. She never tries to force conversation and she is completely comfortable with sitting in silence until I am ready to speak. She never shifts nervously or makes unnecessary movements; she is completely comfortable in her own skin. I wonder if I will ever be comfortable just being who I am. Will I ever stop wanting to be someone else? I clear my throat before trying to speak again. "So do you think that I will get better?"

"Bipolar is not a disease like cancer that can be cured. It can be managed and you will have times in your life where you will function completely normally, and then you will have times in your life that will be a little harder. But you don't ever have to get that far out of control again because you know what is going on now. When you start to sense that familiar feeling of not being able to keep it together you will just let me know and we will see if we need to adjust your medicine or if maybe just therapy will be enough."

I frown at her. "So I will have this for the rest of my life?"

She nods at me but doesn't look worried.

"Why?"

"It's just the way your body is. It sucks, I know that, but it isn't the end of the world. You can and will live a normal healthy life."

I wish I felt as confident as she sounds but deep inside I really wonder if I can ever be the way I was before I lost it. She smiles at me reassuringly.

"When it's time for you to go home you won't be on your own. You will still have counseling sessions with me weekly, okay?"

I nod and try to return her smile.

"Is there anything else you want to talk about before we call it a day?" She asks and my mind immediately jumps to the guy whose name I had discovered through less than honorable channels. I look at Dr. Stacey's expectant face. Finally I let out a groan.

"The new patient that came in today," I pause.

"Yes?"

"She had a visitor…," I'm not really sure what I should say now that I've started. I feel silly for even bringing it up, but the dam has been breached so there was no stopping the water now. "He looked about my age and something about him was…compelling." I don't really know if that was the best way to describe my attraction to him, but it was as descriptive as I was going to get with Dr. Stacey.

"I saw him, and if by compelling you mean good looking, then yes he is." A frown creases her brow as she studies me. "Have you spoken to any of your friends from school since you came here Tally?"

I look down at my hands as I grit my teeth against the immediate pain her question stirs inside. "Just Natalie." Dr. Stacey and I have discussed Natalie many times. She is my best friend and quite possibly the only reason that I didn't kill my history teacher. Since that day I had become the pariah of the high school. I'm *that* girl. I would like to say that I don't care, but that would be a lie and I'm tired of lying to myself.

"I see," she answers. "Well, maybe the next time your mysterious visitor comes you could show him around."

My head snaps up. It wasn't like Dr. Stacey to encourage patients to interact with other people's family members.

She smiles at me. "It would do you good to have a friend who doesn't hear voices but can still relate to you."

I can't help but laugh. It was true that, aside from Natalie and my parents, the only friends I had were here in the hospital. But even as I laugh at her words I know that I will never tell Trey that I'm a patient at Mercy. I don't know what I will tell him *if* I even speak to him, but I don't ever want to see the look in his eyes that others give me, those who know that I'm not normal.

"Okay," Dr. Stacey stands up. "That should do if for today."

I stand up too and toss my tissue in the trash next to the love seat. As I head for the door I hear her clear her throat. "Um Tally,"

I turn to look at her as I grab the door knob. "Yes?"

"Let's try to make group tomorrow, okay?" She is smiling when she asks me but I can see the reprimand in her eyes.

I grinned at her as I opened the door. "You got it boss." I salute her and watch as she rolls her eyes, and I imagine she is remembering that it was how I had originally responded to her, but now I did it out of playfulness rather than as a coping mechanism.

~

I hear a knock at my door as I'm lying on my bed, staring up at the cracked ceiling. I'm practicing being still, something that is very difficult for me. Dr. Stacey says that it's because being still causes me to have to deal with the emotions that are difficult. My response—"why the hell would I *want* to deal with emotions that are difficult?" Granted, I was having a bad day.

"Come in," I say loud enough for whoever is on the other side to hear.

I see Natalie with her long chocolate brown hair and big brown eyes poke her head around the door and give me one of her beaming smiles.

"What's up, my crazy little chickadee?"

I grin back at her. She is the only person outside of these walls that I will allow to call me crazy because I know she doesn't really think it.

"I'm doing homework," I tell her.

She raises a single brow at me. "Err okay, and exactly what is the homework?"

"I'm supposed to be ignoring the people in the room." I glance at her from the corner of my eye and then look back up at the ceiling, "You know, the ones you can't see."

I try not to laugh, knowing that Natalie will try not to act weird about my admission, but it's just too fun to tease her.

"Right," she finally says.

I swing my legs over the side of the bed pulling myself up from my reclined position.

"I'm kidding Nat; I don't see people that aren't there."

She laughs nervously, "I knew that."

"I see dead people, but that's a whole 'nother bag of worms."

Her face pales and I let out a bark of laughter.

"Dammit, Tally," she growls at me once she realizes I'm teasing her again.

"I'm sorry," I hold up my hands as my laughter dies down, "really I'm sorry, it's just that sometimes I have to joke about it or I just might freak out again."

She walks over to my bed and climbs up, leaning back against the wall.

"I know," she tells me simply.

"So how goes it on the outside?" I ask turning to face her.

She shrugs. "It's boring. I never thought I'd be ready for summer to be over, but if it means you will be set free then I'm all for it."

I smile at her. I know exactly what she means; only I'm not ready for school, but I'm ready to be free—I think.

"What's been going on in whacked-ville?" she asks playfully.

I realize that for the first time in a long time I'm actually excited to talk to her about something normal—a guy.

"Well, actually something interesting did happen today." I can't hold back the stupid grin that is pasted across my face.

"Please don't tell me that somebody took off after a nurse with a syringe thinking they were an alien who wanted to probe them."

I roll my eyes. "That has only happened a couple of times, and if you had seen the room they were putting the patient in you would have understood her reaction."

Nat shakes her head and lets out a puff of air. "Okay, if it isn't one of the crazies then what's up?"

"We have a new patient and her son came to visit her today, and let's just say he was easy on the eyes."

Nat grins and lowers her eyebrows, rubbing her hands together greedily. "Yummy, guy gossip and in the nuthouse no less. What did he look like?"

"He is Native American."

"Ooo, so yummy, tan skin, silky black hair?"

"Are you going to let me tell this or do you just want to enjoy your own imagination?" I interrupt her verbal drooling.

"Fine, geez, get on with it."

"Yes to the tan skin and black hair, but that wasn't all. He is just incredible. He is tall, several inches over six feet, broad shoulders, muscular arms and chest, and he just had a presence about him."

"A presence, okay, got it, mm hmm," her eyes are closed and she's nodding her head, savoring every detail. Nat has always been a boy lover, and her taste is wide and varied.

"Okay Nat, bring it down a notch. The last thing I need is you walking out of here putting off major pheromones. One of the manic old dudes might chase after you; they pick up on that stuff; it's creepy as hell."

"Eww, could we please refrain from using terms like pheromones and old dudes in the same sentence?" she cringes.

"Good point," I admit.

"So did you talk to him?"

I shake my head. "Uh, I sort of hid from him."

"What?" she asks with wide eyes.

"I panicked. It's been a while since I've been around a, okay well actually I've never been around a guy as attractive as him before. Plus there was this weird vibe I got from him."

"Vibe? What vibe, you didn't mention a vibe."

"Down girl," I chide. "Let me get there. So when he walked into the rec room I honed in on him like a beacon and I swear it took everything in me not to walk over to him and…," I shudder. "Gah, this is so irrational."

Nat snorts out a laugh. "Did you seriously just say irrational, you?"

"Shut your pie whole," I snap.

"Dude, if the shoe fits."

"The point is," I continue, "it was weird and I wanted to cuddle with…," I trail off, shuddering. I never want to cuddle—with anyone, let alone a perfect stranger.

"Man this is awesome!" Nat throws her fist in the air like a victorious champion. "How romantic would it be to tell your children one day that you met their father in the crazy house?"

"What is with you and Candy dreaming about me procreating with someone I haven't even spoken to?"

"It could happen," she shrugs.

"Whatev," I tell her using our favorite blow off term.

"So you going to talk to him the next time he comes in?"

"Doc thinks I should," I hesitate, "but if I do I'm not about to tell him I'm a patient here. I'll have to make up something. Maybe I'll tell him Candy is my crazy great aunt or something."

She nods. "Mm hmm, I could totally see that working." Nat scoots to the edge of the bed and pushes herself up onto her feet. "So you'll keep me updated?"

I roll my eyes. "Definitely, I wouldn't let you miss one episode of The Young and the Bat–shit Crazy." She hugs me as she laughs at my lame joke.

She's the only one I let hug me besides my parents. When I say I don't like to be touched, it's an understatement. Dr. Stacey says it isn't uncommon for someone with mental health issues to have personal space issues. "Great," I told her, "one more thing to add to my utter weirdness."

"See ya later, k?" Nat waves as she heads out of my room.

I hear the scuffling out in the hall and I know it's time for night time meds. I let out a huff of air.

"Only a month left," I tell myself as I make my way into the hall to join the others and get my nighttime happy pills.

Chapter 4

"Smile for me and I will know that my life has meaning. Smile for me and I will see that all is not lost. When you smile for me, I am complete; I am found." ~Unknown.

~ Trey ~

I open the door to MPF and I'm hit with a refreshing blast of cool air. It's a nice break from the summer heat pulsing at my back.

I walk over to the Information Desk and sign in; just as I had the first time I visited. Mildred is once again planted in the chair on the other side of the desk and she smiles up at me.

"Hello dear; she's in the rec room."

"Thank you," I tell her.

It's been three days since I came to visit her for the first time. My grandmother has visited every day this week and it makes me feel like a jerk for not coming with her. I had somewhat of a good reason; I had been looking for a job. Though my grandmother gets some government help, it's not enough to take care of everything, so it falls to me to pick up the slack. After searching through the classifieds, I came across an ad for a ranch hand. The job is located a few minutes out of town, and it is hard physical labor, just what I need to keep my mind off of things.

Just as I'm rounding the corner to head towards the rec room, I'm jolted back as a small body crashes into mine. I look down and see a head full of pink streaked hair. I put my hands on her shoulders to steady her and I'm surprised to feel how petite she is.

"Crap, I'm so sorry, I wasn't look...," She looks up at me after straightening her shirt and her words freeze in her throat. I'm frozen where I stand as well. My eyes land on the most expressive face I have ever seen. Her eyes are wide and sparkle with surprise, and her dainty nose fits perfectly with her small bone structure and high cheeks. Her generous lips are spread just enough that I can see the straight, white teeth behind them.

To cover my reaction to her, I let out a chuckle. "Are you alright?"

The sound seems to catch her attention and she frowns at me. I'm struck by how utterly adorable it is and feel my pulse speed up.

"Are you laughing at me?" She asks indignantly.

"Well, you did kind of look a little shocked."

"I wasn't expecting to walk into a moving mountain, so I think shocked is an acceptable response." She folds her arms across her chest and lifts her chin defiantly. Her adorableness goes up another notch.

I don't realize that I'm still grinning at her until she points it out.

"You can wipe that grin off your face at any time."

I rub my hand across my chin in an attempt to straighten out the smile. Judging by the single eyebrow raised at me, I haven't fooled her.

"I'm Trey," I finally say and hold out my hand to her. She looks at my hand and then back up at me. For a brief minute I think she isn't going to take it, but then she slips her small hand into mine. Her skin is so soft and warm that I find I don't want to release her.

"I'm Tally."

The name totally fits her. Cute and to the point,

and I like it. I really don't want to embarrass her any more, but at the same time I find that I really like seeing her with her feathers ruffled, so I give into my curiosity.

"Was that you I saw the other day ducking under a table?" I watch as her face slowly blooms a lovely shade of red.

"I, it was, there was...," she stumbles over her words.

I can see the wheels turning in her mind as she tries to come up with an excuse and to my surprise she suddenly clamps her mouth closed. I chuckle. "It's okay, Tally. I think we all have moments when it's just necessary to look for nothing in particular under a table."

She grins at me and quickly looks down at her feet. I'm struggling for what to say next because I'm not ready for her to walk away just yet. She beats me to it.

"I'm not really sure what the protocol is for talking to someone in a mental health hospital without it becoming more awkward."

I watch as she nervously shuffles her feet and I have to cram my hands into my front pockets to keep from reaching out and lifting her chin so that I can see her eyes again. I noticed the first time she looked up at me that they were a striking blue–grey color, like the color of the clouds as they darken for a coming storm. I find myself wondering if her eyes, like storm clouds, become darker and more turbulent with strong emotions.

"Well, let me take the awkwardness out of it," I tell her. "I'm here visiting my mom. She's going through a tough time."

Her face softens as she finally looks back up at me. "I'm sorry to hear that."

I hear the sincerity in her voice and in that very brief moment I see a glimpse of the depth of emotion Tally carries deep inside. Don't ask me how, but something in her draws me and I know that I want to spend more time with her. I want to see just how deep those emotions go.

I raise my brow at her. "Do you have family here?"

Just as she's about to answer, an older woman comes around the corner and stops beside Tally. She smiles up at me and the wrinkles in her face deepen. Her eyes are a tad wild and there is no doubt that this woman is a patient.

"Tally is...," the older woman starts.

"I'm her niece," Tally interrupts, "well her great niece. Candy," she motions towards me, "this is Trey."

The woman called Candy looks me over from head to toe and back again. I might have been a little freaked out by the gleam in her eyes but my attention is caught by the blush that is once again burning up Tally's tan skin.

"It's nice to meet you Candy," I tell her as I hold out my hand. Candy takes it without pause and pumps it up and down vigorously.

"Oh believe me, the pleasure is *all* mine."

Tally tries to inconspicuously stomp Candy's foot as she glares at the older woman from the corner of her eye. Candy doesn't even flinch. She finally drops my hand and takes a step back.

"So you and my *niece*," she emphasizes the word as she glances at Tally, "known each other long?"

"All of about five minutes," I tell her.

"Got any plans?"

"Candy, really?" Tally scolds her aunt.

Candy shrugs. "What? An old lady can't live

vicariously through her great niece's love life?"

"Okay first off, *eww*, second, there is no love life, and third, if there were, the answer would be a big, freaking, fat NO." Tally looks up at me with a small smile. "She has an over active imagination."

"Do I ever," Candy smirks as she continues her perusal of me.

"Okay, so Trey, it was really nice to meet you but I need to take my aunt back to her room before she attempts to rape you in broad daylight."

I choke at her words and can't help laughing when Candy responds.

"It doesn't have to be in broad daylight, and who says I would have to force him, I mean I am much older than you and have much, much," she waggles her eyebrows at me suggestively, "more experience."

"Okay, I think I just threw up in my mouth." Tally grabs Candy's hand and begins to drag her off.

I reach out quickly and snatch Tally's free hand.

"Will I see you again?" I ask her and can tell she is surprised at my forwardness, but frankly I don't care. All I know is that I want to get to know Tally.

"Um…,"

"She practically lives here," Candy snorts. "I'm sure you will run into her again."

Tally throws Candy a look I can't decipher. I'm still holding onto Tally's hand, waiting for her to confirm her aunt's words.

"I am here every day, don't really have anywhere else to be, as sad as that sounds." She admits meekly.

I let my thumb rub across her smooth wrist, as if I've done it a thousand times before, and I see her eyes widen and her breath hitch. "I think it's great that you care so much for your aunt."

She lets out a nervous laugh and I feel her trying to gently twist her wrist free. I open my fingers reluctantly and stand up straight, backing up a step in the process.

"Okay well, see you tomorrow," she frowns as if she doesn't like what she has said. "I mean, you know, not like we're planning it, like a date or anything. I just mean that we probably will run into each other again if you're here and I'm here. It's a possibility. That's all I'm saying."

I smile at her and let my voice drop as I meet her gaze. "I definitely plan to run into you again. If it happens to be with you ending up in my arms, that would just be an added bonus."

"Snap, crackle, pop," Candy laughs. "That boy is off the charts on the smooth and make you want to...,"

Tally slaps a hand over her aunt's mouth as her eyes widen.

"That's my cue, see you later," she smiles and quickly walks away towing her aunt behind her. Before they make it around the next corner I hear Candy's voice.

"If you don't get you a piece of that tall, edible eye candy, I will disown you as my niece."

I smile at her words and think that Candy might not be too bad to have around if she is going to advocate a possible relationship with the lovely Tally.

I resume my quest to find my mom and hope that she is having one of her good days. Tally was a breath of fresh air in the bleak existence that has become my life and I'm not ready to lose the energy she breathed into me.

"Hey, mom." I find her sitting in one of the chairs close to a window. She is staring out at the dead grass and dead trees. The sky is clear and the sun so bright that it is impossible not to squint. I wish that she had a better view, something that would lift her spirit. She has always loved nature so much.

She glances over to me and gives me a small smile. Her eyes are clearer than they were the last time I saw her and that is a good sign. I take the seat across from her and look out the window. I wait, letting her decide if she wants to talk. She is usually more apt to open up if I give her time to gather her thoughts instead of bombarding her with my own. She takes a deep breath and lets it out, the sound reminding me of a deflating balloon. Maybe it isn't as good of a day as I thought.

"Bly tells me you got a job," she finally says.

I nod. "Yeah, out at a ranch. I'll be mending fences, cleaning horse stalls, that kind of thing."

She reaches over and pats my leg. "You have always been so responsible, more than you should have to be."

I cover her hand with mine before she can remove it. The touch brings back childhood memories of a time when it was more common for her to pat me or hug me; a time when my mom took care of me and not the other way around. I push the memories away, refusing to let them get me down.

"I'm doing fine mom. It's good for me to work. It keeps me out of trouble."

She smiles at me and it's one of her real smiles, one of the ones that lights up her face and I can see the beauty that she once was. "You wouldn't know how to get into trouble, even if it chased you like a demon and beat you over the head."

I laugh. She is right. I'd never had the urge to be wild, or rebellious. It was never appealing to me to drink and be out of control or date random girls and use them as many guys I knew did. What was the point? Where would the fulfillment in that be? I wanted more out of life. I wanted to really live, to experience things that alcohol and random lovers couldn't give me. My grandmother says that I have an old soul and that is why I long for things that most guys my age do not. I don't know if she's right, but I do know that there are times when I wonder if I had ever been a kid because I had never felt like one.

"How are you, mom?" I finally ask. My hand still covers her own on my knee and I feel her grip tighten.

"Today is better than yesterday and the doctor thinks the meds they have started me on are going to be a good fit."

"That's good news," I tell her with a reassuring smile.

She nods and slips her hand out from under mine. "I think I'm going to go lie down now. Dr. Stacey has said that initially the medicine will make me tired, so usually I have been taking a nap about this time."

I help her stand and walk with her back to her room. It's small, square, and has a simple twin bed with a grey blanket. The walls are a light tan, probably in an attempt to make it feel less clinical. There is a sink across from the bed and a small dresser next to it. There is no mirror, and I notice that the bed is bolted to the floor as is the dresser. Apparently MPF takes no chances to ensure that a patient will not be able to use anything in their room to harm themselves.

"Thank you for coming today, Trey," she turns and hugs me quickly. Her hugs are always quick as if she can't stand the physical contact. I stopped being offended by it once I realized that I wasn't the only one she refrained from hugging.

"I'll see you tomorrow, okay," I tell her as I step back and watch as she nods and then closes the door. I don't know how long I stand there staring blankly at the door. Part of me wants to go back in, pick my frail mother up and take her home where she can be surrounded by her family, but the rational part of me knows that is not what is best.

As I finally turn to go I feel a slight tingling on my neck, the kind a person gets when he knows he is being watched. I slowly turn my head, attempting not to alarm my admirer. Just as I make a full one eighty, I see pink hair darting around the corner. I grin to myself; apparently I'm not the only one who is curious.

Chapter 5

> "I find myself replaying the scene over and over in my mind. First I bump into him, then I realize who it is and my mind seems to lose all rational thought as I imagine flinging myself into his arms. Then I have the intense desire to crawl into a hole, worried that he is able to see the freakish obsession I already have with him."
> ~Tally

Candy and I sit at our usual spot, poking at the stuff on our plates that they attempt to convince us is food. I'm almost convinced that at any moment it's going to grow legs and walk off my plate, all the while giving me the finger for even attempting to eat it. After my hasty retreat from our encounter with Trey I had been subjected to Candy's endless sexual commentary on my future relationship with said guy. The most important thing to know about Candy is the more annoyed you get with her antics, the more she will provoke you. So naturally I did the responsible thing and ignored her—not. No, instead I had a perpetual shade of red coloring my face, complete with burning ears, which only served to encourage her more. I will admit that, though it was quite embarrassing to listen to an old, crazy lady divvy out details that I did not need, it was educational. But there was no way in hell that I was confessing that to her.

"All I'm saying is that if you were ever going to experiment and explore your feminine wiles, he is the piece of meat you should gnaw on."

Her words hit my ears as I'm taking a drink of water and I choke trying not to spew it from my nose. This is what I've been dealing with all day. You would think that I would know better than to try and eat or drink while she was on a roll.

"I think you have scarred me for life," I say, nodding my head vigorously. "Yep, uh-huh, I'm pretty sure that I will never be able to look at you in the same light again, and there is a strong possibility that I will never be able to have a normal relationship and will become and old spinster reading trashy novels to get my kicks."

Candy freezes in mid bite, her fork stopping just in front of her lips. She stares at me briefly and then erupts into robust laughter. I frown at her as I try to figure out how my words could possibly be *that* funny.

She sets her fork down and wipes the tears from her eyes that the laughter has evoked.

"Oh honey, if you think I get my kicks from trashy novels then I have not given you near enough education today."

I groan and slam my head down on the table. Encouraging her was so not what I was going for.

"Is there even the slightest chance that you might possibly refrain from attempting to sexually enlighten me for the rest of the night?" My words come out muffled because my head is still pressed to the cold table top. I refuse to look up at her and give her any more ammunition, be it shocked eyes or flaming red skin.

"Fine, I'll give you a reprieve," she grumbles.

I let out a sigh of relief, thankful, no matter how fleeting it may be, that she has waved the white flag of peace.

"So, are the 'rents visiting any time soon? I have new material I want to use on them," Candy grins shamelessly.

"Okay first off, where on earth did you learn to speak like that, and second, I don't think you need to subject my parents to any more of your *material*. They are still recovering from their last run in with you."

Candy purses her lips at me and she lets out an annoyed laugh. "Why do you always feel the need to make lists of your questions and comments?"

I blow air out of my mouth making my cheeks puff out and fanning the wispy hairs around my face. "It keeps things concise," I explain, then growl as I realize that she has totally turned the tables on me. "Your turn."

"I watch *My So Called Life.* Even though it's over a decade old, it's still very relevant," she tells me with a shrug.

"Great," I say rolling my eyes. "Just what we need is you watching a show about a messed up teenager hell bent on drinking herself into oblivion, in an attempt to fit in, while constantly trying to sleep with the elusive guy who continually treats her like crap."

"Oh, good, so you've watched it."

Once again I have successfully backed myself into a corner. I stand and pick up my tray as I shake my head at my own nonsense. Only I could act indignant to a crazy lady who watches a teen show of which I have indeed seen every episode.

"Wait!" Candy yells behind me as I hear her chair scrape against the floor in her haste to follow me. "I haven't told you what my new material is."

I look back over my shoulder as I dump the untouched contents of my tray into the trash. Candy's eyes sparkle and her lips turn up in amusement, at herself no doubt.

"Though I am dying to know what embarrassing things you plan to impart on my parents, maybe we should just cut our losses for the day."

Candy knocks her tray against the trash can clearing off any remnants of dinner and carelessly tosses it on the already too full tray cart. "I was going to tell them to stop being insufferable asses."

"Well in that case," I bow dramatically, "impart away my roguish partner in crime."

"You better remember you said that when your mom has her panties in a wad and your dad's face is turning eggplant purple from his need to blow a gasket."

∼

There's no moon out tonight. No soft beam of light penetrating my window and illuminating my tiny cell. That's why it's quiet, I remind myself as I stare out of the glass into the dark night. Dr. Stacey has talked with me about the moon and how it affects mental disorders, the pull of it and the chaos that can result from it. At first I thought she was feeding me some major BS, but after being here for over two months and seeing the difference in the patients, feeling the difference in myself during the full moon, I now know she was telling the truth.

On the night of a full moon it is anything but quiet here. The unadorned hallways that gleam with the reflection of harsh florescent lights are full of pacing bodies. Like deranged zombies they pace and I wonder if at any moment they are going to begin tearing into one another, ripping flesh from bone. Dressed in the signature light green scrubs that compliment no one and wash out every complexion, most mumble incoherently while others cry out, seemingly lost in their own private anguish. The usual number of nurses on duty is doubled and syringes are filled and ready with a sedation drug for those who lose control. I pace those nights as well, only not out in the open with all the others. I pace silently in my room as my mind fills with disarray. My skin feels too tight and I tingle all over with a sensation of ants crawling across my flesh. I scratch my arms and legs until I bleed and though I tell myself that I will be okay, I have this overwhelming sense of doom as the room closes in on me and the air grows thick.

  The memories fade as I feel my body respond to them. My breathing is shallow and the world around me suddenly felt small. I move slowly to my bed and lay down. My body is as rigid as a board and when I blink it feels like sandpaper is glued to the inside of my lids scratching my eyes each time they close and open.

  This is the hard part. I never know when times like this will hit. I can be floating along having a pretty decent day and then like a bolt of lightning the world around me lights up and then plunges into darkness. It's not as bad as it had been before the medication, but it was still too much.

  "Keep breathing Tally, just keep breathing," I mutter to myself over and over. It has become my mantra after my first panic attack while at Mercy. I had passed out because I had literally stopped breathing.

  Now here I lay, struggling again to keep air moving

in and out of my body, wondering how on earth I'm going to make it to morning. I search through the anarchy in my brain, seeking out a positive thought to grab onto, a life raft to keep me a float and finally I see it. Rather, I see *him*. Trey, his firm jaw, straight nose, high cheek bones and eyes that really see me. Gradually my lungs open up and cool, refreshing air rushes in. My back leaves the mattresses briefly as I gasp like a corpse coming to life. I want to question how the mere thought of a guy I just met could possibly bring me down from a rapidly brewing panic attack, but as confusing as it is, it's too precious of a gift to waste on wondering. So instead I close my eyes, shutting out the night around me and allow myself to dream of possibilities.

~

    Morning comes much too soon, although I imagine I only feel that way because of the dreams that I had last night. Never have I wanted to stay asleep so badly, to stay in the world my mind had created, uncaring that it isn't real. Instead, I'm sitting here in my group therapy session listening to Paranoid Pete, Candy's nickname, tell us about how certain he is that the government has put a bug in his room. He is convinced that 'they' are watching and listening to him. When patients say things like that, I realize why Candy always skips group. If she were sitting here right now, she would have Pete clawing at his own skin, convinced that a beetle like creature has been implanted in his body, administered of course, by a top secret department of the United States government because they know he was abducted by aliens and they want to make sure that he hasn't been impregnated by one. And, unfortunately, as hilarious as that would be, poor Pete would probably never recover. Very few do after an encounter with the disastrous storm that is Candy Bush.

My attention drifts as my foot bounces restlessly on the floor. I've been like this since I woke up, as though there is a steady low current of electricity pulsing under my skin. My palms are sweaty and the tension between my shoulder blades could snap a crow bar in half. I'm excited and terrified all at once. Desperate to see him again and dreading the inevitable awkwardness.

It's not until I hear a deep voice, one that I've been replaying in my mind over and over, that I realize that group is over and I've been left sitting among the circle of empty chairs. I tip my chin to look up and have to tip it even further before I finally see his face.

"Is this seat taken?" Trey asks with upturned lips and dancing eyes. He's wearing a grey t-shirt that hugs his broad shoulders and bulging biceps. His jeans are loose, hanging just right on his narrow hips. Instinctively I check my sleeves and hope that he hasn't begun to notice the nervous habit. I swallow with a little difficulty as I try to keep my eyes focused on his face.

"That depends," I tease, "are you going to share about how you carried an alien's baby, were studied by the government, and then dropped in the desert to rot?"

His warm laugh pulls me towards him and I'm hopeless to stop myself.

"I don't have quite that intriguing of a tale, but I might be able to come up with something."

I'm staring like a love struck idiot. One minute I'm flirting and the next all I can do is watch his lips move as he talks and try to breathe in through my nose attempting to smell his alluring scent.

"Tally," his voice and his snapping fingers, draw me from my stupor and I look away pretending to have found something more interesting to look at—as if.

"So why were you in here during a group session?"

I bite my lip as I realize that I hadn't even thought about what he might think if he found me in here. I'm grasping at straws as I try to come up with a suitable answer. Finally, a light bulb.

"I like to sit in on group sometimes just to hear what the therapist has to say, just in case she says something that might help my aunt. She refuses to go to group."

"Oh, that makes sense, and that's really great of you."

I cringe inwardly as he obviously has the idea that I'm some selfless little niece who caters to her aunt instead of a lying fakeazoid. Yes, I said fakeazoid because I'm feeling that *fake* is just not a strong enough word at this point.

"Are you here to visit your mom?" *Did I really just ask that? Why else would he be here?* I secretly hope that maybe he spent the night as intrigued about me as I did him. Perhaps that's why I asked a question that I already knew the answer to.

He nods. "Yeah, I've already seen her this morning." I watch as the smile that seems to come so easily for him slips into tight lips.

"Is she doing alright?" I ask, my voice soft, even

though there is nobody else in the room but the two of us.

"Honestly, I don't know." He looks down and plucks absently at a loose string on the hem of his shirt. "I want to hope that she is going to get out of here, but I'm beginning to think that hope is for those who don't know any better."

My eyes widen slightly at his candidness and I see in a moment that he realizes that he has just been quite open with a virtual stranger.

"Sorry, I didn't mean to get all deep and emotional on you. I don't really know why I told you that." He's staring at me now and his eyes seem to be searching for something: acceptance, understanding, or reassurance that he hasn't freaked me out. I don't know what he sees, but I hope it's all of those things.

"Sometimes things just build to a point inside of us that there is no way of stopping them from coming out, no matter who happens to be in proximity." I hope that my words let him know that I don't judge him. I mean really, who am I to judge, I'm the girl who cuts on herself when she can't cope with her own crap. Granted, I was not about to share that little tidbit with him no matter how badly I feel the need to verbally vomit.

I watch as that easy smile returns. He chuckles as his head shakes. "I guess that's true."

We've reached that place in a conversation where an end has come to the previous topic and a new one has not been brought up. So those involved just sort of wait and hope that they don't look like they are desperately searching for an un-lame, or at least only partially lame, topic. What he finally said, I was totally not expecting.

"You want to get out of here?"

Son of a biscuit, I did not see that coming. His words felt like a slap to the face, though it wasn't his fault. He had no idea that I was an inmate, not a visitor. He had absolutely no way of knowing just how badly I wanted to get out of here and yet I was terrified of that very idea. Maybe I needed to reconsider this little endeavor to keep him in the dark about who I was and why I was here. We hadn't been sitting here fifteen minutes and my brain already hurt from trying to figure out ways to get around his should–be harmless questions.

"Tally?"

I blinked and realized that once again I had been sitting there staring at him, not seeing him, while he waited for an answer. Okay, so I might not need to worry about keeping him in the dark about me if I keep doing totally mental things like that. Add some drool to the absent stare and the absolute wacked-out look is complete.

"Um…." Yep, that was my brilliant reply, *um*, I mean seriously, who leads with that? As I grapple for some way to turn him down without turning him off, I hear the doors behind me slam open. I turn abruptly in my seat to see Candy rushing in. She sees us and grins. I recognize that grin. I saw it in fourth grade, a week before school was out for the summer. Tommy Mitchell, heartthrob of Ms. Tubb's class had that same grin as he came strolling down the hall. We found out later that day that Tommy Mitchell's grin was a result of the five baby pythons he had put in Ms. Tubbs' desk drawers. It was hard to believe that a fourth grader would have access to a baby python, let alone five of them, but it turns out his dad was some sort of reptile expert and his house was lined with glass aquariums full of different reptiles. So yeah, Candy's grin was totally *I set baby pythons loose on your ass* worthy.

"Hi," I clear my throat as I catch myself and remember to add her fake title, "Aunt Candy, everything okay?"

"Everything is excellent, just brilliant," she tells me breathlessly. "What are you two kids up to?"

"Oh, well, Trey has just invited me to go *out*," I emphasis the *out* hoping she will catch the significance of it. My hope fizzles out when I see her eyes narrow and her mouth quirk up in a saucy smile.

"Want to show my niece your tee-pee, hmm?" She says grinning from ear to ear.

I slap my hand to my face ignoring the pain I register a second later. I shake my head as my eyes close and pray that at any moment the earth will open up and swallow me, and Candy for that matter. I hear Trey chuckling and try to focus on his deep rumble instead of my intense embarrassment.

"Actually, I just thought she might like to go get something to eat," Trey tells her.

Candy's face drops into a frown. "Oh, well that's not nearly as exciting."

"The point is that he wants me to leave," I pause, "as in walk out of the building." I don't look over at Trey for fear of seeing the look on his face. He has to think that I am an absolute looney tune, no the irony isn't lost on me considering where I'm sitting. I can tell by the lack of acknowledgement that she isn't even listening to me. Her head is cocked to the side, her eyes narrowed, listening to whatever was happening beyond the door.

"I know how you get anxious when I leave Aunt Candy," I grit my teeth as I talk and resist the urge to stomp my feet and yell *pay attention you crazy old bat*. "I want to make sure that you are okay with me *leaving* you here, in the mental hospital…alone."

"Ohhh!" Her eyes light up and I can see the light bulb flicker.

Finally

"No, no, no!" Candy begins shifting from foot to foot. She is wringing her hands and her eyes begin to look wild. If Candy did anything well, it was turn on the crazy. "You know I'm not good when you aren't here. I feel lonely when you aren't here and I worry that I might do something dangerous like blindfold Paranoid Pete and poke him with sharp objects so that he thinks he is being probed by aliens. You remember what happened the last time you left me during the day, I…,"

I begin making a cutting motion across my throat, trying to signal her to stop. I glance over at Trey to see what his reaction is to her confession and I have to give it to him, he's handling it pretty well.

"Okay, Candy," I cut her off before she can say anything that might send Trey running. "I'll stay here."

Just as I begin to ask Trey if he would be interested in staying here, a loud crash rattles the walls just beyond the closed doors. The doors Candy had just come rushing through.

"Um, Candy, why exactly were you in such a hurry when you came through those doors?"

She smiles at me innocently as she glances down at her fingernails as if they suddenly need a good grooming. "Oh, I don't know. I might have played a teeny, tiny prank on dear Ms. Sheila." The glow in her eyes tells me that it's more than just a tiny prank."

My eyes grow wide as my insides begin to squirm. "What exactly did you do?"

She shrugs nonchalantly. "Nothing she doesn't deserve, the thieving old biddy."

"Candy…," I warn.

"I may have…traced my hand shooting her the bird on her desk with permanent marker, and then maybe I glued Xanax pills to the top of the desk as the outline of the hand." she laughs, "Man I wish I could have stuck around to watch her try and pick them up."

I can't help the snort of laughter that bubbles out of me.

Candy grins at me. "And I left her a message with the pills."

"I'm scared to ask."

"Underneath the hand I wrote 'Xanax is for nutters, silly rabbit.' Think she'll understand the reference?"

I glance over at Trey to see his reaction to her and to my relief, instead of looking on in horror; he is smiling, obviously enjoying himself.

"Probably not," I answer. "The hair coloring fumes have more than likely fried her brain cells."

"Who is Sheila?" Trey asks.

"Oh, she's the nurse who passes out the medicine to the patients," Candy explains, "but she has a bad habit of slipping a few into her pocket when she thinks no one is watching."

"Has someone reported her?"

Candy shrugs. "They know."

Trey frowns. "And they don't fire her?"

"Not many nurses want to work in the crazy house, Tonto."

I feel my face heat up as I close my eyes and shake my head. "Could you please refrain from derogatory comments for, oh, I don't know, like ever?"

"Psht, quit your whining. Trey is a big boy. If he doesn't appreciate my humor then let him be the one to speak up."

Both our heads swing over to look up at Trey.

He shrugs. "It takes a lot to offend me."

"There, you see, he's not going to run crying and hide in his wigwam."

"Ugh!" I groan as I grab Trey's arm and begin pulling him towards the doors. "Okay Aunt Candy, we're going to leave you to your pranks. Try not to get put in the strait jacket today okay?"

"Are you leaving?" She asks as her brows rise worriedly.

"No, just going to have a sit outside."

"Zeke is at the back door, so you might want to go that way. He won't ask a lot of questions, if you know what I mean." She winks meaningfully.

"Right." I wave over my shoulder as I tug Trey through the doors and turn right to head to the back door. I hear yelling in the direction of the front of the building and realize that it's Sheila shrieking about how *that* woman needs to be locked up and not allowed to roam free, as she so kindly says, to drive everyone bat shit crazy. I roll my eyes at her words and secretly commend Candy on her antics.

My mind is racing and my heart beats against my chest like steady drum. I know the pounding rhythm is partly because of the tall guy walking with me and partly because I'm going to somehow keep Zeke from outing me as a patient. For one brief instance I wonder if going through all the trouble to keep Trey in the dark is worth it, then I glance back over my shoulder to look at him. I catch his eyes and see his lips quirk up in a sexy smile. Yes, yes, it is definitely worth all the trouble and a whole lot more.

Zeke is sitting in a metal chair, and though to an average size person the chair would have looked normal, Zeke makes it appear as if it was built for a toddler. His massive hands hold a magazine, and on closer inspection, I see that it is a about crocheting. Since living in the mental hospital I've learned not to questions things, not even about the staff. I figure we all have to cope somehow and if crocheting is Zeke's thing then more power to him.

"Hey Zeke," I say and realize too late that I sound a tad manic.

"Oh, hey Tally." He looks up from his magazine with a warm smile and then his eyes land on the figure behind me.

Before he can say anything more I blurt out, "This is Trey and we are just going to sit outside and talk. You know how *Aunt* Candy doesn't like me to leave during the day, even though I come and *visit* her every day. We aren't going any further than the bench there." I point to the wooden bench across from the doors. Zeke's eyes keep jumping from my face to Trey's. I'm pleading with my eyes for him to just go along with my story. I guess my face must have conveyed my desperation because he finally answers,

"Alright, if Candy, or anyone else, happens to ask for you I'll just let them know that you haven't *left* for the day just yet."

I let out a quiet sigh of relief and mouth, "Thank you."

Zeke gives me a slight nod of his head and then turns back to his magazine and as I push out of the door I can't help but notice the slight smile on his lips.

Chapter 6

"Have you ever wished you could fast forward? As I stare into her blue-grey eyes, all I can think is how I wish we were beyond the awkward phase and to the part where I have the right, the privilege to hold her, to kiss her, to call her mine." ~Trey

I know that I must be making her feel uncomfortable as I stare at her, but all I can think is how I want to memorize every feature, every facial expression, so that I can bring her perfectly to mind later when she is no longer before me. *Creepy much, Trey,* I think to myself.

"So you just moved here?" she asks me as she sits down next to me on the wooden bench.

"Yes, we moved here from Arizona."

"You like it?"

I smile slightly as I look into her eyes. "More and more each day." I love the flush on her skin. I love how she isn't sure how to take compliments, no matter how subtle.

"You don't beat around the bush do you?" she asks coyly.

I even love how she calls me out. Yes, I have it bad and it's only the second time I've talked with her.

"Not when I see something I want. Life is too short, and too unpredictable, to leave things to chance." I watch her closely, needing to see her reaction to my words, wondering if I'm pushing too fast and too hard.

"I guess I can understand that," she finally answers.

"So what's your story, Tally," I let my words trail

off as I hope that she will give me her full name.

"Baker, Tally Baker."

I notice her voice shake just a bit and watch as she twists her hands in her lap. Have I asked the wrong question? I wasn't trying to pry, but I desperately wanted to know more about her.

"I'm not trying to be nosy," I tell her hoping she will hear the sincerity in my voice.

"It's alright. I...well," she stops and takes a breath letting it out slowly. "I'm seventeen and will be a senior this year."

Okay, vague, but at least it's something.

"Do you have any hobbies or a job?"

She grins. "I use to be an assistant pet photographer."

She must see the question on my face as she lets out a small laugh.

"Basically I dressed the dogs, or cats, up in cute little outfits and then posed them for the photographer to take pictures of them."

"People really brought their pets to you for these kinds of pictures?"

She nods her head. "Yep. Mostly really rich people with no kids."

"Did you enjoy it?" I ask.

She thinks about it for a second before answering. "Yeah I did. It was fun, and I really enjoy animals. Do you have a job? She asks as she leans down and plucks a piece of dead grass from the ground. I watch in stupid fascination as her small hands play with the blade. Something so insignificant, and yet all I can think about it how I wish her hands were on me instead of the lucky little piece of grass.

"I actually just got a job as a ranch hand."

Her face lights up and I feel my breath catch at the sudden ray of light that she has bestowed upon me.

"So you get to be around horses and stuff?" She is nearly bouncing in her seat.

I chuckle as I nod my head. "Yeah, but it's not as glamorous as you are thinking. I will be mucking out their stalls."

"Still, you will get to see horses." she says wistfully.

"Have you never seen a horse?"

She shakes her head. "Not up close. I mean I've seen them out in pastures when driving out in the country, but I've never gotten to touch one."

I realize then just how different our lives must have been growing up. I had grown up around horses. We had several on our reservation. In fact, horses were considered sacred to our tribe as they had served our people for generations, taking them through dangerous times and often saving them when traveling on foot would have meant death or capture.

"Maybe I can take you out to the ranch. I'll ask Mr. Taggert. I imagine he will be fine with it." If I thought her face had been bright before, now it was practically glowing.

"Really?"

I raise my brow at her. "I told you, life is too short to pass up opportunities. When would you like to go?" Just as quickly as her face had lit up, it suddenly fell. Again I find myself wondering what I have said wrong.

"Oh, well it will have to be later, maybe when summer is over." she answers, again vaguely.

I decide that I won't push her now, maybe after we've known each other a little longer.

"Alright, we can revisit it later."

She looks up, obviously surprised that I didn't

press her for more information. I watch as her shoulders relax.

"So what's *your* story?" she asks, her head turned slightly to the side and her forehead wrinkled in question.

"What do you want to know?"

"Well," she begins, "you are obviously Native American."

"Obviously," I interrupt with a crooked smile.

She rolls her eyes at me. "What kind?"

I let the humor I feel from her question show on my face as I lean back against the bench and stretch my arms across the back of it.

"You mean what tribe?"

"Um, well if that's the correct way to ask, then yes, what tribe?"

"I'm White Mountain Apache," I tell her. "My tribe is in North Western Arizona."

"Wasn't it hard to leave?"

I think about it. I think about my friends and my family I left behind and realize that since I met Tally, I hadn't missed them. "At first, yes," I agree. "But not so much now."

"Are you about to make one of your, I'm not going to beat around the bush, statements?" Again I watch as heat floods her skin.

"Does it bother you?" And I realize then that even if it does, I have no plans to change my approach. I don't want her to have any question of my intentions.

"It's just different from most guys our age. They aren't usually quite so bold." she explains.

"Most guys fear rejection."

Her eyes narrow at me. "And you don't?"

"There are worst things in life than rejection." I see

the moment that thoughts of my mother run through her mind as her face softens and her eyes drop.

"Yes, there are."

Something in her voice catches my attention, and I realize that its knowledge and understanding. Tally has experienced something worse than rejection, but I don't yet have the right to ask what that something is.

"To answer your question, a certain girl has taken my mind off of those I have left behind on the reservation."

She looks back up at me and to my relief, her smile has returned. "One of those amazing horses is a female?"

Her teasing has caught me off guard. "Tally Baker, you are trouble." I laugh and enjoy her laughter mixing with my own. Something in that moment causes her to relax even more and rapid fire questions begin to flow from her.

"Favorite color"
"Grey"
"Favorite artist/band:"
"Coldplay"
"Greatest fear"
"Loss"
" of what?
 "Anything."
"Longest relationship": (this question brings a deep scarlet blush to her face)
"Only been on a few dates, no one I would claim as a girlfriend."
"Favorite food"
"Italian"

Two hours pass in the blink of an eye and when

she asks me the time and I tell her it is two o'clock I find myself nearly begging her to stay when she jumps up.

"Oh crap," she exclaims. "I have to go."

"You need to leave?"

"Yes well…I mean no, I have to go with my aunt to her therapy session with the doctor."

"Oh, okay." I couldn't help but find it a little odd that she did so much with her aunt when no one had said anything to me about joining my mother in therapy or group sessions.

"Alright," I tell her as I stand up. She turns to go back inside and once again I find myself reaching out and grabbing her hand.

"Will you be here tomorrow?"

She smiles like she has a secret and I would be a liar if I said I didn't long to know what that secret is.

"Yes." she answers simply.

"Can we do this again?" I motion towards the bench. She glances back at the door and then to the bench and I can see that she is considering turning me down. Not going to happen.

"I'll meet you here tomorrow at noon," I tell her, taking the choice out of her hands. Her eyes narrow and she opens her mouth and I know that she is about to argue with me.

"Don't you need to get to that session with your aunt?" I ask her and smile.

She laughs. "Fine, I'll see you tomorrow."

She turns and I let her hand go and watch as she hurries through the door. I stand there watching her, mesmerized by her graceful movement and the gentle sway of her hips.

I had told her that I didn't fear rejection, that there

were greater things to be frightened of—I had lied. For the first time in my life I felt the dread of knowing that someone I was deeply attracted to and longed to know more would have no interest in me.

~

    I find my mind continually drifting back to my time with Tally as I drive to the ranch. Mr. Taggert had agreed to allow me to work in the evenings. I wanted to be able to visit my mother during the day, and take care of any errands my grandmother might need me to do for her. I find as I'm mucking out the stalls with sweat trailing down my back that it is a perfect time for me to work off all the pent up energy from spending time with Tally.
    I finally reach the fifth stall of the horse stable and, though the sky has begun to darken, the air is just as hot as it has been all day. I grab the leads of each of the horses and go to gather them up and put them in their respective stalls. With the last horse locked safely away, I look in through the slats. This one is my favorite, Rosa, a female Bay with sorrel colored hair and a black main and tail. She is very affectionate and often stands at the edge of the stable watching me as I work. I try to imagine what Tally's face will look like when she meets her. I hope that her face lights up as it did today, giving me a break from the shadows that have begun to be my constant companions. A brief flash of my mother's face enters my mind and I wish that it was the face from my childhood. That face was beginning to fade, replaced by the lost stare of glazed over eyes and the slack mouth

that didn't seem to remember how to smile.

    Once in my truck, I roll down the windows but I keep the radio off. My muscles are tired and sore, but it's a good feeling, a feeling that tells me I have put in a hard day's work. I take comfort in knowing that my father would have been proud of the job that I am doing, caring for the animals that give so selflessly of themselves and not settling for a meaningless job regardless of my age. I find it interesting that Tally and I both work with animals, and though I am not one to believe in destiny, I wonder if it is a sign. My people believe that our ancestors who have passed on watch over us, their spirits guiding us. Maybe my father's spirit was indeed watching over me, and just maybe he was guiding me to my future, to Tally.

Chapter 7

> "If I wasn't crazy before, I definitely am now. My heart is filled with possibilities, but my mind is filled with reality and it's telling my head to wake up and get a freaking clue. Meanwhile, I'm walking around smiling like a damn fool and it's not because of the little pills I take like candy. No, this drug is living, breathing, and so very, very addictive."
> ~Tally

I have no idea what time it is when the knock comes. I rub my eyes groggily and drag myself from the bed. Before I make it to the door it opens slowly and the wide eyed face of Candy pops into my room.

"Hey lover girl," she grins at me.

"Candy, what time is it?" I growl.

She swings the door open all of the way and grabs my wrist. She catches me off guard and I stumble forward. Did I mention crazy people are crazy strong? Well, they are, so take note of that if you are ever faced with a deranged psychopath.

"It's time to live," she cackles over her shoulder. I realize then that Candy is having one of her highs and after this she is bound to fall. I don't know what Candy's official diagnosis is. I've never asked and she's never offered, but I've learned her patterns. The greater the high, the lower and more painful the crash will inevitably be.

"And just what do you have planned?" I groan.

"Have you ever ran full speed towards a pond and

jumped as hard and high as you could?"

I inwardly groan as I realize her plan.

"I'm taking your silence to mean you have not," she continues as she throws her free hand up in the air dramatically. "Pinky, you are so young, so innocent, with so much life ahead of you. You have yet to experience all the things that you must in order to make your teenage years worth remembering and I only have a month left to squeeze it all in."

I decide to address the most pressing question first and deal with what she has said later.

"And how do you plan to get us out?"

"Oh ye of little faith. One thing you should know by now, my sweet protégé, is that everyone has a price and everyone can be bought."

I do not fail to notice that she has not answered my question. We reach the back double glass doors on the farthest side of the building, where the employees go to smoke.

Her head swings back to look at me and she smiles wickedly.

"Turns out that Bob's price was something that I could easily pay." She winks at me and I slap my hand over my mouth and feel my eyes widen. Bob is one of the nightly cleaning crew and is known for whistling annoying tunes while running his floor waxer thing. I kept waiting for the night when poor Bob's whistling would finally land him as quarry for one, or goodness forbid, several of the utterly lost souls who could no longer separate reality from delusion.

"Please tell me that you did not provide a sexual favor just for us to jump in a bloody pond." My words come out muffled because my hand is still covering my mouth.

Candy lets out an annoyed huff as she raises a brow at me. "He wanted Sheila's number. Good grief Pinky, you might as well just roll around in that gutter you seem to have found yourself in ever since Sacajawea came swaggering in."

"You do realize that Sacajawea was a princess, as in, not male." I point out.

She shrugs. "If you want to get technical, but since you have yet to examine the goods, for all we know he's just a poser and could very well be a princess. He does have lustrous long hair." She pauses and then smiles slowly, "Unless that bench out their got consecrated." She waggles her eyebrows at me and I try very hard not to allow the picture she evokes to pop into my mind. Successful? Plead the fifth.

"Could we please get on with breaking the rules so that you can rest assured that I have *lived*." I make air quotes around the last word as I follow her out of the door and into the hot summer night.

"So, I got Bob Sheila's number and I might have accidently written her address on the piece of paper as well. I kind of get the stalker vibe from him, but Sheila will probably be too high to even notice if he is lurking outside her window."

My mouth drops open gaping at her words as I stop in my tracks.

"You gave Sheila a stalker?" I squeak out.

Candy lets out a huff that puffs out her lips and makes her wrinkled face smooth for a brief moment. She stands their looking at me for a moment and, other than the chirps of crickets, the night is quiet.

"There," she says motioning with her hands quickly, "we've had a moment of silence in honor of the weirdness that Sheila is bound to have to endure with Bob's advances. Now can we *please* continue on with my brilliant plan to corrupt you?"

With nothing to be done about it now, I nod and begin to follow her again. To my surprise, when I arrived at MPF over nine weeks ago, I discovered a beautiful pond about a quarter of a mile behind the building. The perimeter of the pond was adorned with a concrete walking trail, impressively manicured shrubbery, and a cornucopia of perennials. I wondered at the time, though I didn't ask, why on earth they would put a pond so close to people who just might entertain the idea of throwing themselves into it in hopes of ending their miserable existence.

As I see the pond come into view I admit that the moon shining off of the rippling water is very tempting. Remembering to be thankful for small victories, I take relief in knowing that the temptation is not to seek the depths of that pond and never resurface. A gentle breeze caresses my skin pushing me forward, beckoning me like a siren.

"Okay Pinky," Candy stops and stares out at the water longingly and I wonder if she feels the pull as well. "This is where we run. We feel the wind rushing across our skin, blowing our hair behind us like the manes on wild horses and then we jump for all we're worth."

"I didn't know you were so descriptive," I tell her and smile.

"Yes you did, you just didn't know that describing terrifying scenarios for the paranoid and delusional crack pots wasn't my only talent." She motions me to follow her as she takes off in a surprisingly quick run for a sixty year old. "Now quit stalling and come on!" She yells.

I hesitate for one, two, three beats of my heart and then mutter, "What the hell." I'm running, my arms are pumping and my breath begins to speed up as my lungs push for more oxygen. All I can hear is the wind rushing past my ears and the pounding of my heart. Just before I reach the pond I push with all my might, my legs kick wildly as if running in midair. I'm not sure but I think I let out a yelp and it's abruptly cut off as my body hits the water and I'm swallowed up. The darkness is absolute as even the moon does not penetrate the surface and illuminate the depths. I feel peace envelope me and sink even more into the warmth of the water. The peace only lasts a few seconds as I suddenly feel the water convulsing around me. I lower my legs so I'm vertical and kick frantically to get to the surface. When I break through I feel the warm air hit my skin. I rub my eyes as I kick with my legs to stay above the water and look around to find the source of the commotion.

"CANDY!"

To my horror, she is bobbing up and down as her arms flail rapidly, vainly attempting to keep her head above water. Her eyes are wide with fear and I gasp as I realize she can't swim.

Shaking off the shock I dive forward, kicking hard and circle around to her back. I've taken one lifeguarding class, enough to know that you don't approach a drowning victim from the front. They will latch onto you and drag you down with them. I quickly move in behind her and wrap an arm around her neck pulling her onto her back. She instinctively grabs my arm with both hands and, when my other hand supports her torso to keep her above water, she stops fighting me. I lean in, dropping my shoulder just below the surface and begin scissor kicking my legs.

"I've got you Candy," I tell her in the calmest voice I can muster. I kick harder, and though we've only jumped a few yards into the water, I'm exhausted by the time we finally reach the edge of the pond.

"I need you to turn and grab onto the ground Candy, I will not let go of you. I need you to try and pull yourself up."

She starts to shake her head 'no' and I feel her shutter.

"Dammit Candy! Quit acting like a frightened kitten and get out of this water!" She stiffens briefly in my arms and then she begins to sit up. I help her get vertical and, as she grabs the ground pulling with everything she's got, I push her. I sink under the water and grab the backs of her thighs and lift her so that she can get one leg up on the ground. From there she takes over and pulls the rest of her body out. She's panting hard as she lies on her side and then rolls onto her back.

I hoist myself up out of the water and stare down at her.

"Are you alright?" I ask as I bite back the emotion coiling inside me preparing to strike like a snake.

Her eyes close and she coughs, and then to my utter shock she begins to laugh. First it's just a chuckle, but then it's a full on, rolling on the floor, laugh. I suppress my desire to strangle her and take several deep breaths. I try to remind myself that Candy isn't a normal person; she's in a psychiatric facility and for good reason.

"You should have seen your face," she says through her laughter. "I'm serious it was so, so," words elude her as she continues to laugh.

If I thought I could keep my calm because she's a nut job, I thought wrong.

"WHAT THE HELL CANDY!" The tone of my voice has penetrated her bubble and she abruptly stops laughing and looks up at me.

"How can you find this funny?" I'm gritting my teeth and I think that if I clench them any tighter I just might break my jaw.

"Whoa, wait a second," she holds her hands up as if to hold me off, "you're mad? At me? I was the one who nearly drown, how can you be mad at me?"

"You could have DIED!" I motion wildly to the pond.

"But I didn't." She looks at me like a child beaming with pride and looking for approval from a parent.

"That's not good enough for me. You jumped into that pond knowing that you can't swim. You didn't stop to think about how that would affect me. You didn't consider the consequences of doing something so reckless, so incredibly irrational!"

"Who are you to preach at me about being rational?" Candy snaps as she clamors to her feet. Though her soaked clothes stick to her skin, she seems unfazed. "You, who turns to a blade or flame with every emotional plunge. Really, Tally? You want to start comparing our crazy notes?"

I step back feeling the sting of her words like the slap of a hand across my face. She's right, which only pisses me off more.

"I don't drag others down with me," I counter. "I keep my crap contained in my own messed up bubble. But you vomit your crap all over everyone and then you run and hide, leaving the rest of us to deal with your mess." The minute the words are out I see her face change and the glaze of indifference that is so common here, film over her eyes.

She starts to back away from me and she begins to nod. "Okay, I hear what you're saying. You think I pull you down, I *vomit* on you." I take a step towards her, but she keeps moving backwards. "I can't pull you down if you're not tied to me, so consider yourself untied."

"Candy wait," I call out to her as she turns and walks briskly towards the back doors we had only a little while ago slipped through.

I stand there alone, dripping wet. I am so confused as to how the night went from us doing things to help me experience life to saving Candy from death. How's that for irony?

The next morning I stand in front of the cork board where I have taped the positive statements that Dr. Stacey tells me I need to ingrain in my mind. My eyes lock onto my least favorite one. I want to grab it and crush it in my hands but I don't. I push the words from my mouth even as I loathe saying them.

"Today is hard, it's lonely, it's crappy. Today is a day that you want to crawl in a hole and never come out. But today you will smile anyway." I can't help myself; I give the saying the bird. Yes, I know, real mature.

The morning is a blur as I get my meds, go to breakfast, and then to group. I haven't seen or heard Candy and the hole that she fills is beginning to open up. My time to meet Trey is nearing and I'm so desperate to talk to Candy, to have her distract me from my nerves with one of her outlandish statements.

I'm walking back towards my room when I pass Zeke.

"Hey have you seen Candy?" I ask him.

Zeke's face falls, and for a split second I feel my heart drop into my stomach as I fear the worst.

"She won't leave her room and the only thing we can get her to tell us is that she will keep her vomit to herself."

"Thanks, Zeke," I tell him quickly as I hurry towards Candy's room.

I knock on her door, more out of politeness than necessity, as there are no locks on the doors in the nut house.

"Go away," she snaps.

I open the door and slip inside, closing it quickly behind me. Candy is sitting on her bed, her back against the wall, knees bent and feet flat.

I smile tentatively when she looks up at me.

"I know your diagnosis is bipolar, but when did your co-diagnosis become dumbass?" She glares at me.

"Okay, I deserve that one."

I walk further into the room, thinking that at any moment she just might cause me bodily harm. Hey, it could happen.

She lets out a slow breath and as her shoulders slump. I see the sixty years of life that has weighed her down. "What do you want, Tally?"

She's using my name, not a good sign.

"I came to apologize for last night."

"For being an asshat?" She retorts.

"Yes, for being an asshat."

"And a bitch?"

"Yes a bitch."

"And…,"

"You've made your point Candy," I cut her off before she can continue her long list of adjectives. "In my defense, I was scared." I take another step closer and another until I'm able to sit on the end of her bed. I turn my body towards her and meet her stare. "I spoke out of anger. You are my friend and I don't want anything to happen to you."

Candy chuckles as her lips turn up slightly. "You do realize that the death rate in a mental hospital is higher than that of a regular hospital."

"No it isn't, you're just making crap up now." I say as I roll my eyes.

Candy leans forward, her smile fades, and the same longing I saw the night before is flooding her eyes.

"I die a little more each day," her voice is soft and I have to lean forward to hear her. "I've lived with this disease that has robbed me of my sanity, has stolen any real life that I could have had for more years than I care to admit. I have no family, no friends, no children, and no husband. I have nothing but these white walls."

I feel her words deep inside me and I know a little of the emptiness she must feel, though not for the same reasons.

"I just want to live, Tally. Being around you has made me see all the things that I never got to experience, all the things that I want you to get to experience. I don't want you to wither away in this place scared of who you are."

I nod, letting her know that I understand. "You've never jumped into a pond either?"

"Now I have," she smiles and for a brief moment

she is the Candy I know, not this broken woman before me.

We sit in silence, both of us lost in our own version of hell, unsure of how to escape. It's in that moment that I remember I'm supposed to meet Trey.

"Crap," I say jumping up.

"What?" Candy asks as she too climbs to her feet.

"I'm supposed to meet Trey at the bench." My eyes widen as I think of the possibilities. "Candy what if he asked someone about me? They would tell him to check my room, MY ROOM!"

Candy grabs my shoulders and pulls me to face her.

"You have got to pull it together."

I nod my head but know my eyes must still look frantic.

"I will go and see if I can find your Geronimo and you stay here and get a grip." She gives me a firm shake as if it would help sink the message into my brain.

"Okay," I nod, feeling slightly better now that we have a plan. The feeling quickly evaporates as I hear a knock at the door and then a familiar deep voice.

Candy turns and looks at me and winks. "Found him."

I scamper around to the farthest corner from the door where he would have to look around Candy to spot me. I fill with worry as I wonder if he knows that I'm a patient and has come to confront Candy about it.

"Well hello handsome," I hear Candy say and I can tell by the sound of her voice that she has a thousand watt smile plastered on her wrinkled face. "Did you finally come to your senses and realize that there is something to be said for playing with a cougar?"

I slam my hand over my mouth as a combination

gasp/laugh attempts to jump out of my throat. I let my breath out slowly, trying to keep it quiet so that I can hear Trey's response.

He chuckles. Have I mentioned I love his deep chuckle?

"I am flattered, Candy, truly I am, but I'm afraid my heart belongs to another."

My shoulders tense at this news and I wonder if he's had a girlfriend all along. Maybe he wasn't honest with me the other day. My heart beats frantically and I feel like a fool for ever thinking that someone who looks like him, could ever be interested in someone like me.

"Zeke told me that Tally hasn't come in today. I wanted to make sure she was alright," he paused briefly and when he continued I could tell he was unsure if he should. "I was also wondering if you might give me her phone number or address. I know that sounds creepy, but I promise that I am not a stalker or axe murder."

Candy laughs. "I'm not worried that *you* will kill her. No, Tally's going to die of natural causes. Most likely it will be from Virgin-itis."

I feel myself sliding to the floor as I continue to listen to Candy's words. I feel torn between laughter and embarrassment and then wonder how I will ever face him again.

"This is a disease?" Trey asks. "Then how is it natural?"

"Disease is relative in this case Tonto. The important part is how it kills. See, knowledge is power. She won't realize she has Virgin-itis until it's too late; it's what is known as a silent killer. One night she will be lying in bed in her tiny apartment and she will hear banging on the wall behind her. She will feel the wall shake and maybe even a picture or two crash to the floor. With a final muffled, albeit satisfied," she adds with a sultry tone, "scream, silence suddenly envelops her and she dies."

Trey is quiet and I begin to wonder if maybe he has left, totally outraged by Candy's ridiculous story but then I hear his voice again.

"How does she die?" He asks and I can tell he has figured out her ruse. "She's just lying there and then just— dies?"

I watch as Candy huffs. "You know what? Just ask Tally when you see her, k? She will be glad to give you all the gory, sad details. She isn't here today because she went to a lake last night with some friends. Apparently her clothes got soaked so she stayed at one of their houses overnight to use their dryer. She was tired this morning and I told her to get some rest."

"She went swimming with her *girl*friends?" It was obvious that he was fishing for details and my insides did a happy dance.

Candy shrugs. "She didn't give me an itinerary with the list of participants. But since the house she stayed at last night was occupied by a person named *Nate*," she drags the name out with a knowing voice, "my incredible deduction skills would tell me that it wasn't a *girls–only* wet t-shirt party." As Candy starts to close the door she adds. "So having her address would be pointless seeing as how she isn't there and she mentioned her phone went swimming as well." Just when I think the horrifically embarrassing scenario is over, Trey's foot slips between the door and the wall.

"Will you give her a message for me?" He asks and I hear his voice rumble with anger.

Candy nods and her usual grin has disappeared.

"Please tell her that next time I expect pictures, and that it is unacceptable for her to sleep at Nate's house," he pauses and the air feels thick with anticipation as I wait for him to continue, "or any other guy's for that matter."

I hear his heavy footfalls getting farther from the door and slowly look up from where I have collapsed on the floor.

I see Candy's grinning face and wait for it. "You have *got* to jump his bones."

And there it is.

Chapter 8

> "For a brief moment I feel a strange kinship to the predators of the animal kingdom. I realize that I am not so different from the wolves, the great cats, or the bears. Like them I find that I am possessive of what I consider mine, I long to tear into one who would dare enter my territory and I have a need to provide for the female who belongs by my side. We men deceive ourselves when we claim civility. At the core of our being, we are animals." ~Trey

It's been three days since I have been to the hospital, two days since I put a hole in my wall, one day since I worked for sixteen hours straight at the ranch. And still I burn on the inside. I have gotten in too deep, too fast. My father told me once that the men of our blood only know how to love one way: with our complete being, with the depths of our soul, with the beating of our hearts, with the marrow of our bones and with every thought that invades our minds—we love completely. It was in that same conversation that he also told me to be very careful who I gave that love to, that giving it to the wrong female would be the death of me. I didn't fully understand then, though I could see *that* love in my father's eyes when he looked at my mother. The intensity of his emotions for her was lived out in the little things that he did for her. I'm not ready to examine how deep my feelings go, not just yet, but I know that very soon I will need to face them.

I asked my grandmother to visit my mom so that I

could go and work some extra hours at Mr. Taggert's. I'm not nervous to see her; I'm not scared or insecure. Those are emotions that I refuse to feel when it comes to Tally because I have already decided that she is mine. I avoid the hospital because I am angry. It's irrational and I know that. She went out with friends and had a good time, so what? She was wearing soaking wet clothes in mixed company; it's not my business. She stayed at some guy's house because she needed to dry her clothes. It doesn't mean they were together. I have repeated these facts to myself a million times. I have tried to reason with myself, but I can't get her out of my mind. I can't let go of the feeling that it is wrong for her to be with anyone else.

"Can you spell retaining order?" I mutter to the empty house. My grandmother told me that she would give me one more day, but tomorrow I was to stop running. She told me that my spirit was restless, searching for something. I never fully understand her when she starts talking about the spirits and nature around us. But somehow, she always seems to hit the nail on the head.

I don't hesitate as I walk towards the Mercy facility. I thought about her all night. I thought long about what I would say to her, but more about what I would not say. I thought about how much I still didn't know about her and how much I wanted to know. As I lay in my bed last night, I made up my mind to find out if Tally Baker was the female who I could love completely, and would I be the one she chose?

"Hi Mildred," I smile at her as I walk past without signing in. I'm not sure why she's allowed me this leniency but I wasn't going to complain. It just meant that I might see Tally that much faster. Now for the first time it crossed my mind that she may not be visiting her aunt today, so I silently prayed to the Spirits that she was here. But first I need to see my mother. I need to talk to her and I hope that she was having a good day.

She isn't in her usual spot in the rec room so I head for her room. When I get there I find her standing in front of the window. She looks tired, I think to myself. Staring at her frail form, I feel shame wash over me at not seeing her for three days—all because of a girl. Not just any girl, I remind myself.

"What has you so troubled son?" Her voice comes out stronger than she looks.

I walk into the room and stand next to her. I smell the familiar scent of vanilla on her skin and I wonder if my grandmother has smuggled her in some lotion. She turns to look at me and I exhale as I see that her eyes are clear and bright. I want to wrap her in my arms and beg her to stay, to tell her that I can't stand to see her in bondage to a disease that I can't see and I can't save her from. I think she sees all of those emotions in my eyes because she reaches up to pat my face gently. She motions for me to sit next to her on the bed. Once she is settled she again looks at me, really looks at me and my jaw nearly hits the floor when she speaks.

"Who is she?" Her question is so matter of fact and so dead on that it takes me a moment to collect my thoughts.

"Am I so transparent?"

"You are my son; I know you better than anyone. You are just like your father—you only know one way to do things."

I smile as I nod. "All the way," I answer her statement though she didn't ask for it.

"Bly tells me that you worked sixteen hours in one day. A man who works like that only has a few reasons to be doing so: he's broke, he's running from something, or he's trying to fill an emptiness inside." I see tears gather in her eyes and my chest tightens because I don't want to hear what she will say next.

"I know that you are empty, because of me. It is only natural for a child to one day need the emptiness to be filled with a different kind of love than that of a parent. But it shouldn't happen like this." Her voice wavers and I reach out and take her hand, hoping that somehow I can give her strength.

"I don't blame you," I tell her. "I miss you, but…,"

"You need someone," she interrupts, "to be strong for you too child. You need someone you can fall apart with. You can't always be the rock, even rocks chip and break. Is she that someone?"

I close my eyes and finally say the words that just last night I had denied, words that I know can never be taken back, words given that are written on the heart that go with them.

"Yes, she's the one."

She pulls me to her and I feel like the little boy who at one time climbed up in her lap while she sang to him. My eyes sting and I clench my jaw, trying to hold back the tears because the other half of that statement is one that I won't voice.

"Don't be scared," she whispers in my ear. "I spent one day with your father during a harvest and that night when I went to sleep I knew he was the one for me. So don't think it isn't possible. Your spirit is so strong and you are so faithful. Trust in your choice, Trey. Don't trust your heart because emotions will rise and fall, but trust in the choice you have made to love her and then do it with everything inside you."

I can't remember the last time that I truly cried, but there in the middle of my mother's room, in a mental hospital in Oklahoma I weep in her arms. I wrap my arms around her and hug her. I don't know if it would be the last time that she will invite such intimacy and I treasure it.

When I finally pull back, I wipe my eyes and let out a deep, cleansing breath. There was just something freeing about telling my mother the things that I knew that only she could handle because her love for me is unconditional.

"Are you going to tell me about her now?"

I smile and I know that it's one of those absurd grins worn by smitten men.

"She's beautiful, funny, and at times very shy. She has fight in her, but attempts to keep the peace before letting it loose." It dawns on me then that my mom might have seen her because Tally was at the hospital all of the time.

"You might know her; she's up here every day visiting her aunt. Her name is Tally and she has pink streaks in her hair. She's pretty hard to miss."

My mother's face suddenly goes white and her eyes drop from mine.

"Mom what's wrong? Are you okay?" I ask her, remembering that staying calm was very important to helping her stay calm.

She swallows and then clears her throat. I can tell

that she's trying to gather herself, but I don't know what has unraveled her.

"Pink hair?" she smiles though it doesn't meet her eyes. "Yes, I have seen Tally around here. She seems sweet."

"I'll have to bring her to meet you."

"I would like that. Can I tell you one more thing before you go?" The clarity that I see in her eyes and through her words is so refreshing. At that moment I could listen to her talk forever because in that moment she was my mother.

I frown at her. "Of course, you can tell me anything."

"Every relationship has its dark times, Trey. Even your father and I had our moments. Don't give up on her during those dark times. Take time to step back and remember the choice you made. Never, ever forget that, though initially it was attraction, infatuation, and falling in love with her that brought you together, it will be the choice to keep on loving that will get you through those dark times."

"I'll remember," I tell her, and I mean it.

I glance at my watch and see that it is nearly noon. I'm not sure where to look for Tally so I go to the only place that I think she could be. When I reach Candy's room, I try to mentally prepare myself for the, no doubt, entertaining, albeit slightly embarrassing, comments. I knock on the door and then step back and wait. I hear scuffling on the other side and then the door swings open dramatically.

"Look who has finally decided to show his fine aaa...," Candy is cut off by the voice that I have so longed to hear.

"Candy...,"

I hear the warning in Tally's voice and wish that Candy would move so that I could see her.

"What?" Candy asks with an innocent bat of her eyes. "I'm just pointing out that Running Bull here hasn't bothered to grace us with his presence for a while."

Tally pushes around Candy, who gives her a dirty look and sticks her tongue out at her behind her back.

"Candy if you don't put that tongue back in your mouth I will super glue your lips shut."

Candy laughs. "Totally loving the snarky, though threatening, comments. I have taught you well!"

I look down at Tally and in the three days it has been since I saw her last I'm struck at how small she is. Her eyes dart from my face to the floor to the hall around me and I realize that she is nervous and unsure.

"I want to talk to you." I see the surprise in her eyes at my bluntness and she lets out a sharp breath when I reach for her hand and begin to gently pull her from Candy's room. I have to stop abruptly to keep from running Candy over as she steps in front of me.

"I think it would be better for you all to sit in my room," she says sweetly as she pushes on my chest.

"Why?"

"More privacy," Candy retorts and pushes harder.

I look back at Tally. "She's right."

So I turn back towards Candy's room and follow Tally, who has already stepped through the threshold. I hear the door close behind me but don't bother to check if Candy has followed us.

I watch as Tally climbs up onto the bed and pushes herself until her back is against the wall. She glances up at me and then down at her hands. I'm not really sure how to open up the conversation, but she saves me the trouble.

"How's your mom?"

The question surprises me. I had been expecting her to say something about my conversation with Candy, because I had no doubt that Candy had conveyed every detail of it to Tally.

"Today is a good day."

She smiles. "That's great."

Finally I just dive in. "How was your night out?" I try very hard not to growl the question but as her eyes snap up to mine I know I have failed.

"It was eventful." Her words drip with sarcasm and I watch her defenses go up as she folds her arms across her chest.

"What exactly does that mean?" I take a step closer.

"Why do you care?"

"Since that first day I saw you ducking behind that table you have intrigued me. And then after spending time with you, I just want more time. I want to know about you, about what you like, what you hate. I want to know what makes you smile and what causes you to have that frightened look that you sometimes get." I'm not sure at this point if my words are going to have her throwing me out of the room with her yelling at me for being the stalker I claimed not to be. "I like you Tally." My mouth says the words but my heart is screaming something totally different.

"Candy said you acted like a jealous and sexy nut

job. Those were her words," she quickly explains.

"I don't know about the sexy part, but I might have felt a little jealous."

She raises an eyebrow at me. "A little?"

"Well it might have been more than a little."

"Trey, you told Candy to tell me that I couldn't stay at guys' homes. And then you don't show up for three days, all of which I'm thinking that you've decided I'm a floozy because of my night out and now you don't want anything to do with me." Her words are sharp and cut me deep. I hadn't thought about how my actions would affect her. All I had thought about was how I was feeling and what I wanted.

"I would never think that about you Tally, I," she cuts me off before I can finish.

"To be honest I really shouldn't feel that way, I mean it's not like we are dating. Hell, we barely know each other. You don't owe me an explanation, just forget it."

I clench my jaw so tight that I'm sure I'm going to crack some teeth. The pain of her words is shredding my insides, but what was even worse was seeing the pain in hers.

"I was angry." I decide to ignore her dismissal and give her what I know she wants and needs, a reason and assurance. "I'm trying to crawl before I run, but my emotions and what I feel for you are sprinting full speed ahead." I'm so screwing this up. I pinch the bridge of my nose and squeeze my eyes closed. I need to get a grip and speak plainly, but when she looks into my eyes like she is doing now, words escape me. When I finally look up, my eyes search for something in hers, a sign that my words are not wasted on silent ears. I see her eyes narrow as she bites her bottom lip, there is life in her face; anger—yes, but she was listening.

"When I left here that day, Candy's words were like a broken record playing over and over in my mind. I tried to turn it off, but the more I tried the worse it became. I was angry because I had wanted to see you. I was angry because I couldn't stomach the idea of you with another guy. I was angry because I can't tell you what I feel. I can't ruin this before it has even begun." I tear my eyes from hers, not wanting to see the look of fear at hearing the intensity of what I feel. My chest aches and tightens as I wait for her to say something, anything.

"You didn't want me to see you angry?"

I let out a relieved breath as I hear her words, so thankful that she isn't screaming at me to get out and never come back—yet.

"I'm sorry, Tally. I should have thought about how it might make you feel, but all I could think about was you swimming with a bunch of guys and then staying with that Nate guy."

Her eyes flicker with something: guilt or shame but it's gone so quickly that I think maybe I just imagined it.

"Nothing happened, I mean, if you are wondering or whatever." she shrugs. Her lack of concern for a potentially dangerous situation ignites the flame of anger that had begun to simmer down.

"How well do you even know this Nate?" I snap, but don't give her time to answer. "And do you know what a guy is thinking when he gets a girl to sleep at his house—in wet clothes?"

She waves off my concern with a small laugh. He didn't find it funny that she could have been with a guy who took advantage of such a tempting situation.

"Nate is harmless."

"He's a guy," I counter.

"He's gay."

That pulls me up short. Tally's smile is smug as she watches my reaction.

My brilliant come back, "Oh."

Her smile fades as she bites her bottom lip and shifts uneasily on the bed. I know she is uncertain where we stand.

"I'm not leaving, not until I get what I want."

She smiles, but it's tentative, like a frightened mare unsure of whether she should make a run for it or trust the man before her.

Seconds seem to crawl as I wait for her response. Finally, she pats the spot next to her.

"What is it you want Trey?"

I move slowly, denying the urge to pull her into my arms and beg her forgiveness. I was sure that wouldn't get me what I want. I sit down beside her and slide back against the wall. The cold of it seeps through my shirt, but where my shoulder touches Tally warmth shoots through me. I wonder if she feels it as well and I have my answer when she shudders and moves closer, until our leg and hip are touching as well.

"I want you to give this a chance," I say.

"Okay," she whispers and I turn to look at her, wanting, needing to see her face after having gone three days without her.

"Now that we have that covered. I want to know you."

"What do you want to know?"

"Everything," I answer quickly.

She laughs at my obvious eagerness.

"Alright, well my name is Tally Baker. I love animals but loath sports because I'm so bad at them. I have no clue what I want to do with my life when I grow up. I live with my parents, side note, they are jerks, and I am an only child. I don't have a favorite color, I like them all. I prefer singer/song writer music. I love scary movies but won't watch them by myself. I've been kissed twice in my life and the second guy tried for second base. He stopped when he realized I was laughing at him. When he asked me why I told him that if he ran the bases like he kissed then I forfeit the game."

I cringed. "Harsh." For a brief moment I feel sorry for the guy but then I remember that she just told me he had been trying to touch her, okay now I want to kill the guy. I tell myself not to say the words that pop into my mind, but I enjoy her reactions way too much. "I'll remember that."

"That I'm harsh?" She asked and her eyes flicker with curiosity.

"No, I'll remember to make my kiss worthy of the bases."

I watch her closely and for a brief second shock has her mouth dropping open, but it is quickly replaced with the light of interest in her eyes and a wicked grin on her full, tempting mouth.

"I've upped my standards since then, so you might want to consider making that kiss worthy of the whole game."

Chapter 9

"I feel guilty for being so happy even though my mother is in a psychiatric hospital. I almost feel like I don't deserve what I have been given with Tally, even if it is a few short hours every day. I'd like to say that I'd give it up if it was the right thing to do, but saying and doing are very different things." ~Trey

"Don't even try to pick up where we left off yesterday," Tally teases me as I sit down next to her in what we have silently claimed as our spot. I hold my hands up letting her know I'm waving the white flag already and she flashes me one of her quick, but heart stopping grins. It's been one day since I apologized for not coming to see her and I kick myself for missing out on that grin during the three days I was a "no-show".

"If the bases are off limits, then what do you have in mind?" I ask as I playfully nudge her shoulder. She has never initiated any sort of touch with me, and I have never been an overly touchy person, but I am constantly looking for subtle ways to touch her, to be able to have that small privilege. But I can tell it's going to take time.

She produces a deck of cards from her back pocket. Lucky damn deck of cards, I think and then try to feel bad about thinking it, nope not going to happen.

"I figured we could play cards." She takes the deck from the box and begins to expertly shuffle them.

"What game do you have in mind?"

She laughs and I see the blush crawl up her neck. This ought to be good.

"I was thinking we could play slap jack, and for every jack you slap you get to ask a question."

"Any question?" I ask as I let my voice drop suggestively.

She shrugs and looks up at me from under her lashes as she deals out the deck. "Scared?" she asks.

"You should be," I wink at her and enjoy the effect as she pauses in her dealing.

I can see now that I could use sex appeal to my advantage in this game. It seems she is every bit as attracted to me as I am to her. Would that be unfair of me? Yes. Is that going to stop me? Absolutely not.

"Okay here's your stack," she hands me half the deck. "The rules are simple. We flip over cards from our deck and lay them face up in the center between us. If a jack comes up then the first person to slam their hand on it wins that pile and a question."

"Simple enough." I agree.

"Maybe, but are you fast enough," she says with a wink of her own.

The game begins. Back and forth, we go and it seems like forever until a jack finally is laid down.

"Got it!" she smiles as her hand rests triumphantly on the jack under mine.

Her smile is infectious and I find myself grinning even though I'm the loser. We pull our hands back from the center and she gathers all the cards up into a neat pile. That's when I notice that she is wearing bracelets at the end of her sleeves so they won't move up while she plays. Leave it alone Trey, I tell myself not for the first time.

I look back up at her face and see that her head is tilted sideways and her eyes are shifted up, thinking I presume.

"Surely there is something you want to know."

She holds her finger up at me and I use my hand to make a zipping motion across my lips. And there's the smile. I've decided that if I die today, it would be alright because I've seen her smile.

"Okay, we've pretty much asked all the typical, get to know you questions, so I had to really think about it. I'm going with, what's hanging on the walls of your bedroom right now?"

I simply stare at her, not moving my imaginary zipped lips. When she picks up on what I'm doing she rolls her eyes and reaches across the make shift table. I hold perfectly still not wanting to scare her away as her finger glide across my lips, as if to unzip them, I fight the urge to playfully bite her. I see the moment she realizes what she has done as her eyes widen and she jerks her hand back.

"Are my lips that revolting?" I ask calmly.

She shakes her head, "No, I, it's."

I let her stumble for a minute before saving her. "I have a dream catcher that my grandmother made for me."

"That's all?" she asks, her embarrassment obviously forgotten.

"Too many things on the wall make me feel closed in. I would rather be outside anyways."

"Oh," she seems to consider that, then nods, "I guess I can understand that."

Without another word she begins laying cards down again. This time only four sets are laid out before a jack comes up. I win.

I give no reaction to my victory as I pull my winnings back and join them with the stack in my hand. I'm learning things about Tally without her even having to tell me. Like, when I do not respond at what most would think is the appropriate time, instead of being uncomfortable like most are, she just waits. Unless I'm staring at her, then she fidgets. Like her, I have to think about what to ask. I know the everyday things. The things I want to know we haven't reached that point in our relationship for.

"How much do you like me?" I ask more out of curiosity of what she will say, than wanting to know if she likes me at all.

To my surprise she laughs. I was expecting blushing and squirming and maybe some stuttering, not laughing.

"I'm not sure I understand what's funny about my question."

"Ahh," she lets out a final sigh and her eyes are dancing with delight. I take a snapshot in my mind of this time and place, of that look, so I can see it again in dark times.

"What's funny, Swift, is you presume that I like you at all," one side of her mouth is quirked up in a crooked smile and they are pursed just a tad, her expression has challenge written all over it.

"Swift?" I ask.

"Well it's better than teepee boy, or totem pole—both of which are nicknames from Candy," she points out quickly.

"Agreed," I lean back against the bench and cross my legs. "Are you going to find another way to avoid the question Baker, or are you scared?" I throw her words back at her and find that I like the easy teasing that comes between us.

"I like you enough."

I turn my head to look her in the eyes and see the

blue-gray storm swirling in them. She's scared. Of me? Of her emotions? I don't know of what, but I see it there.

"That's enough for me." I tell her gently.

Our time is over for the day and she says good bye so that she can go do therapy with her aunt. I stand there, just like yesterday and watch her walk away.

"For now, Baker, that's enough for me." I say to her retreating figure.

~Tally~

I watch from the bench as Trey walks towards me. It's been two days since he apologized to me and I've almost forgotten the pain we caused each other. I decide that it should be a sin to look that good. He's wearing a t-shirt for goodness sakes, but man he is wearing the hell out of it. He has his hands in the pockets of his jeans and has on a pair of brown work boots. I don't think many guys could make a girl drool in something so plain. His hair is pulled back so I imagine he must have braided it today. Bummer, it's easier to fantasize about running my fingers through it when it's down.

I barely have time to close my mouth when he raises his head and looks at me. A small smile plays on his lips. He knows I was staring. Well it's his own fault, he shouldn't look so edible. "Hey," I say, attempting to play off the fact that I was getting hot and bothered just because he was walking, seriously Tally, who does that?

"You look lovely," his voice is deep and I would die if he knew that with everything he says, I hear 'have your way with me Trey.' Kind of like how Patty on Charlie Brown only hears the teacher say 'Whawhawha.'

I'll just keep that as my little secret.

"Thank you. I dressed up for you; I wore a black long sleeve shirt, instead of my usual black long sleeve shirt." This gets a laugh from him and I try not to close my eyes and enjoy the deep rumble. He sits down next to me, giving me my usual few inches that he seems to notice I like. I'm not sure how to correct this because truth be told that rule never applied to him. But I guess I can't very well pat my lap with a goofy grin and say 'come here boy.'

We sit there in our usual comfortable silence, well comfortable as long as he isn't staring at me.

"Tally," his voice is soft and I realize he is leaning on his arm that is draped on the back of the bench. "What is it you dream of?"

I'm caught off guard by the question. "Do you mean like a literal dream while sleeping, or do you mean a vision of what I want to happen?"

"Is it ever both?" he asks.

"Well maybe sometimes but it seems like what we dream, or at least what I dream is more fantastical than real life could ever be."

"Do you want your life to be fantastical?"

Okay he is getting deep today. I wonder if I should be worried. I'll just go with it for now but at the first sign of entering the danger zone, I will panic. I repeat I- will- panic.

"I want my life to mean something,"

He interrupts before I can finish. "Your life does mean something Tally."

I look down at my hands. I think about what is under those sleeves, and I want to cry. I want to break down right there, crawl into Trey's big, safe arms, and ask for my life to mean something to him.

"I want my life to mean something to someone else," I finish.

His eyes widen just a little at my admission. In that moment, I see the protectiveness that seems to live and breathe inside of him rise up and choose me as one he would shelter. I don't know how long we stare at one another, silent words being sent between us; it is more intimate a time than I have ever shared with another human being. He clears his throat and the moment is broken, but the connection is still there. "You never answered my question."

"I dream of living, of being whole, happy, and bold." He's quiet and I wonder what he thinks about my answer. I won't ask; I'm not wondering that hard. "What about you, Swift, what do you dream?"

Something in the way he looks away from me tells me that he isn't going to tell me the truth, or at least not the whole truth.

"I dream of a life that is real, full of all its joys and all its darkness. I dream of being complete."

Aaand that concludes our time today boys and girls, please don't stomp each other when you run for the exit. He sees that I have checked out, that my mind is in *find a hole and dig it deeper* mode.

"Tally," his voice is stern and confident. He isn't worried about hurting my feelings. He is simply gaining control of a situation where I feel out of control.

My eyes come back into focus and I'm looking into big dark brown eyes. Some of his hair has come loose from his braid and is blowing around him making him look wild and untamed. His eyes are focused and alert, but he doesn't look panicked.

"We good?" He finally asks.

I nod. And just like that, we move on.

"Good because I have a game I want to play." He smiles and there is rare, boyish quality to it.

"Why do I have a feeling this isn't going to turn out good for me?"

He simply smiles in response and pulls a black case from his pocket. As he opens the case, my eyes widen at what's inside. I can't help it; I'm laughing so hard my side hurts. This stoic, over six feet tall, stern looking guy brought me *Pass the Pigs* to play.

"What?" He asks innocently.

I finally pull myself together and shake my head, "Nothing, I'm good."

"You're ready to listen now?"

I nod.

"You're sure you're going to behave?"

Eye roll.

"We are going to play it a little differently than the conventional rules. During your roll, for every pig that lands on its feet you will have to write down something about yourself,"

"Wh," I start to interrupt not liking the sound of this at all.

"At the end of the game, you will write down your secrets and then give them to your opponent in your own time." He watches me, quietly waiting for my answer.

I know I shouldn't agree to it because I will not be able to uphold my end. Once I am released from MPF, I won't see Trey again. My body seems to ignore what my brain is telling me and I nod.

I feel like the beginning of a relationship has a lot of potential if pig throwing is a common interest.

Chapter 10

> **"There's this feeling that happens when a relationship is so new that it's even questionable that it is a relationship. This feeling of constant ache when you are apart, and then breath-stealing joy when you are together again. It's exciting and exhausting at the same time." ~Tally**

It's been two days since I essentially issued a challenge to Trey to make a kiss from him so good that I lose all inhibition and throw the game. Don't ask me why I'm sticking with baseball analogies. Right now, I can barely keep up with what is happening and why I'm letting it happen. I'm still hurt over the fact that he avoided me for three days. I haven't told him how much it affected me. The wondering, the speculating, finally telling myself that there was no way I was good enough for him. Then out of nowhere, he was back, and he came every day to just sit and talk while Candy helped us evade the staff. It has been the best two days, well, three days counting today, of my life, and undeniably the worst as well.

I throw myself down into one of the chairs of Dr. Stacey's office. At this point I'm tied up in knots, fluctuating from needing to throw up to asking for a conjugal visit. Doc is already seated across from me: cool and composed. She has a file in her lap. I wonder just how composed she would be if I told her of my two dilemmas, though I have an idea of how she would react to the visit.

"How are you today, Tally?" Her voice is calm as usual.

I look up at her, meeting her eyes and doing something that I have never done. I open up and let her in. "I'm confused, frustrated, angry, elated, excited, and scared."

Her eyebrows raise and she clears her throat before she speaks. "That's a myriad of feelings."

I'm not in the mood to deal with her open ended statements that are really disguised questions. My eyes dart around the room and my legs begin to bounce up and down. I know this feeling. I dread this feeling.

"Could you please, for once, just drop the psychobabble? I need to talk to someone who isn't going to make sexual jokes or dream up my future and how many kids I'm going to have. So please, can you be that person?" I'm hovering on the edge of a panic attack but I'm clawing at the ledge trying not to fall.

"I can do that," she eventually says, laying the folder down on the floor. She waits patiently, body relaxed, hands in her lap and eyes showing genuine interest in what I have to say.

I suck in a deep breath and the words come with it as I exhale. They pour from me like a river, its dam failing and raging water that has been set free. I tell her it's the visitor—Trey, that he doesn't know that I am a patient and that Candy has been helping me keep him in the dark. I tell her about our first meeting on the bench and about the day that Candy told him I went out swimming with friends, implying that other guys were there as well. I tell her that I'm glad he was jealous, but then he was gone for three days. I explain exactly how low and hurt I had felt. I know that I'm smiling foolishly when I tell her about our talk when he finally came back and about his honesty regarding his feelings.

I feel the words flying out of my mouth, one right after the other, and frankly some of them might be so jumbled that she misses them entirely. I cannot help it. I need to get it out, to get it off my chest so that I can breathe.

My heart speeds up as I tell her about today, about the past two days. How he had come every day and just sat with me. Sometimes we talked non-stop and then sometimes we just sat, both trying not to get caught staring at one another, until Trey ultimately just said, "to hell with it, you're beautiful and I want to stare at you." Yes, I inwardly swooned and I'm not ashamed.

Finally, all of it is out. I watch doc's face and can tell that she is searching for something un-psychobabble-ish to say.

She clears her throat before she speaks. "You like him."

Okay, so it's not the earth–shattering, squealing response I would normally get from Natalie, but I accept it. It isn't a question. But I treat it like it is. "I do. Very much."

"He's kind, attentive, funny, intelligent, and obviously very caring since he comes to see his mother every day."

I'm not catching on to why she is stating the obvious, so I just nod.

"You feel a close, strong connection to him because you have spent time getting to know one another but haven't taken the next step of becoming physical."

I frown. "Doc, this is starting to sound like babble."

"I am simply trying to understand you and because I am not the type of person to tease you with sex talk or fantasize for you about what your babies would look like. I will try to help you break down the walls and separate the feelings that are overwhelming you."

I roll my eyes and toss my hands up. "Well, you tried. I'll give you that much. So, get on with it. Examine, peel away, carve out, or whatever other description you like to use."

"You're being released in two days. You have shown that you have the ability to reasonably cope with difficult situations. You have developed relationships instead of seeking solitude. Your medicine is working. You will have a week and a half to acclimate yourself back into everyday life before you start school. You need that time, Tally. You need to see that you are in the driver's seat and the disease is no longer in control."

I sit there staring at her, unblinking, still as a statue. My mind is still stuck on the words, *You're being released in two days.* I feel as though a baseball bat, swung by the world's greatest batter, has just nailed me in the stomach. I try to catch my breath, try to get even a millimeter of air into my cut-off wind pipe. My mind is screaming at me, telling me that I should be ecstatic. I should feel proud that I have come so far from that scared, broken girl who crawled in here nearly three months ago.

"Tally!" The demanding tone of her voice snaps me back from my growing fear.

"How can you be sure that I'm ready?" I sit staring at her. My veins feel like they are filling with ice and my heart feels that at any second it will cease beating.

"You have been able to maintain a friendship with a guy that hurt you and you didn't lash out. Instead, you reacted in a rational manner. I know that it's hard, but you are taking control."

"I've lied to him so that he would think that I am normal, that I'm not some F'd up girl who cuts her arms when she can't cope anymore. How's that for rational?" My words are sharp and I'm shaking: with anger, fear, or pain. I don't know which. Possibly all of them.

"I don't think that was irrational behavior. I think that was a girl who has been rejected by her peers and her parents because of something that is beyond her control. That girl saw an opportunity to have someone see her as something other than a mental health patient."

"And that makes it okay?"

"I didn't say that," she tells me as she leans forward in her chair. Her eyes are filled with fierce determination, but also with hope. "You need to tell him the truth before you leave. He deserves that much and you need the closure. He has been good for you, even if he didn't know the truth. He has helped you to realize that you are still a human being with feelings that can be good. He gave you something nobody else has bothered or could give you."

"What?" I choke out, not realizing that tears are slowly falling from my eyes. "What has he given me?" I ask again, attempting to control my quivering lip and hiccupping breaths.

"That is for you to figure out. Consider it your final assignment." She stands up and I realize that the session is over. It's over and I still don't know what just happened. One minute I'm pouring out my heart about Trey and the next I'm told that I'm leaving.

As I leave doc's office, I walk slowly, as if on

autopilot, retreating to my room, the only place that I can call my own. As I turn the corner, my eyes land, not on my door, but on the figure standing in front of it.

Trey's mom is standing there, her arms folded across her chest, leaning against the wall as if she has nowhere else to be, which, she didn't. As I reach her, I mentally say a quick thank you to Trey for telling me her name yesterday. I try to smile and I wonder if it is convincing, but suddenly I don't care.

"Tally," Lolotea says curtly.

"Hi Lolotea, it's nice to finally meet you." I'm begging her in my mind to just go. We've met now please go. Apparently, she can't read minds.

"It is time that I speak with you." Her words sound oddly formal and I realize that I don't want to speak with her. I want to hide. I want to run. Fight or flight. Candy already pinned me as a flight kind of girl. Instead, my feet are moving of their own accord, following Lolotea down the hall.

We reach what must be her room and an ominous feeling envelopes me as she closes the door. The feeling is heavy and I think that it just might drop me to the ground.

"You are lying to my son."

Okay, we're just going to skip the pleasantries. Fine. My day has already gone to shit. Let's just top it off with a good verbal thrashing from Trey's crazy mom.

"It's complicated." I cannot believe I just said that and the tightening of her lips and narrowing of her eyes tells me that she can't believe it either.

"I may be in a mental hospital, but I am not dense. So please, un-complicate it for me."

This was not my plan for tonight and I fight the

urge to stomp my foot and tell her how I was supposed to be curled up in a ball on my bed freaking out. But I won't say that, not to Trey's mother.

"I have bipolar disorder. Everyone knows it: my parents, my friends, the entire freaking school. The fact that I am in a mental hospital is the gossip of the century. People whisper around me and refuse to look me in the eyes, like at any second I'll snap and start screaming that the voices won't shut up." I'm crying again and it pisses me off. I wipe my eyes, frantically trying to clear them, to remove the evidence of how badly all of it has hurt me, is still hurting me.

"Trey treated you normally." Her voice is softer, gentler, and when I look at her through the wetness in my eyes, I see understanding in them not the condemnation from minutes ago. "He saw you, not the disease."

My knees shake with the effort to hold my body up and I reach to the wall for support.

"He loves you."

NO, I scream inside, but outside I calmly shake my head. "No, he doesn't. He can't love me. We've only known each other a week. Plus, he doesn't know me, not really. He knows the Tally I wanted him to know."

"I disagree. He knows the Tally who doesn't have to pretend to be okay because everyone is judging her every move, her every word. He knows the Tally who is able to be exactly who she really is because, in his eyes, she is not broken. She is whole."

"But I'm not. I'm not whole."

"With him, you are."

Her words reverberate in my head as a sob escapes my erratic breathing. That's it, that's all I can take. Without looking back, I turn, fling the door open, and rush into the hall. I reach for the rationality that Dr. Stacey is so sure that I have and collect myself enough to not be a spectacle. I hold it together just long enough to reach my room. Now, all bets are off. I let the tears loose and give in to the shame of what I have done. Pain, as though a knife were plunging into my chest, rips through my heart. But would I bask in that pain? Physical pain: that I can handle. Physical pain I would welcome with open arms. But this anguish, terror, and indignity that is running through my veins, wrapped around my nerves, and invading my mind, I can't handle. This pain stays once the tears have run out. The dull ache of it stays with me like a festering wound that refuses to heal.

I don't hear the door open and only vaguely register the arms wrapping around me, offering me comfort that I do not deserve. I have no idea how long I lay on the cold floor. I don't care anymore.

"Pinky," I hear the worry in Candy's voice. "The dumbest thing a person asks in these situations is 'are you all right,' because it's obvious that you definitely aren't all right. So I have concluded a better question is, 'who do I need to kill?'"

I want to laugh, I really do, but there is no laughter in me. The laughter left once I decided to accept that what I had done was selfish, and so very, very wrong.

"Sit up, Tally." she uses her firm, *I won't take any crap*, voice. Out of habit, I obey. I lean back against the wall and she sits beside me.

We sit like that, no words, just nothing, and I feel myself putting up the walls that had taken months to tear down. It was the only way I was going survive what I knew I had to do.

"You're not going to tell him are you?" Candy

finally asks.

"I can't." My voice is hoarse from the tears and weeping. I try to clear it but it's useless.

"It doesn't have to end just because you're leaving."

"Yes, it does. He would find out the truth if we kept seeing each other."

"And that's a bad thing?" she asks.

I look over at her, feeling lost by her words.

"You of all people should understand. I would not survive seeing the revulsion, or worse, the pity, that I would see in his eyes. I'm used to seeing that look every day from my parents. I need to remember the way we have been together. I need untainted memories of the tiny bit of time I stole with him."

I can tell she wants to argue, but she stops herself and just pats my leg. "Okay," she relents. "Do you have a plan for leaving?" she asks me.

"Haven't really made it that far, yet."

"Do you want to see him one more time?"

"No." My answer is swift and rings with a finality that I can't escape.

"Today is Tuesday. You aren't leaving until Thursday." She points out unnecessarily.

"Then I guess I need to leave sooner."

I see Candy's wheels turning as she considers my words. "We'll need Zeke. Are your parents coming?"

"No, I'm eighteen, I can sign myself out, and Dr. Stacey agreed that that would probably be best."

Candy nods and then stands up, moaning and groaning and mumbling something about getting old being a bitch. "I'm going to go get Zeke, we're going to get this planned and then you are going to get some sleep."

"Yes Aunt Candy," I say as I roll my eyes and cringe because they hurt from me digging my hands into them trying to stay the tears.

~

Exactly twenty two minutes from the time Candy left my room in search of Zeke we have a plan. It sucks, but unless I'm ready to bear my shame and truth to Trey, which by the way that's a big freaking *hell no*, then this is the best I've got.

"I'm glad you're getting to leave Tally, but I'm going to miss you." Zeke's smiles at me and I wonder again how someone so large can be so gentle. He hugs me and because I'm falling apart, I hug him back. "You don't worry about a thing, Candy and I will make sure he doesn't find out."

"Thank you, Zeke," I whisper to him before I finally let go.

I look over at Candy, not really expecting any sappy words.

"You aren't really leaving tomorrow brat, so I'm not giving you any blubbering or goodbyes."

I smile at her and realize that not only am I going to miss Candy, but I was losing a piece of myself. Candy holds a special place in my heart, and so that piece will stay with her when I leave. That's what sucks about giving away your heart, whether to friends or lovers, if you love completely then you never get that piece back.

They both begin to head towards the door. "Hey," I step towards them, my head is screaming at me to shut up, but my heart is yelling louder. "Um, can you get me a piece of paper and pen?"

Candy shakes her head knowingly as Zeke reaches into his breast pocket and pulls out a piece of paper that had been folded one too many times and a pen. He hands them to me but before he lets go his eyes meet mine, "Some things only come once in a life time—remember that."

Chapter 11

"When my mom told me to remember my choice during dark times, I didn't know those dark times would come knocking at my door before my choice had even been declared."
~Trey

"I'm headed out to see mom, Shichu." I grab my keys off the counter and slip my phone in one pocket and my wallet in the other. My grandmother comes around the corner of the kitchen doorway, a single brow raised.

"Just your mother?"

"Don't start grandma," I tell her dryly.

She shrugs, "It's not my business, but you seem to be spending a lot of time with her. You haven't bothered to introduce her to your mother… or me for that matter."

I walk over to her, lean down, and wrap her in a hug. "I'm not going to rush things with her. She seems…," I take a breath trying to pick the right words, "fragile. Not all of the time, but sometimes when she doesn't know I'm watching, I see the pain that she hides from whatever it is that has caused it."

She reaches up as my mother has always done, pats my face, and looks into my eyes. "Well, if she is a wounded animal, then it is right to take it slow. Then again…," I see worry suddenly frame her features and her eyes drop, "You've dealt with so many wounds in your young life. Maybe it's time to find someone who doesn't require so much of your strength."

I feel my body tighten. There have only been a handful of times that I have been angry with my grandmother, and those moments didn't last very long, so I'm surprised to feel the rush of anger that fills me from her words.

"Our hearts don't choose their match based on the baggage they may or may not have." My words are nearly a growl. I turn to look at her as she clasps her hands beneath her chin and a smile stretches across her face.

"You would be such a fine Chief."

"You were just testing me?"

She nods. "A lesser man would agree with me. I'm glad to know that your experiences with your mother haven't warped your ability to love."

I blow out an annoyed growl and squeeze my eyes shut. When I open them, she has walked away and is humming a favorite tune.

As I'm driving to the hospital, I consider what my grandmother has said. There is definitely something in Tally's life that has caused the lost look that I sometimes see. She is too young to have something so terrible to happen and I can't imagine there is anything that would keep me from her. There isn't much that is worse than watching a disease destroy your own mother to the point that she attempts to take her own life.

As usual, my mom is in the corner of the rec room, only this time she is holding a book in her hands. When I get closer, I realize that it is a Bible. I find it odd because she has never shown any interest in the Christian religion, though she does believe there is one creator of all.

"Planning to convert?" I tease, taking a seat next to

her.

She glances up at me and there is such sorrow in her eyes.

"What's wrong mom?"

She closes the book and gently sets it in her lap, folding her hands on top. Her shoulders slump forward while she drops her head forward briefly before finally looking at me.

I can tell something is really wrong and I feel a prickle of fear crawl up my spine. "Are you okay? Do I need to get a doctor?" I'm desperate to figure out what is happening because the anguish I can feel coming from her worries me.

"No, I don't need a doctor," she answers at last.

"Okay, can you tell me what's going on?" I ask wanting her to elaborate.

"I'm just sad today. It's nothing to worry about."

She's lying to me. I don't want to upset her so I decide to let it be. The rest of our time I tell her about Tally and the conversations I've had with her.

"You look tired," I say after a long pause in the conversation.

"Yes, but I want to sit just a little longer. You go ahead and go on. I love you."

"Do you think your meds are working?"

She hesitates, but then finally nods. "Well enough, I suppose."

"Mom…,"

She cuts me off. "Trey quit worrying about me. You have enough to worry about."

"Okay," I tell her as I reach over and hug her. I stand, glancing back once while I walk out of the rec room. I only have a second to consider mother's last statement when Candy's door flies open even faster than usual and she storms out.

"We need to have a powwow," she tells me gruffly.

"Can it wait until after I see Tally?"

Candy gives me a look that shouts, *you did not just say that* and then adds, "If I thought it could wait til after you see Tally I would have said, 'Hey we need to powwow, *after* you see Tally.'" Turning away from me, she cups her mouth and yells, "Zeke!"

The big man that generally sits at the back doors comes striding towards us. His usually smiling face is masked now with a tight jaw and narrow eyes.

"Candy, I'm not asking. I want to see Tally, now." I start becoming agitated with her, but I tell myself *I've never man-handled an old lady and I don't want to start now.*

I am trying to think of reasons that Candy would have for doing this and one hits me, "Is she alright? Has something happened to her?" When she doesn't answer, I ask another question that occurs to me, "Have I done something?"

"Well if you did, I hope you at least enjoyed it." she cackles at her joke and then grabs my arm and turns us in the opposite direction of Zeke. With his long stride, it doesn't take long for him to catch up. Candy's footsteps quicken and I'm surprised that she can keep up with my own long strides, but she doesn't seem to even be out of breath. As we turn a corner, I realize where we are. The pair is leading me to the back doors, to the bench where Tally and I always sit. Maybe Tally is waiting there for me and Candy insists on playing a joke on me to make me think that something is wrong. That is, after all, something Candy would do.

As soon as we are at the doors, Zeke reaches around me, pushes it open, and Candy tugs me through the passage. The bright summer sun makes it hard to see and my eyes take a second to adjust. When I can see what's around me, I definitely don't see a girl named Tally. Now I'm just plain pissed. "Where's Tally?" I snap at Candy. I see Zeke take a step closer to me and turn my head to look at him.

"There is nothing about you I fear, so you can give up the scare tactics." He must see truth in my eyes because he simply shrugs and steps back. His face relaxes as he folds his arms across his broad chest.

I turn back to Candy and see that she's holding out a worn, folded piece of paper. I feel my stomach drop to my feet and I know that I don't want to take that paper. I don't want to know what it says and I know that is irrational because it's just a piece of paper, right?

"Take it, Trey," Candy tells me with an unusually kind voice.

My eyes snap up to hers and the sorrow in them tells me everything that I need to know.

"Where is she, Candy? I'm not playing around. Where is she?" My jaw tenses and I feel every muscle in my body become rigid. There I stand, Candy's own personal Indian Totem pole, staring at a piece of paper that is going to crush me.

"Please, Trey, she wanted you to have it. Please don't make this any harder. Just take the paper and go." Candy's words sound like they're coming through a tunnel as I hear the blood rushing through my veins. My heart pounds in my chest and I feel it all the way to my throat. She continues to speak, but I can't hear her over the throbbing. Then a word finally breaks through the noises in my head. *Gone*. I heard the word gone.

"Wait." I shake my head, waiving my hand in front of her. "What did you just say?"

Candy huffs, "I said she's gone. You asked. I'm

telling. So would you please take this damn piece of paper so that I can go terrorize the delusional patients who are playing Bingo?"

I reach out to take the paper and feel as if I am moving in slow motion. I feel every movement from the extension at my elbow all the way to my hand's grasping motion and then I feel the paper's texture in my fingers and a burning sensation making me want to drop it but not being able because it's from *her*.

I unfold it slowly, hoping that the worn creases do not tear. I see my name hastily scrawled at the top. Knowing she thought of me when she wrote it makes my mouth and throat begin to feel like sandpaper as I try to swallow. My eyes drift slowly down, not wanting to get to the other words that I know are there. I notice splotches all over the paper that could only be from her tears. My jaw tenses and I squeeze my eyes closed. I have to force my hands to relax so that I don't crush the note. With nowhere else to look, I land on her words.

Trey,

There is so much I need to tell you, but I can't. I've known you all of a week and all we ever did was sit on a bench at the back of a mental hospital and talk, yet ours was the most meaningful relationship I have ever had. I will never know what I am to you, but I figured out what you are to me, what you give me, and it's something that only you could. You gave me hope. It may not sound like much, but it could mean the difference between life and death. With you, I was able to really be me. Because of you I know that when I can't find the real, whole, untarnished Tally, it doesn't mean that she is gone.

This might freak you out because you barely know me. And I wish that I could see your face when I say it, but I can't, so I'm saying it anyways.

I love you Trey Swift
Y.A.~ Tally

I stand there reading the letter over and over hoping maybe it will change and say something different. I finally look up from the letter and realize I'm alone. I look back down with frustration that she hasn't left an address or phone number, something…anything. I know she felt what I did when we were together. Why would she not even at least want to keep in touch and where the hell was she going? She never mentioned moving. I feel anger stir as shock begins to fade and realize that she didn't explain in her letter why she left. My body freezes as I look at the back doors. There is one person who would know everything because she makes *everything* her business.

I'm trying to get my raging emotions under control and a little surprised that I'm responding this way. *Are you really?* I ask myself. Fine then. I'm reacting exactly as a man who has just lost his world.

I reach Candy's closed door and knock on it a little harder than normal etiquette dictates.

The door opens, but only wide enough for Candy to squeeze out. She pulls it closed tightly behind her and slaps on one of her many smiling faces, choosing one that basically says *why are you still here?*

"I need her address or phone number. Preferably both." Being the man of the house for so long now, I have learned that you get more accomplished when you tell instead of ask.

"Why would I have that information?" she asks. I notice that she seems even more restless than the other times that I have seen her. She scratches her leg and then tugs at her shirt as if to make sure it is on straight.

"Because you are her aunt and you seem very close to her. Surely you plan to keep in touch with her." My eyes narrow at her and I get that stabbing feeling in my neck that I have been played.

"Yes, well, we had a falling out. There was yelling, scratching, all sorts of name calling, and then, just like that, she was giving me the finger and walking out of here." She folds her arms on her chest and begins tapping her foot as she looks up at me.

"You do realize that I'm not that dumb, right?" I start to clench my hands, only to remember I'm still holding Tally's letter. I fold it up, slowly using the time to get my ire in check.

"What harm…?" I start but she cuts me off holding her hand in the air.

"Look, I didn't want to have to tell you this. You seem like a nice guy and I'm sure you have an incredible teepee, but Tally didn't want you to have her number. She said it's over, a summer thing. She starts school back soon and she needs to get ready for the stress." Candy cringes and bites her bottom lip. She obviously thinks she's said too much.

"That's an awful lot of crap, Candy. How did you fit all of it in your mouth?" I mock. My control is gone. Candy, and Tally for that matter, are trying to play me like a fool.

Candy suddenly bends over and at first, I think something is wrong but then I realize she is laughing, correction, hysterically laughing. She stands with tears from her laughter running down her cheeks. Several seconds later she lets escape a contented sigh, "Oh, man, that was so good. I mean, that was like something I would say." She lets out a breath and another chuckle, "It's a shame," she says shaking her head.

"Tally might very well have said those things. If she did, she was lying to herself and me. There is no way she only thought of me as a summer thing." I can feel my chest tightening as I allow myself to briefly consider it but dismiss it just as quickly. I know that Tally didn't think of *us* as just killing time.

"Damn it!" Candy snaps and stomps her foot. She sets her jaw and stares directly into my eyes. "I'm not going to let you leave here wondering or thinking she didn't care." She leans forward and motions for me to bend closer. She puts her mouth close to my ear and whispers softly, "It may take a little bit for her to realize that she can't live without you; she can't breathe without you."

Candy steps back and has her annoyed look back in place, she clears her throat and then points to the exit. "Do what you gotta do, Tonto! Personally I think she's a squaw worth fighting for."

"It usually helps to know who your opponent is," I say, ignoring her references.

"Tally is fighting herself, and a past that might as well be plastered on a damn billboard, and you are fighting Tally." She explains ticking them off on her fingers.

"I'm fighting Tally to have her?"

Candy's eyes widen and then I realize how that sounded.

"You know what I mean, Candy. How do I fight her to keep her? Seems like a futile battle."

"You know how we tell kids that they don't know what's good for them?"

I nod.

"This is one of those situations, only we're dealing with an almost adult woman who has assholes for parents, only one friend she can trust, and self-esteem the size of the hairs on a flea's butt." She takes a deep breath and just keeps going, "Those things might not seem like a big deal, but there are other factors that can make those things unbearable. Now I've said way too much and if my niece finds out, she will gut me in my sleep.

 I step out of my truck and out onto the dusty road the Taggerts live on. With the sound of the creaking door slamming closed behind me, I look up and for the life of me can't remember driving here. I remember Candy telling me to leave and shoving me in the direction of the front doors. She wasn't unkind about it. I think she was worried that I was going to lose it. She wasn't far off the mark. I remember getting in my truck and reading her letter again. I look down at my right hand and see that my knuckles are bleeding; I vaguely remember punching the dash board. But from there on, I don't remember. It was like I was on autopilot.

 I head towards the horse stalls. I'm glad to be doing something, especially something that would take a lot of energy. Mr. Taggert let me know the day before that he had square bales of hay he wanted stacked. That was fine with me. Throwing something, even seventy-five pound bales of hay, was better than just sitting and thinking about Tally.

 I was dripping with sweat by the time I threw the last bale. It had worked for the most part; Tally had only come to mind every ten unbearable seconds instead of the excruciating five. What was even more ridiculous about my reaction to her leaving was that I hadn't even held her hand, hadn't kissed her, hugged her, or run my fingers through her hair. I didn't even know what she smelled like. But that's how strong our connection had been. Just being near her, listening to her talk and laugh, she was such a bright spot in my day. I was able to talk with her about my mom and I wasn't afraid to tell her my fears, my anger, and my worry.

"Five damn days, Trey," I growl into the empty barn. "Five days and I did exactly what my father warned me not to." I close my eyes and hear my father's voice. I respond as if he can hear me. I gave my heart to a woman who I believed could love me just as completely and she just might be the wrong woman.

She might be the right one, the voice counters. My eyes snap open. There is no way that I just heard my father's voice. No, I reason, it has to be because I want him here, need him here to tell me what to do.

When the eagle goes hunting, he does not expect to catch his prey quickly. He is patient and he chooses carefully the one he will take. Then he watches, follows, and watches some more. This can go on for days. He is patient, waiting for the right time to swoop in and take it.

My eyes widen and my mouth falls open. I try to reason out how on earth my father's voice just said something that my father would indeed say. In fact, I'm pretty sure he's said it to me before. "Dad?" I ask out loud, waiting for it. Several minutes tick by and still no voice. Deciding not to examine it right then, I decide instead to focus on what he said and what he is trying to tell me to do. It's very straightforward, but also very eye opening. Tally is who I have set my sights on; she is the one, out of all the others, that I have chosen. He's telling me to be patient and to realize that what we want the most in life does not come easily.

The revelation does not take the hurt away. The ache that has made itself comfortable in my chest is there still. But it's given me perspective. Candy said that Tally couldn't breathe without me, so at some point she's going to need air, and that means she is going to need me. And whether she knows it or not, I need her.

Chapter 12

"Have you ever done something, and literally two seconds later realized that it was the wrong something? That's not when I realized it. I realized it the moment that I met Trey Swift. I realized that ever walking away from him would always be the wrong something." ~Tally

"Tally, you've been sitting in that same spot since Running Eagle left. You have got to get up."

I pull my head up from where it lay on my knees. My eyesight is blurry from tears, so I blink several times before she finally comes into focus.

"I know. I'm sorry, Candy. I can go back to my room." My movements are slow and my muscles ache from the intensity of the last few hours.

"What time is Nat picking you up?"

"The earliest she would agree to was eight, and that was after begging."

Before I make it to the door, Candy suddenly wraps me in a hug. It catches me off guard because Candy, like me, only touches out of necessity.

"I don't do goodbyes. So don't expect me to be standing outside waving to you, saying good luck, throwing rice, and what not?"

"Rice is for weddings, not leaving mental institutes, you old bat." I'm trying to sound playful, but with my voice dry and hoarse, I only sound like an old smoker.

"Brat," she mutters.

We step back from the hug at the same time and I see Candy's eyes glistening. She looks away and wipes nothing from the wall. "We didn't get to do all the things on the 'really live' list," she pauses and eventually looks back at me. "You do them, Tally. You go out there and really live. If not for yourself, then for those of us stuck here, trapped in our minds. I know you're scared that you will have to come back. You won't. You're young and you've started treating it so young. You fought the worst of it and you won. Just stay in front of it, okay?" she takes a step back not realizing that she had moved closer to me. I see the pain and loss in her eyes and I don't know what to say, so I don't say anything. Sometimes that's best, to just not say a thing. I pat her gently on the arm and turn the door knob. Just as I step in the hall, I hear her say, "I expect pictures, and I don't mean boring ones with you and your friends painting your toes. Make'em good ones."

    It's seven fifty in the morning. I have not slept at all and for some reason I can't get my legs to stop bouncing up and down as I sit on the edge of my bed. I haven't cried since I left Candy's room last night. I don't know if it's a defense mechanism or if I have simply run out of tears.
    I hear a knock on my door and jump up so quickly that I fall forward but catch myself before planting myself face first. "Stand up much?" I mutter.
    I pull the door open slowly. The reality that I'm leaving has really sunk in. There is relief, a little, but mostly there is fear and the dull ache of love lost.
    Nat's smiling face is on the other side of the door.

"You ready to blow this joint?"

Her perky voice and cheerful face make me want to vomit, preferably on her. Then we'd see how perky she would be. Holy crap! Did I just think that? I feel my heart speed up as I consider that maybe I'm not ready. Maybe I only seemed ready because of Trey.

With him I *felt*, sounds weird I know. But before him, I was surviving, *just* surviving. The meds are working, yes. I haven't been crying all the time, recent events notwithstanding. I haven't had the urge to play 'cut the crazy girl.' I'm eating, sleeping, and socializing even though it's been mostly with the black sheep of the hospital. I've been doing everything they needed to see in order to release me. But I didn't feel anything, not until him. In my letter to Trey, I had told him that I figured out what he gave me and I meant it. So why am I feeling like this if I have hope?

"Tally? Hello?"

I turned to look at her and realize that she's asking me a question. Okay, Tally, I tell myself, put on your big girl panties, and, as Candy would say, 'add a garter just in case and go back to your life.'

"What did you ask?" I lean in so she knows I really am listening.

"Is this all you have? Just the one bag?" She looks mortified that I didn't have a year's worth of clothes to choose from every day.

"Yes, Nat, just the one."

She stands up straight and looks at me, really looks at me. It's a rare moment for her not because she doesn't care, she's just easily distracted.

Her lips tighten into a straight line and she pulls her shoulders back, "You're going to be okay, you know. And I'm not saying that because I want you to be different or get over it, or whatever other crap your parents spew. I'm saying it because you are my best friend. We've made it through tough times; we will make it through this." She follows her statement with a curt nod.

I'm touched and I know she means every word, but I know something she doesn't. I'm tired of being just okay and there is only one person who makes me better than just okay.

I'm surprised when Dr. Stacey comes out of her office and gives me a hug. I'm going to see her once a week for a month and then she said the sessions won't be so close together, so a goodbye isn't really necessary. As Candy promised, she is nowhere in sight. I feel that absence already in my heart.

The drive to my house is a quiet one and I appreciate that Nat seems to know that I need that silence. As she pulls into my driveway, I gather my bag and purse, ready to climb out. Her hand on my arm stops me. She has tears in her eyes and she bites her bottom lip trying to hold it in. I know that feeling well.

"You okay?" I ask.

"I just want you to know that I'm so glad you're home. And I don't think any differently of you. You are still my Tally, whether you're smiling or not, okay?"

I swallow back tears of my own. Apparently, I haven't run out.

"Oh, and I bought a book."

"A book?"

"About bipolar disorder. I don't want it to be the elephant in the room with us, Tal. It is what it is. You have bipolar disorder and I want to know how to help you and when I can. I mean, I've read some of it already and I know there are going to be times that I can do absolutely nothing and that's okay, but I won't know if I don't understand." She's talking fast which is something she does when she's nervous. I'm looking at her wondering where my flighty best friend went. She squirms in her seat and once again, I'm just sitting in silence.

I say, "Thank you," but it sounds so inadequate to my ears, "I mean it, Nat. I don't want it to be awkward either. It's going to be hard enough with my parents."

The smile is back and though I can't return it, I hope she sees the gratefulness in my eyes.

"It's okay. I know. You have more going on than just your BP, and I have a feeling it has to do with a certain tall and yummy guy you met."

"Yeah," I nod. "I'll talk to you about it. Just not today, okay?" I say tentatively.

"Okay. I'm here when you're ready."

Impulsively I reach over and pull her into a hug. I need this. I need someone who would accept that this is me now. She hugs me back and I hear her sniffle. The hug ends and there's something different between us, something stronger.

"I'll text you later," I tell her as I climb out of her car.

"Sounds good." she waves and backs out of the driveway.

I turn to look at the large house that my attorney parents bought even though they only have one child. I love my parents, I do, but somewhere along the way they got caught up in the lawyer way of life: work too many hours, stay after and have a few drinks to unwind, wake up early to get to court or wherever they need to be, and repeat. It's why they didn't notice my slide into depression and it's why they won't be any help in what Dr. Stacey calls 'shoring up.' Basically, 'shoring up' is building a support system. Have people around me that I trust, people I can call if I get into a crisis situation, people that care. "Well, crap. I left all those people at the damn mental hospital," I tell the empty yard. The humor lasts about ten seconds and then I realize exactly how alone I am.

I knock on the front door and then turn the knob. It's open. I step in and I'm a little creeped out that nothing has changed in three months. I mean, I don't know what should have changed, but it's almost like even the dust hasn't moved, like the house is holding its breath. I square my shoulders trying to fortify myself to face my parents.

"Mom?" Even though I don't say it very loud, it sounds like I've yelled into the high ceiling that travels up with the staircase. I walk towards the kitchen, my footsteps too loud to my ears. The silence is making the hair on my neck stand and my palms are beginning to sweat. My eyes land on the kitchen counter on the little pink paper that has a B at the top of it. I have to bite my cheek to keep the tears from coming. Now I wished I had run out of tears. I snap up the paper from the counter and see my mother's unusually pretty handwriting for an attorney:

Tally,

Dr. Stacey called us and told us you would be coming home today and your father and I are so sorry that we couldn't be home. We both had to be in court and it wasn't something that we could

reschedule. I hope you understand. There's some money for you in your room along with your car keys. You know the rules, be home by curfew. Love you,
    Mom

As soon as I read the last word, I drop the paper and run for the foyer bathroom. I get the lid up just in time to throw up. I groan when I realize my hair has fallen forward. "Ugh, gross," I mutter. You know you've hit rock bottom when you have no one hold your hair while you puke. I'm not sure if I'm done yet, so I don't get up. I've come home from being gone three months, and not on some vacation or summer camp. I've come home from a freaking mental hospital and my own parents aren't home to greet me. How's that for building a support system?

After several vomit free minutes, I slide down on the floor and lean back against the wall. The cold of the tile seeps through my jeans and I fight back a shiver. I'm really not sure what to do and that's beginning to bring on the familiar shortness of breath and clammy skin.

"Okay Tally, think about what you learned. What do you do when there's no plan, no order?" I'm talking out loud now because I can't stand the quietness. I'm so used to the noise of the hospital that the lack of it is suffocating.

"A list. She said to make a list of things that I need to do and then mark them off one by one." The other tidbit that doc shared with me about the list is to only leave one task showing at a time because there are days when just looking at a list can cause you to just give up and go to bed. I push myself up to my feet, wipe my mouth on the hand towel, and then head back to the kitchen. I grab the pink letter my mother left me and flip it over quickly so that I don't have to see her words again. There's a pen lying haphazardly nearby as if she had written the note quickly and then tossed it down.

"Okay, what do I need to do?" I ask out loud. I click my tongue as I think of something.

One: Stop talking to yourself

I chuckle as I think about Candy and what she would say to that, "but it freaks people out and that is totally worth being deemed crazy."

Focus, Tally. I don't say this out loud. I tap the pen against my cheek and try to get my thoughts in some semblance of order.

Two: Shower

The longer I stare at the paper, the more frustrated I get at not having anything to write down. Finally, I drop the pen. I've already accomplished number one, so it's time to take care of number two. I let out a small laugh as I realize how that sounds. "Take care of number two, that's awesome."

Damn, I think, maybe number one is going to be more difficult than I thought.

~

Clean body, clean hair, and clean clothes, that about covers it. Holy crap! I'm an old person. I'm ticking off the little things I have to do and the most difficult one is to not talk to myself.

I sit down on my bed and pick up the money, my keys, and my phone. I stare down at them in my hand. I have a choice: go out and be social or curl up in the bed

I haven't slept in for three months and let sleep swallow me. For most teens my age, it's a no-brainer. Go out, duh. But for me, the bed is looking very nice. I'm about to set the contents in my hand on my bedside table when the song "Stronger" by Kelly Clarkson comes blaring out of my phone. I smile because I know that Nat had to have been the one that programmed it. I look at the screen and sure enough, her silly face is on it.

"Hey," I answer.

"Hey, I know you just got home, but I was wondering if you wanted to have a sleep over." She laughs, "That sounds so 'junior high', doesn't it?"

"Regardless of how it sounds, yes, I would like that," I tell her and inside I do a teeny, tiny dance. Don't judge. I'm celebrating my little victory.

"Your parents won't care?"

I swallow hard to keep from blubbering all over the phone. "They aren't here."

I have to hold the phone away from my ear to keep from busting my ear drum as Nat breaks into a string of expletives.

"What happened to your parents, Tal? They weren't always asshats." She finally says now that she has calmed down... somewhat.

"I don't know. They just both have really busy jobs." The excuse sounds lame, but it's all I have.

"I'm going to head over now, so I'll see you in a few."

"'Kay, see ya." I hit the end tab on my phone and take a deep breath and let it out. We've never been a religious family, but in this moment, I am saying thank you to God for Natalie. *You could have had Trey, too,* I hear that little voice that sometimes pops up at the most inconvenient times, and I shake my head. No, I answer. I couldn't have had him. If he found out I was actually a patient at Mercy, he would have turned for the hills and not looked back.

I realize I have another thing to add to my list:
Three: Don't respond to the nagging little voice
Nice.

~

"Can I just say that your parents are asshats"? Nat tells me as she flops onto my bed.

I laugh, "You already have. Twice."

"Oh… Well I'm sure I'll say it more. You should make an asshat jar. That way every time I point out they're asshats, a dollar goes in the jar." She looks pleased with herself and I find myself smiling. It's small, but hell, it's a smile, and that means a victory dance. Of course, I don't bust out dancing in the middle of my room.

"What are you smiling about?" she asks me.

I think about it for a minute, then shrug. She said she wants to know and learn, so here goes.

"I'm doing an inner victory dance," I tell her and hold my breath, waiting for the laughter to come. It doesn't.

"What's the dance for?" she asks and I can see in her eyes that she's genuinely interested. She's not laughing. Man, three victory dances in a few hours. That's got to be a record or something.

"Get comfortable," I tell her as I stretch out on my stomach on my bed, head propped up on my hands. "You're fixing to get the Cliff notes on pretty much every therapy session I've been in."

~

"Wait," Nat interrupts me for the umpteenth time in the last forty-five minutes. I'm surprised to realize that she really wants to know what is going on with me. What's even stranger is that I *want* to tell her.

"You actually told your psychiatrist that you had lied to Trey? *And* that he thought you were skinny dipping with mixed company, but really you were rescuing an old, crazy lady from a pond?"

"Yeah, but I didn't tell her the part about Candy and going on our little field trip."

"So what happened with Trey?" She asks, "Did he come back?"

I told her about how he stayed gone for three days and enjoyed her gasps.

"That was such a butthead move," she says, "but it definitely doesn't rise to the level of asshat."

I giggle and continue. But then I tell Natalie how he treated me the last three days we were together and she says that he is forgiven.

I'm getting to the difficult part and I'm not sure that I am ready to relive those feelings.

"Did you tell him you were leaving?" she asks and takes the choice right out of my hands.

I shake my head, "I would have had to tell him the truth. Nat, you don't understand how amazing it was for someone to treat me like a normal person."

Her face falls and I realize how my words sound.

"No, I didn't mean that you don't. You totally do.

You've been great. It's just that he isn't tainted by the memory of what I looked like, you know, on that day." I grind my teeth and stuff the memories back into the cage. Dr. Stacey has been pulling them out gradually, but I keep the ones we haven't dealt with safely locked up in that place in my mind, that place we all have and that we all avoid.

She reaches over and takes my hand and gives me a reassuring smile, "I get it. He's your 'you had me at hello' guy." I smile at the reference she uses to describe what she believes is another person's soul mate. I don't know what I believe, but I know that what Zeke said was true. Trey was a once in a lifetime kind of love.

"I left him a letter," I look up at her and then back down at my hands. I realize that the sleeves of my shirt have ridden up a little and Nat hasn't once looked at them. I tug the sleeves back down anyway.

"Go on; give me the cliff notes of that, as well," she says as she motions with her hand for me to continue.

"I told him what he means to me and what our relationship did for me. He gave me hope, Nat. Hope that I can have normal relationships that I can live, really live. And I told him that I love him."

There are tears in her eyes. "That's the most beautiful thing ever. You could totally make a movie about it. And it would be awesome, accept for the lead chick who is a dumb ass."

Okay, not what I was expecting. "What?"

"If he is as wonderful as you say he is, he would still have wanted you. He doesn't sound like the type to judge. And it sounds like he was good for you and in case you forgot, you don't have a whole lot of good in your life right now. I mean, I'm *it*, Tally and I love you with all my heart, but I won't be enough."

I think back on Dr. Stacey's words. *"The medication is only ten percent of controlling the disease. The other ninety percent is you choosing to fight."* The sound of her voice is so clear in my head it's as if she is sitting right in front of me. *"Tally, bipolar disorder is something you have, not something you are. You control it, not the other way around and the way to do that is to keep people around you who can help you see signs that your sliding too far one direction or the other."*

"You're right, Nat, I know you love me, but I'm going to need more than one person."

"Correction, Batgirl, we are going to need more people. We are a package deal, okay? Well, except for guys."

That makes me laugh.

"Tally," her voice is softer now, "I need you to know something."

"Okay, it can't be worse than what I've been through, so quit worrying and just tell me." I try to sound light hearted to ease her nerves.

"Dr. Stacey called me at the beginning, when you went to Mercy. You're parents gave her permission to talk to me. She told me that she wanted me to considerably limit visits and phone calls. I didn't like it, but she explained that even though we are best friends and she knows that I don't see you any differently. At that point, I was a reminder of what had happened and who had been there. She just wanted the best for you. That's why I didn't call much or come see you." She looks at me and I know she is waiting to see if I'm going to be upset.

"I was never angry at you about not coming around much. I figured you were working and busy and that was okay. I didn't expect your life to go on pause just because mine did."

She lets out a relieved breath. We both become statues as we hear the garage door opening. My parents are finally home. Woo-hoo.

"Just so you know, I'm staying tonight even if they don't like it." Nat snaps, though I know it's not directed at me.

"Thank yous" just don't seem adequate anymore, but I say it anyway.

I hear the familiar click of my mom's heels on the stairs and my dad's deep voice as well. Wonderful, they've decided to make a dual appearance. I sit up and the tension that Nat had helped relieve was back in full force. My spine is straight, my chin jutted forward, and my lips stretched in a thin line across my face. I imagine if my eyes could shoot lasers, now would be the time they would be fully operational. There is a small tap on the door and then it opens as usual without my saying to come in.

I see my mom's face first and a small part of me wants to run to her and beg her to never leave. But that part was smaller than the part telling me to protect myself from rejection.

She smiles, and for a slight moment, I think I see fear in her eyes. Then she opens her arms. It would be rude not to hug her so I get up and let her wrap her arms around me. To my surprise, it is a fierce hug, like she's trying to convey to me what she can't say with words. When she finally lets go of me, I see that she has put her mask back on. The 'we are a perfect family, no crazy daughters live here' mask. My dad steps around to stand beside her and I can see that he is uncomfortable. He shifts from side to side on his feet and looks everywhere but at me.

"We're glad that you're here." he says.

I look behind me at Nat and then back to my dad. I can't really figure out if he's talking to me or her.

"Er, I'm glad to be here?" I say though it comes out more as a question.

"How are you feeling?" my mom asks tentatively and I wonder if she's worried that I'm going to suddenly start screaming that the voices are telling me to write 'red rum' in red lipstick on the mirror.

"I'm alright," I finally say honestly and realize that in that moment it's true. Ask me in five minutes and my answer might change.

"Hi, Mr. and Mrs. Baker," Nat says cheerily from behind me. "I think it's great that Tally is home. I'll probably be spending a lot of time with her, since we have school starting in a little over a week. We're going to be planning evacuation plans and crisis intervention times. Just a little planning ahead."

I'm biting my cheek so hard to keep from laughing, but it is extremely difficult. From the seriousness in Nat's tone to the look of utter shock on my parent's faces, really, it's a moment I wish could be captured on film.

"She's kidding, Mom," I say, trying to sound flippant about the whole thing.

"You are welcome here for as long as you want, Natalie." My mom smiles and my dad just sort of mumbles his agreement. "Okay, well we don't want to intrude. Is there anything you need, Tally, anything we can get you?"

She's trying, I tell myself. Cut her some slack. She's my bloody mother, she shouldn't have to try. It should just come naturally, I argue. Great, now I'm arguing with myself *while* others are in the room. Way to show that you're sane, Tal.

"Thanks, Mom, but I think I'm good."

"Oh, alright. We'll just leave you to it then." As my mom is closing the door behind them, I hear her whisper to my dad, "You could have said something more." I don't hear his reply, nor do I think I want to.

"So where were we?" Nat asks as soon as the door is shut.

"Well, according to you we are devising ways to insure that I don't let my alter ego loose on unsuspecting students and faculty."

"Oh, that. Naw, no worries there. We were talking about Trey. Tall, delicious, *going to get him back*, Trey."

I'm already shaking my head before she even finishes her sentence. "Nope. I've already told you why I can't. Not to mention, I don't even know where he lives."

"Maybe not, but you know where he goes every day. Not to mention, did you find out if he is in our senior class?"

My insides immediately freeze. "He's eighteen. He's done with school."

Nat frowns, "Is that what he told you?"

"N-n-not exactly." I stutter realizing the mistake I made.

"Then what did he tell you?"

"Oh, crap," I groan. "He told me his age, but never if he was in school. I told him I was going to be a senior. I just assumed that since he was eighteen,"

"You know what assuming does...," Nat starts.

"I know that if you finish that statement you're going to get a boot in your mouth." *Or a dollar in the jar,* I think.

She laughs. My threats have never accomplished their intended goal with Nat. Probably because she knows I would never follow through, at least not with her.

"Okay, so here's what we know," she raises her hand, "you've met your match," ticks off a finger, "you want him, he wants you," tick, "said match quite possibly will be joining us in our senior year."

"That about sums up the coming disaster," I say as I lay flat on my bed and cover my eyes with my arm. "My only hope is that he is already graduated, or that my parents suddenly decide to move."

"Not happening while I'm still breathing," Nat says dryly. "What are you going to do when he shows up on the first day of school?"

"What I do best," I peek out at her from under my arm, "flight."

She shakes her head at me, "Not this time, Tally. This time you are going to stay and fight. You deserve something good and good things come to those who fight."

"I thought it was good things come to those who wait?"

"Yeah, yeah, whatever. The point is you aren't going to crawl in a hole and lick your wounds or become a chicken just because you've had some tough things happen."

"When the hell did you become the voice of reason?" I grumble.

"When you went bat shit crazy."

A small smile lifts my lips, "Oh, yeah. Good point."

Chapter 13

"I don't have anything profound or eye-opening to say. What I feel right now is very simple, but very painful. I miss her; I want to see her. I want to know she's okay, I need to know she's okay." ~Trey

"Tomorrow I won't be by until the afternoon, Mom," I tell her as I sit next to her in the rec room of MPF, "remember, because I start school."

She nods but her eyes are blank. The nurse told me that she had a rough night and it was blaringly obvious in the exhaustion written across her face.

"You're sad," she tells me, and it's something she has said every day this week.

"Just got a lot on my mind."

She reaches over and pats my hand. "She will come back to you."

I smile at her though I know it doesn't show in my eyes, because the eyes are the window to the soul and my soul is lost.

"Mom, are you okay?"

She looks away from me and I watch as she mumbles something under her breath, but she isn't speaking to me. She isn't speaking to anyone *I* can see. I reach out and take her hand. She jumps a little but doesn't pull it away. I sit two feet from my mother, but she is in another world in her mind, a world I can't enter and a world that she can't seem to escape.

"Can you hang in there for me? Just let the doctors get your medicine worked out." I know that my words aren't getting through. She looks up suddenly and she looks frightened.

"I don't think that's a good idea." she says.

"Mom, who are you talking to?" I ask gently.

"They're back," she whispers. "They followed me here and I've been ignoring them. I promise, Trey. But I'm so tired."

She won't let me pull her close so I just hold her hand and sit with her to let her know that I'm real, and I'm with her and not going anywhere. She clings to my hand and I watch as she shakes, staring at nothing and being terrified of it. I see the nurse out of the corner of my eye and know that they are going to give her a sedative before she becomes too upset.

I lean close to her ear before they give her the shot and whisper, "You aren't alone, no matter what they tell you. I love you and need you here with me. Remember that."

I think she nods, or maybe it's just that I hope it so badly that it's what my mind tells me I see. Maybe her mind isn't the only one upon which tricks are being played.

~

As I walk down the hall towards the front desk, I hear my name, or one of the names Candy claims is mine.

"Tonto," she grins as I turn and I see her walking up the hall towards me. She's wearing the hospital issued scrubs, but instead of shoes, she has on slippers that look like sharks. She looks down at her feet and then back up at me. "It really wigs them out when I start singing the *Jaws* theme music."

I smile at her and for a brief moment, feel a small amount of relief because being near Candy makes me feel close to Tally. Crazy, yes, but then look where I'm standing.

"How's your mom doing?" she asks. It feels weird for her to ask such a normal question without adding a typical Candy tag to it.

"Today's not a good day," I tell her honestly.

"I'm sorry to hear that."

"At the risk of sounding like a pathetic loser," I grin halfheartedly, "have you… heard from Tally, that is."

She's shaking her head before I even finish, "I haven't heard from her. I wish I could tell you I have. Turns out I miss the brat."

"She's not really your niece is she?"

Candy looks away from me, but I see the truth. "Trey…"

"It can't be good Candy if you're calling me by my given name."

She smiles at me and for a second the half crazed look in her eyes is gone. "I'll always claim her as mine. She's a good kid and she just got dealt a lousy set of cards. She's young, though, and that means she is going to be able to make the best hand out of what she's got."

I don't know what to say to that because I don't really understand what she's saying. So I just nod. I tell her I'll see her around and as I'm walking away she yells, "Tell her I said 'hi' and she better come visit her aunt."

"I don't know when I'll see her, Candy," I tell her as I turn, walking backwards as I look at her.

"Don't worry, you will."

By the time I'm in my truck, I'm running my conversation with Candy through my mind, replaying every look, every move and twitch, every word trying to decipher if there was some hidden meaning in it. With Candy, you just never know.

The only thing I know for sure is that Tally is not Candy's niece and they are both hiding something important from me.

I drove out to the Taggert's to put in my last full night. Mr. Taggert had told me that I could still work for him, to just let him know my schedule once I started school. I was thankful because I really did not want to have to look for another job, not to mention I really like what I did, even if most would consider it hard, dirty work. It paid the bills and kept me in shape.

When I got home, it was late and my grandmother was already in bed. She left a note for me saying there was a plate of food for me in the fridge and to make sure I ate and got to bed since tomorrow was my first day of school. I smiled at the fact that she sometimes still treated me like I was a kid and not eighteen. Although yes, tomorrow was the first day at a new school, it was the least of my worries.

By the time I ate, cleaned up, and showered, I was ready to crash. I lay down and closed my eyes and though I fell asleep almost immediately the last thing I saw in my mind was her face... her beautiful, sad face.

~

The first thing I notice when I walk into Broken

Arrow High School is that I'm going to stand out. Not just because of my traditional Native American look with my long, dark hair and jewelry but also because of my six foot three height. Thankfully no one seems to pay much attention to me as I walk past and into the office. Part of that I attribute to the fact that I am several hours late. My mother had been hysterical all night and the hospital called, so I went and sat with her most of the night and into the morning. Sometimes just hearing my voice was enough to calm her down, sometimes not. So, I had called the school and they had been very understanding. Of course, what are they going to say when your excuse is because your mother is in a mental hospital?

I step into the office and a woman who looked to be in her thirties, though dressed as if she was one of the teenage students, was standing behind the counter. I walk up and the smile she gives me makes me feel like I need a shower. Yeah, it was that bad.

"I'm Trey Swift. I need to get my schedule." I don't elaborate more than that simply because I want to get out of the office as quickly as I can. For a second as she stares at me, I think she just might reach across the counter and run a finger down my chest.

"Um, ma'am?" It must be the ma'am that snaps her out of her stupor. She frowns at me. Yep, it's the ma'am. I smile coolly. "My schedule?"

"Right, Trey." Her voice is high and nasally and reminds me of the woman who played the nanny on some sitcom.

"I'm Liza French. You can call me Liza." She pronounces her name as Lee-za and says it with a little too much tongue flapping around. I'm pretty sure she's going for sexy, but really, it could also be that she has a lisp. Her shoulder length bleach blonde hair looks as if she has sprayed a can of hair spray on it while holding her head upside down. And although she may have been pretty, it was hard to tell under her war paint she was trying to pass off as make-up.

"Thank you, *Ms.* French." I stress the Ms., making it very clear that I am the student and she is not. She hands me the schedule and I take it making sure to avoid any skin contact.

"If you need any help finding your classes, I am happy to show you to them."

Yeah, I think to myself, a little *too* happy. "I'm sure I'll be fine," I tell her and turn to leave the office. I decide right then and there never to be caught alone anywhere with that woman. I glance down at my schedule and see that I am due in Calculus. The room number is two hundred and twelve, so I'm betting it's on the second floor. Yes, I know my powers of deduction astound even me. I wander around until I find a flight of stairs and take them two at a time. Not because I'm in a hurry, just that my legs are that long. I notice that there are a few stragglers here and there and even one couple involved in some pretty heavy kissing and maybe more around the corner from a group of lockers. I don't give them longer than a glance and keep going. If I've learned anything about keeping a low profile, it's avoiding eye contact and not staring at people who are obviously engaged in something that is better kept behind closed doors, or at least the seclusion a car.

Why do I want to keep a low profile? It's pretty simple. I don't have much time for a social life and I definitely don't have time to listen to people's judgment on my mother being in a "psych" facility. I don't have much patience with people who stereotype on a good day, but when it comes to my mom, my patience is non-existent.

I finally find my classroom and open the door. I walk in and of course, all eyes turn to me. The teacher, a portly man with glasses barely holding on to the tip of his nose, looks over them at me.

"You must be the new student."

I nod, "I must." I can tell I'm going to like this guy because he doesn't take offense to my curt attitude.

"I'm Mr. Styles, of which I have none." The class chuckles collectively, "Have a seat and enjoy my ability to make calculus the most riveting subject you've ever taken."

My lips quirk in a slight smile. Yeah, definitely going to like him. I look out into the class and find an empty seat towards the back. As soon as I sit down, I see my mistake. The girl in front of me turns in her seat and smiles. She's your typical, blonde cheerleader type. Based on her smile and the flirtatious gleam in her eyes, she likes new shiny things.

"Hi, I'm Amber."

She looks at me eagerly and I'm not sure what she expects of me. "I'm Trey." I tell her and then look right past her to Mr. Styles and his riveting teaching. I see her frown out of the corner of my eye, but she turns back around. I feel eyes on me and turn my head to the right. A guy, who looks to be the closest I've seen to my size, gives me a nod, and then looks at Amber and rolls his eyes. I let out a huff of laughter to see that this guy must have been at the receiving end of her wiles at some point. I return the nod and we both look back to the front. Just like that, I know I have at least one ally.

Class passes quickly and with Mr. Styles' quick wit

and, albeit, ridiculous jokes, it's not too miserable. As soon as I stand up, the guy from earlier walks over and holds his hand out. I was right about the size. He's only an inch or two shorter.

"Hey, man, I'm Bobby." The first thing I notice about Bobby is he doesn't stare at me like I'm some anomaly or even look at me like I'm any different, though I stand out like an orange among apples.

"Trey," I tell him as I shake his hand.

He nods over to Amber who is steadily talking to a group of girls. A guy walks in and puts an arm around her. She looks up at him, her eyes vacant of the same adoration, but more like she's telling him that it took him long enough. She glances back over her shoulder at me and gives me another grin.

"Oh, man, you're on her radar." Bobby chuckles as we release hands.

I look back at him, "Let me guess, she's trouble."

He nods, "Of the worst kind."

"No offense, but you look like the type to be with *her* type," I frown inwardly as I realize I've done exactly what I hate. I've stereotyped based on what Bobby looks like.

He takes it good-naturedly as he laughs, "I've known Amber all of my life and that means I know way too much about her to ever go shaking that peach tree."

I can't help but smile. I like Bobby already.

"I've got lunch next, what about you?" he asks.

I take my schedule out of my back pocket. "Yeah, I've got lunch."

"Come on, then. I'll maneuver you through the waters and try to keep you from the piranhas."

As we're walking down the halls, I hear a commotion over by the lockers where the couple had been earlier. I notice a crowd has gathered around one locker in particular. "What's going on over there?"

Bobby frowns and his eyes narrow, "Assholes doing what they do best, being assholes."

"That's pretty obvious by the obnoxious laughter, but what's so funny?"

"I don't like to tell other people's business. Let's just say that something happened last year and the person it happened to is going to relive it the rest of the year if it's up to that bunch." I can tell that whatever it is, it really bothers him.

"That sucks," I murmur.

I'm not sure, but as we walk into the crowded cafeteria I think I hear Bobby say, "Especially for someone like her."

Whoever it is he's talking about, I already feel sorry for her and I don't even know her.

Chapter 14

"Have you ever been hit so hard that the wind gets knocked out of you? The more you gasp and gasp, the harder it is to get air in, and there is that moment of panic when you really don't think you will ever breathe again. That feeling sucks. It sucks even worse when it happens and it isn't because you've been hit, at least not physically." ~Tally

"So far, so good," I tell Nat as we head towards my locker. Half the day is over and I haven't heard anything about a hot, tall, yummy, new guy. Yes, that would be my description if I saw him, but I'm pretty sure anyone with a uterus would feel that way, and probably several people without a uterus. And yes, I did just think that.

"It's not good," she grumbles.

"Don't be cranky just because your dream to save me by pushing me into the arms of—," my words trail off as we come around the corner and my locker comes into view.

"Those pieces of shi-,"

I reach out and grab her arm as I feel my legs start to give. I'm sucking in air, but nothing seems to be getting into my lungs.

"Oh crap, Tally," she grabs me and helps me stay on my feet.

"Thanks," I mumble as I stare at the mess that is my locker. As we walk closer, I see that razor blades have been glued to it and something red has been painted on them. A name plate has been made and is stuck to the center that says, "RIP, T.B. when she finally does the job right." That's not the worst part. The absolute worst part is a picture of me on the bathroom floor, blood all around me, and the look on my face is that of a dead girl.

"What the hell is wrong with people?" Nat is cussing a blue streak and attempting to pull off the picture and name plate, but they aren't budging. I just stand there staring, in shock. I knew that there would be talk, stares, the usual high school crap, but this—this I did not expect.

"I can't do this today, Nat," I tell her as I begin to back away.

"Don't leave Tally. If you do, then they win."

I shake my head, "Then today they win because I don't have the energy to deal with this."

She grabs my arm and turns me towards the office, away from the noise of the cafeteria.

"Okay, today you go home, you collect yourself. Think of ways to get even with those sacks of swine. Then tomorrow you walk in here with your chin held high."

I look at her and try to smile, "You're kind of the best, you know."

She grins, "Of course I know."

"Don't be humble or anything, Nat." I roll my eyes.

"Don't worry. There is no risk of that."

We walk into the office and Ms. French and her too tight clothes are sitting behind the counter. She looks up and when she notices that we don't have more testosterone running through our bodies than estrogen, she looks back down. Nat can't stand her and doesn't hide it. Then again, I can't stand her either. Usually I try to be respectful, but that's on a day when my locker has not been turned into a sick memorial.

"Hi, Ms. French," I say and she doesn't bother to look up, "my locker needs to be cleaned and I need to go home." She still doesn't acknowledge me. I feel Natalie getting restless next to me. But I'm not going to let her fight all my battles. That won't help me get stronger.

I step forward and slam my hand down on the counter, and for a minute, my mind flashes back to the day I caught Sheila stealing Xanax and yelled at her. Man, those were good times.

"HEY! I'm talking to you. I realize that because I don't have the right body parts you think you can ignore me. But if you would stop sniffing nail polish, or guys for that matter, long enough to do your job, we would get along a whole lot better." I have her attention now. I paste a smile on my face as she stares at me in shock. "Now, I said that I need my locker cleaned off. And I'm going home. Did you get that or do you need to write it down?"

"I got it," she snaps.

"Good, I'm Tally Baker if you need to know whose locker."

"Oh, I know who *you* are." she sneers at me.

I smile and I know it must be one of those wild-eyed smiles because she pushes back from the counter in her chair. "Excellent. Then we won't have to have another one of these little talks."

I turn and walk out of the office and my chin is a tad higher. Am I still going home? Heck, yeah, but at least I didn't totally cower in a corner.

"That was awesome!" Nat grins.

"I learned a few things at MPF." I tell her just a

little smugly.

"You going to be okay?"

We step through the front doors of the school and squint at the midday sun. "I will be, but right now I'm a lot of things other than okay. But I will be. I'm going to head over to see Candy. I don't feel like going home to an empty house."

She nods, "I'll make sure your locker gets taken care of."

"Could you maybe get my books out of there?"

She tilts her head to the side and raises a brow at me, "Like you have to ask."

"Thanks, Nat."

"Text me later," she yells after me as I descend the stairs and head towards my car.

As soon as the door is closed behind me, I take a deep breath and fight off the tears. I refuse to let anyone make me feel worthless. I was good enough at doing that myself.

"Get a grip, Tal," I tell myself. I even tell myself to go back in the school and finish the day which makes me laugh. "Why would I go back in there when I can go see Candy? Good point." I answer myself. I groan as I start up the car. There I go talking to myself again and it's getting worse if I'm actually having a full conversation with myself. It could be worse, I think. I could be talking to voices that weren't my own.

~

"You just couldn't stay away, could you?" Candy smiles at me as I walk into the rec room of MPF.

"Nope I was having withdrawals from your constant abuse."

"That's good because these nut jobs around here don't understand that they are supposed to do whatever I tell them." She stands up from the table where she was playing cards—with no one.

"How dare they?" I smile. I take a deep breath and let it out. Candy watches me closely and I see the moment that she knows something isn't right.

"This is one of those moments where I need to ask who I need to kill, isn't it?" She walks over to me and motions for me to follow her. We walk to the back door and slip out to sit on the bench. My stomach aches and I feel a burn in my chest as I think about the last time I sat on this bench and who I sat with.

"Go on and tell me. You will feel better. And if you don't, we'll do whatever we need to do to get there."

My eyes swell up with tears because the one person who truly understands me is a sixty year old woman in a psych hospital and I would rather be with her than anyone else. At least that's what I tell myself.

I tell her what happened and she sits and listens intently. I even tell her about Ms. French. That gets a good cackle out of her.

"So you're telling me that these kids, who are obviously taking up precious oxygen from the rest of us, have nothing better to do than try and make you feel like a whacko?" She narrows her eyes at me, "And when I say 'try' it's because only you have the power to let what they do drag you down. Is it going to hurt, well, hell yes, but what you do with it from there is totally up to you."

"I know," I lean forward placing my elbows on my

knees and rub my face with my hands. "It's just so irritating because it's like they think they have to point it out to me, like I don't know. Hello, I'm the one who spent the summer here and not on some damn vacation."

"Oh, come on, you know this was way better than any vacation you have ever been on," she nudges me with her bony shoulder. I look at her, then really look at her, and notice that just in the week and a half that I've been gone, she's lost weight.

"Candy, are you okay?"

"Uh uh, don't you try and deflect onto me. I'm fine, and we're talking about you." She looks away from me and though I notice that she has some fresh scratches on her arms, I don't bring it up.

We sit in silence, but I know it won't last long. Candy can't stand to be still or silent for more than a minute or two.

"You up for a game?" she asks me with mischief dancing across her face.

"Are we going to be vandalizing, jumping into ponds, or making prank calls?"

She looks appalled, but I know it's not real. "Good grief, Pinky, if that is your idea of a game, I think they let you out a little too early."

I laugh, "Right."

"I was just talking about a little game of poke'em."

"Don't you mean poker?"

She purses her lips, "No, I mean poke'em, as in poke'em with a fork."

"Poke who with a fork?"

"Em'! Geeze, don't you listen? Poke'EM."

"Has anyone ever told you there is something wrong with you?" I tease with my usual question.

She winks at me and grins, "No one who matters."

Chapter 15

"I feel her, just beyond my reach, but she's there. I would question it, but then I already know the answer. There isn't anything supernatural about it, but it isn't easily explainable either. Her heart and soul call to mine. Her pain, her fear, they are mine. But I need her to understand that her joy, her safety, and her heart—they are mine as well."
~Trey

I sit with Bobby and some of his friends during lunch and it's all pretty comfortable. They only ask me a few questions and nothing real personal, almost as if they can tell they wouldn't get any answers anyways.

"What's your next class?" Scott, a short, stocky guy that Bobby introduced me to asks.

"Health," I answer.

"That's any easy class. You don't even really have to do anything, just show up," Bobby tells me.

"From what I can tell, none of my classes are going to be tough." I tell him, "You won't hear me complaining."

"Same here," Scott says. "It's a good thing because between football, my job, and my girl, I don't really have time for classes." Everyone laughs. Scott is easy to be around and talks constantly, which is great because it keeps me from having to.

The bell rings and everyone begins to gather their things. Bobby and Scott walk with me out and I have to admit that it's nice not to walk around looking like a lost idiot.

"Hey, Bobby, there's Nat," Scott points out a curvy girl with long dark hair. Her back is to us and she appears flustered as she stands in front of a locker. I see Bobby's face change subtly and know that this is a girl he's either dating or interested in dating. He heads towards her and Scott follows. I shrug and follow. It's not like I know where I'm going anyways.

"Hey, Nat," Bobby says at we get closer to her.

She doesn't turn to look at him as she speaks, "Hi, Bobby." Her voice is filled with irritation.

"Is everything alright?"

Her shoulders drop and she turns around. Her lips are tight and her eyes are narrowed. If looks could mutilate, then our bodies would be shredded.

"No, things are absolutely not alright. I need to get into this locker and those bloody mother….,"

"Whoa, hey," Bobby steps forward and puts his hands on her shoulders. "Let me help okay; don't kill anyone just yet." As Bobby moves her aside, the locker in question comes into view. I feel my gut tighten as my eyes narrow. My jaw tenses and I feel like my blood just might melt through my skin as the anger within me heats it up.

"There won't be anyone left to kill when I'm done." I say so low that I'm surprised they hear me. Bobby's Nat suddenly notices me and her eyes widen.

"Freaking A, you're him!" I hear her, but I can't take my eyes off the locker. I can't take my eyes off the picture of the bloody, broken girl, my girl, with tears streaming down her face and cuts all over. I see the initials above the picture and I feel my heart pounding all the way to my head. I can't remember a time in my life when rage has consumed me until I couldn't see straight. I step forward and Bobby steps aside, smart guy.

I reach up and grab the edge of the picture and rip it off. The name plate comes next. My hands are shaking as I shove them both into my back pocket.

"Trey, man, are you alright?" I hear Bobby's voice but in that moment I can't speak. I don't know if anything that would come out would be rational.

"Trey, exactly." Natalie's voice comes from my right, "You're Tally's Trey."

My head whips around and my eyes land on her. She takes a step back and Bobby moves closer, almost in front of her, as if she needed protection from me.

"You know Tally?" I knew the answer had to be yes since she had obviously been trying to get into the locker.

She nods and her eyes are wide as she stares up at me.

"Would someone please tell me what is going on?" Bobby asks.

"Tally met Trey over the summer, and they… she… he…," She can't seem to get her thoughts together and her words are a mess.

"Tally's my girl," I tell them using the words Scott had used to refer to his girlfriend.

A smile spreads across Nat's face. "Yeah, exactly, Tally's his girl." She lets out a breath, "You have no stinking idea how glad I am to see you. And damn, you are one big dude."

Bobby glances at her and frowns. Nat blushes under his stare and shrugs, "I'm just pointing out a fact." she shakes her head in agitation, "The point is that Tally needs you. She won't admit it because she's as stubborn as a bloody mule."

"Where is she?" I ask impatiently.

"She left, she went home, wait, no, that isn't right," Nat rubs her hands up and down her legs and Bobby wraps an arm around her waist pulling her close. She leans into him and finally seems to pull herself together, "Sorry, just a tad pissed. She said she was going to see Candy." I could tell that she hoped that I knew what that meant because she obviously didn't want to mention Mercy.

I started to turn to go, but I felt a hand on my arm. I glared down at the hand and then up at its owner. Nat pulled it away quickly, "Do you really think it's a good idea for you to go see her like this?"

I knew she was referring to my anger, but there wasn't anything on earth or anywhere else for that matter that was going to keep me from finding Tally.

Nat must have seen that in my eyes because she held her hands up, "Okay, I get it. But if you hurt her I swear I will, I will," she growls and narrows her eyes at me, "I don't really know what I will do just yet but believe me it will be utterly horrific."

I don't have anything to say in that moment because frankly, if I hurt Tally I would want Nat to do something utterly horrific to me.

~

My foot presses heavy on the gas petal and I have to force myself to slow down. I know it would only slow me down if I get pulled over and make it that much longer before I see Tally. My wheels screech loudly as I turn into the parking lot and whip into a space. My truck is barely in park as I open the door and slide out. I take a few good deep breaths as I try to calm down. I don't want to scare her, but I can't stop and get myself fully under control. I *won't* be fully under control until I see her, see that she is alright.

I don't give Mildred a first glance, let alone a hello as I stride past her. The first place I check is Candy's room. It's empty. I go to the rec room next. I notice that my mother isn't there and neither is Candy or Tally. I'm heading towards the only other place I know to look when I hear Zeke's deep voice.

"She's walking out now." I turn and look at him. He points to the front, where I had been only minutes ago. I must have literally just missed her. Zeke points to the back door. "Go out and around, you can head her off."

"Thanks," I give him quick nod.

"Take care of our girl," Zeke tells me.

I bite my tongue from saying *you mean my girl* because I know he means well and he cares about Tally.

I see her just as I round the building. She's walking up to a white BMW.

"Tally!" I yell across the lawn.

Her head snaps around and her eyes widen. I can tell she was definitely not expecting to see me. She's backing up and I know that she is considering bolting.

"Don't," I say a little more sharply than I intend.

She stands still and watches me cautiously as I continue towards her. As soon as I'm within reaching distance, I pull her to me and wrap her in my arms. I've never taken this liberty; I've never really touched her because she always seemed so frightened. In that moment I don't care, I just need to hold her. I need to feel her against me. She is stiff and doesn't return the hug, but I hold on. She must realize that I'm not letting go anytime soon because she finally relaxes against me, wrapping her arms around me. I close my eyes as I feel her arms tighten and I can't help but wonder when the last time was that she had been held. I lean down and press my mouth to her ear. "We need to talk.

She shakes her head and tries to pull away. "No, Tally, I'm not letting go. We are going to talk."

"There's nothing to talk about," her words are muffled because her face is pressed into my chest.

"I'm going to pretend that you didn't just say something that ridiculous. You're going to get in my truck and talk to me."

She pushes against my chest until she can look up at me. I see her tear streaked face and my heart clenches painfully.

"You don't get to tell me what to do, Trey. There is nothing to talk about. I'm going home and Nat's going to bring me my assignments and then I will sleep, get up, go to school, and do it all over again the next day." She's shaking as she talks and I can't help but run my hands up and down her covered arms, hoping to comfort her.

"I'm sorry, but that's not acceptable to me. I've spent the last week and a half in hell wondering if you were okay, wondering if I would see you again. Did any of that time together mean anything to you? Did you care about me at all?"

I see the battle waging in her eyes as she struggles with what to tell me. Her lips tighten and her forehead wrinkles.

"Don't you dare lie to me."

"Uhh!" She groans, "Why the hell are you so bossy? Can't you just let it go?"

"No. Just talk to me, Tally. What is the harm in

that? Can't you at least answer the questions?"

She looks down at her feet and I stop myself from reaching out and lifting her face to look at me. I've missed her so much. I just want to see her face, but I've already pushed and maybe too far. I need to calm down.

"Yes," she finally whispers.

"Yes, what?" I ask trying to soften my tone.

"Yes, it means something to me. Yes, I care about you." She looks up at me and takes another step back. "But it doesn't matter. We can't be together, if that's even what you're saying you want."

I can't believe she even has to wonder what I want. Haven't I made it blaringly obvious?

"What do you mean it doesn't matter and we can't be together?" I glance around her to the BMW behind her and then back at her. I realize that she must come from money. How else would she be driving a brand freaking new Beamer?

"Am I not good enough for you? Is that what you're saying?" Anger laces my voice because the Tally I know would never think something so shallow.

"NO!" she gasps. "Of course not. How could you even think that?"

"What else am I supposed to think?"

"I think it would be obvious, Trey. Has it escaped your attention that I lied to you or have you not figured out that Candy isn't my aunt and I wasn't just visiting this place every day?" She motions towards the Mercy's building. "I was a patient, Trey, a freaking patient in a psych hospital."

"I am angry that you lied to me, but I understand why you did. What I'm trying to tell you is I don't give a damn. It doesn't change who you are to me."

"Why aren't you listening to me?" She rubs her forehead and her other hand clenches and unclenches. "How can you possibly want to be with someone like me, when you already have your mom who needs you? Can you honestly tell me that when you leave this place from visiting her that you would want to then have to deal with me?"

I'm speechless. She has rendered me speechless. I only thought I was angry before. She honestly believes that I am so shallow? Her eyes grow wide as she watches my face. I feel my nostrils flare as I try to take in air and I glance away briefly in an attempt to get the rid of the look on my face at the utter horror at her words. "You think so little of me?" I finally grate out.

"Trey," she says gently as if she is attempting to calm a raging beast, which is not far from what I am in the moment. "I wasn't meaning to insult you or question your integrity. Please understand that."

"Whether you meant to or not doesn't matter. What matters is that you did."

"I'm sorry." she says and I know she means it. I can see it in the slump of her shoulders and the forlorn look on her face. Tally doesn't want to hurt me, but she's also afraid that I will hurt her.

"I will accept your apology as long as you let me prove you wrong."

She stands there quietly. Her eyes look everywhere but at me. She lets out an exhausted breath and I think she is finally coming to her senses. "Then I guess I will just have to live with the fact that you won't forgive me." She turns and is in her car, backing out of the lot before I have time to even register what has happened. Her words say one thing, but the look in her eyes says something totally different. She wants to be with me, I know she does. It is written all over her beautiful face. But I also see the terror there. She's scared to death that I will walk away, that at some point I won't be able to handle whatever it is that is going on with her.

I pull the picture from my back pocket and look at the girl, devastated and bloody.

"Tally, baby, what happened to you?" My voice is soft, but even I hear the ache in it. Whatever it is that put her in that bathroom on that floor, whatever it is that brought her to this place, it isn't enough to keep me away. She may not believe me now. She may expect me to just accept what she's said, but instead she's going to learn that she has just met her match. And after seeing what was done to her locker, there is no way on earth or hell that she will go through that again.

Chapter 16

"I have never wanted to believe somebody more in my life than I did Trey. As he stood before me offering me himself, offering for me to be held in those arms again. I nearly caved. I nearly said fine, I'll take my chances. But if I let him in any further than he already is and then he decided to jump ship, I'm not sure I would ever get over that.
I'm not a stranger to pain and at one time, I welcomed it with open arms. But it nearly killed me. I won't do that again." ~Tally

I hear the knock on my door and as much as I wish I could just tell her to go away, I know I can't do that to my mom.

"Come in," I tell her, surprised that she didn't just walk in.

"Tally?" she says tentatively. "I just wanted to see how your first day back was."

I close my eyes remembering my locker, then Trey. "It was fine," I lie.

"Can I talk to you for a minute?" She walks farther in and then sits on the edge of my bed where I'm lying on my back looking at the ceiling. What am I going to say? No? My heart is broken; some buttheads vandalized my locker; so please leave me the crap alone?

"Sure," I tell her.

"I just need you to know that I realize your father and I haven't handled this in the best way. It's just really hard to see your child go through something like this, especially when we don't understand it."

I know she means well, really I do, but does she think that I understand it any better than she does? Didn't she stop to think that regardless of whether or not they understood, I needed them? I needed them to tell me that it didn't matter what was going on that they loved me no matter what?

"It's alright, Mom. I know it's hard." I try to sound as understanding as I possibly can, but with everything that has happened today, my level of sincerity is about as high as my level of patience, which is to say, nonexistent.

"It's really not, but I want you to know that we love you very much, even when we aren't good at showing it. Parents make mistakes, and when we do, we have no idea how to fix them." I look up at her face and see sincerity there. I love her. I want to accept her apology and part of me does. But it will take time for me to let go of the hurt they caused.

"Okay." That's all I can say. That's all I have in me right now.

"Alright," she says after a moment. She stands and walks out, closing the door quietly behind her.

I glance over at my books that are sitting on my desk. Natalie had brought them over just as she said she would. Then she proceeded to drill me about Trey, after she swooned over how good looking he was. "You said he was hot, Tal. You did not say he was not even on the temperature scale because of said hotness." she had told me. I had to agree, the guy was amazing. But he was off limits, at least to me.

I hear my phone vibrate and Nat's ring following. I reach over and grab it off my bedside table.

"What's up?" I ask her.

"You don't sound devastated. Why don't you sound devastated?"

I frown at the ceiling, "Did you ever think that maybe I'm tired of being devastated?"

"If you were tired of being devastated you would be on the phone with that big hunk of Native American yumminess and not with me." she points out helpfully.

"Nat?"

"Yes."

"What do you want?"

She huffs, "I'm hurt that you would think that I want something. I'm just calling to say hi and see how you are doing. Also to point out that Trey ripped that crap off your locker. I forgot to mention that earlier."

"WHAT!" With everything that had happened in the parking lot of Mercy, I hadn't even thought to ask how he'd known where I was.

"I was trying to get it off, but it wouldn't budge and then Hercules comes in and just rips it off. I thought he was going to kill someone. Seriously, Tal, you should have seen the look on his face."

"I think I know the look you're talking about," I tell her as I remember the look he had given me when he thought I had insulted him and questioned his integrity.

"I just thought you might want a heads up. I can't believe he didn't tell you when you saw him today."

"Things were a little tense when we talked today," I remind her.

"Right, well, I'm not going to quit telling you that you're making a mistake and that you will be pissed once one of the other hussies snags him up."

I don't even want to think about Trey with someone else. It actually makes me ill to even consider it. Thank you, Natalie, for that.

"Okay, Nat, I'm going to bed now."

"Fine. Ignore me, but you know I'm right."

As I lay there in my bed I close my eyes, willing myself to sleep, but it wouldn't come. Instead, all I can think about is what I would do if Trey did move on and started dating someone else. I decide then that I would do what any girl would do in that situation. Slash the girl's tires, of course.

I grin to myself as I think of Candy's smiling face, then wonder if it was the best idea to be happy that my decision would please Candy.

~

"Hey," I say to Nat who is standing next to my car as I climb out.

"Hey back," she smiles.

"I know that smile, Natalie, what's going on?" I narrow my eyes at her.

She shrugs. "I have no idea what you're talking about," she says a little too cheerfully.

She grabs my arm and tucks hers into it as we begin walking towards the front doors of the school. She's chattering on about how she thinks Bobby Reynolds might be into her. Which I already know, but Nat is just so oblivious it takes her a couple years to catch up to what the rest of us have figured out. I listen intently, enjoying some normal conversation that for once doesn't pertain to me, pscyh wards, or guys beyond my reach. Just as we're nearing the lockers, we see a crowd.

"Bloody hell, not again," I groan.

"They're not doing anything to your locker, Tally," Nat tells me as she holds me back.

"Then what's going on?" I ask her as my eyes stay glued to the group of people. I can't see through them to what so exclusively has their attention, but it's not a fight because no one is chanting or acting like idiots.

"It's a warning," she tells me. Bobby walks up beside us and smiles warmly at me.

"Hey, Tally." I've always liked Bobby, in a completely platonic sort of way. He's always been kind to me and though he looks like he would hang with the "haves,", those are the ones that think they are beyond the reach of even the gods, he pretty much is his own crowd. He has friends in just about every social circle and if he doesn't care for a person's attitude or actions, he just doesn't hang out with them, regardless of who it is.

"Hi Bobby. What do you mean, a warning?" I ask quickly after acknowledging him.

"I might have told Trey who was involved in the locker incident because he might have asked." Nat confesses.

"You did not." My eyes widen as I stare at my best friend.

"Tally someone needs to scare the crap out of these jerks and who better than your huge boyfriend."

"He is not my boyfriend," I snap in a whisper. Why I say it in a whisper I'm not sure, and even if I am, I will not fess up.

Natalie starts walking towards the group and Bobby stays with her, so I quickly move to catch up. She pushes through the crowd ignoring scowls until we are finally at the front. My mouth drops open as I see

Trey holding a very pissed off looking Carter Evans, Amber's on-again-off-again boyfriend, and unspoken leader of the "haves." Trey's got him by the throat, pressed against a wall of lockers and to my utter surprise, Carter's feet are not touching the ground. Trey's hair is in its usual braid down his back and his gray shirt hugs his body. His forearm and bicep bulge as he holds his prey. He looks relaxed, oddly enough. His long, powerful legs encased in faded jeans that fit a little too nicely, are spread just slightly to brace his body because of the extra weight. He's magnificent, truly, and though I don't want to be, I am totally crazy, ignore the pun, for this guy. My attention is drawn back from his body to his face and then to Carter's.

"If I ever see you near her locker, her car, her house, or her, I'll...," Trey leans forward and whispers in Carters ear so softly that no one else can hear. But when all the blood drains from Carter's face making him now resemble a corpse more than a living being, I decide that it's a really good thing that no one heard what Trey said.

Just as Trey is letting Carter go, Amber pushes through the crowd and saunters, yes, literally saunters, up to him. I watch as she raises her hand and lays it on Trey's chest and leans forward. I don't have any idea what she was planning on saying because I'm across the space that was between us and standing in front of Trey faster than I knew I could move. I smack her hand away and glare at her.

"Back the hell up," my voice is surprisingly calm considering the jealousy and anger that is pulsing through me. Amber stares at me with utter disdain and if I could even bring myself to care, I wouldn't. I feel a strong arm come around me and pull me back against a firm stomach. I feel warm breath on my neck and nearly pass out when I feel lips just behind my ear.

"Good morning." Trey whispers against it. "Breathe Tally," he tells me and I realize that if I don't do as he says, I just might pass out. The crowd clears as they realize the action is over and I'm left standing there alone, in Trey's arms.

"What are you doing?" I whisper back.

"Saying good morning to my girl," he responds. I pull away and he lets me go, but steps closer when I try to back away.

"I'm not," I start to speak, but he stops me.

"Regardless of what you think, Tally, you are mine… and now they know it as well," he motions out to the hall where people are milling about. "The quicker you come to terms with that, the easier this will be."

"We've already talked about this," I grumble at him. He wraps an arm around me and starts to pull me along beside him.

"What's your first class? I don't want you to be late."

"English," I answer automatically.

He grins down at me, "Me too."

This is not happening, I think to myself. I am not going to let this happen. I really am trying to tell myself that, but as we walk down the hall together and people turn away instead of stare at me, I have to admit that it is so nice to feel protected and safe. And I know that with Trey I'm safe, physically, that is. But with my heart, that's a whole different story.

We walk into English and Trey guides us to the desks on the right side of the room all the way to the back. He ushers me into the second to last desk and then takes the one behind me. The bell hasn't rung yet, so I turn and look at him. His lips twitch as if he is trying to hold back a smile and his eyes smolder into mine. I raise my eye brows at him, "What are you doing?"

"This," he whispers and motions between us.

"No, we are not doing this." I tell him for what feels like the hundredth time.

He leans forward in his desk until his face is less than an inch from mine. "I asked you to give this a chance. We were in Candy's room. You were sitting on her bed. Remember?"

I close my eyes as I see the moment he is talking about. I nod.

"You said, 'Okay'. So yes, we are doing this."

To my complete and utter shock he wraps his hand around the back of my neck and pulls me towards him. He closes that half inch between us and presses his lips to mine. It was quick, but it was potent. I'm still staring at him when he lets go of my neck and leans back in his chair. The bell rings. I'm still staring. Mrs. Potts begins speaking and I am still staring at the smirking guy behind me.

"Baby, turn around," he whispers and then winks. WINKS! I was saying we weren't doing this. I know that's what I was saying and now he has kissed me, is calling me baby and winking at me. What the hell?

I turn around slowly and tell myself that it is NOT because he told me to. I have no idea what is being taught in English. My neck and face, I'm sure, are stained a permanent shade of red as I feel the dark eyes on my back.

After class, I stand, and before I can grab my bag, Trey has it slung over his shoulder. I look up at him with an attempt at being stern, but based on the smile he flashes me, I don't succeed.

"Where to next, beautiful?"

Okay, is he trying to make me cry? Does he want me to just melt to the floor? Because if he keeps saying things like that, then that is exactly what is going to happen.

I sigh deciding I will just have to argue with him later. "History," I tell him and try not to flinch. "History class and I don't have good history together." Ha, I made a joke, lame, but a joke nonetheless.

"You okay?" he asks. Of course he does. He notices everything about me. He always did when he came to visit at Mercy, as well. He is watching me closely and at times, it un-nerves me.

"Yeah," I tell him with a nod and small smile.

Natalie is waiting for us as we walk out of the classroom. She grins at us like an idiot when she sees Trey carrying my bag. I am shaking my head at her with narrowed eyes while she simply ignores me.

"Hey," she says smiling, "I thought I'd walk with you to History since we have it together."

I knew the real reason she wants to walk. She is being supportive and I really appreciate it. And I really appreciate the arm that comes around my waist as we get closer to the room. It was like Trey can sense that with every step I feel like I am getting closer to my own doom.

As we walk into the class, just like yesterday, it takes everything in me, and Nat pushing me, to not turn around and bolt. Yesterday, eyes had followed me all the way to my desk. Today, no one looks up as I walk past, my hand in Trey's as he leads me.

By the time lunch rolls around, Trey has shown me his schedule and it turns out that we have every class together except third period, which thoroughly annoys him.

"It's one class, Trey," I tell him as he frowns at me, "not to mention, it shouldn't matter because we aren't doing this."

I start to sit down in my usual spot at lunch but he snags me around the waist and pulls me onto his lap. I shut my mouth just before a startled yelp starts to emerge. He moves me so that my back is to the room and I'm as far as I can turn without straddling him. I nearly jerk my arms away when I feel his hands on my sleeves, but when I look down I see that he is tugging them down where they had slid up, something he had done once before. My eyes dart up to his and I see such incredible compassion and understanding that I can barely swallow.

"We are so doing this," he whispers and then turns back around and places me next to him like I weigh nothing at all.

As we're sitting there eating lunch, Bobby, Scott, his girlfriend, Hannah, Natalie, and Jill are all talking to Trey like he has been there forever. Trey is constantly sneaking in little touches here and there. And by the end of lunch, my nerves are humming like a low electrical current, overwhelmed by so much contact. I don't think that I have been touched so much since I was an infant and it was required.

The bell rings and just as he has been doing all day, Trey grabs my backpack and my trash from lunch and disposes of it for me. Natalie walks over to me while we both watch Trey like some sort of groupies.

"He's just…," Nat begins.

"Shut it, Nat." I snap.

She snickers, the traitor.

The rest of my day continues on just the same. Trey with me everywhere I go, carrying my bag, holding my hand, keeping me safe. How can I possibly say no to this, I question myself. How can I turn away from someone who is willing to be there for me? But what if… that's my problem. All I can think about is the what ifs. Doctor Stacey told me a hundred times in therapy to stop thinking about the things that are out of my control, and that it could become an obsession that would keep me from having meaningful relationships. Easier said than done, doc.

At the end of the day Trey, Bobby, Nat, and I all walk out to the parking lot together.

"I'll see you in five, chick," Natalie tells me as she heads towards her car. Bobby follows her and I have to hold back a smile. The boy was gone for that girl.

Trey walks me to my car and I turn to face him. I don't know what to say. I've never been treated with such care in my life and I've never felt more secure.

"Tally, look at me," he says after I attempt to look everywhere but at him.

I relent and look up at him. His hand reaches up and he tucks my hair behind my ear. I try to suppress the urge to lean into him, to reveal to him just how much his touch, no matter how slight, affects me.

"So, how was your day?" he asks.

I grin, "You've been with me all day. You tell me."

"I would say that it was awesome."

"Oh, really?" I say as I fold my arms across my chest. "And why would you say that?"

"Because you were with me," he says flirtatiously.

"And how was your day?" Did I just ask that in a sultry voice? No, of course not. I wouldn't do that.

He takes a step closer to me. There is nowhere for

me to go unless I want to climb over the hood of my car, which I am not ruling out as an option just yet.

"Best day I've had in a little over a week and a half," he tells me.

I feel the sharp stab of guilt over leaving him high and dry the way I did. Though I still think it was for the best. But then again, maybe I'm not always right—maybe.

"Have you finally resigned yourself to this?" he asks.

I decide for honesty, since that hasn't been my usual course of action with Trey.

"I don't know. I'm not going to pretend that I don't want this. I won't pretend that today wasn't the best day that I've had at school in a very long time. I'm not going to say that I haven't felt safer with you than I have ever felt before." I can't believe I'm spewing all of this out in the school parking lot, for crying out loud, but then Trey has always had that effect on me.

He smiles, but it isn't an 'I told you so' kind of smile. It's genuine.

"Then let me keep you safe," his words are soft and filled with such passion that they resonate deep inside of me. "Let me in, Tally."

I realize then that, even though he has seen the picture and knows that I was in Mercy as a patient, I have yet to tell him why. My stomach feels as though it has been filled with a thousand bees buzzing around inside, churning up the bile and stinging me up through my throat. I don't want him to know. I don't want to share my humiliation, my shame, and my brokenness with him. I don't want to taint him with the stench of my soiled past. Honesty, Tally, I remind myself, you're going for honesty.

"I don't want to tell you," he starts to interrupt me, but I stop him with a finger to his lips, the first touch I have initiated between us, "but I know you deserve to know." I finish.

He takes my hand, the one that has my finger pressed to his lips, and flips it over, palm up. He kisses the center of it gently and then closes my hand around it. His eyes never leave mine as he tugs me to him, and just as he did the day before he wraps me in his strong arms. He is so much bigger than me that I feel like he engulfs me, every inch, from the tips of my toes to the top of my head. In his arms I am cocooned safely away from the world, away from eyes that stare and mouths that spew ugliness. I shouldn't allow this. I shouldn't give in to his demands. But it's too late, it was too late the moment I saw him as I ducked under that table.

Chapter 17

> "She is mine. She always has been, but now she has admitted it. With all the darkness and ugliness in my world, all my pain and anger, she is my sun. She shines on me and warms the coldness that has slowly seeped into my body over time. If she is my sun, then I am her storm, washing away the stains with my rain, deafening the lies with my thunder and crushing any who would hurt her with my lightning. She is mine as she always has been."
> ~Trey

Walking away from Tally in the parking lot is the hardest thing I have done all day. I didn't want to leave her. I didn't want to give her time to think about her choice to reconsider it. As much as I want to be with her constantly, I can't. I would smother her and she would grow to resent me. So, I got her number, kissed her forehead, and told her I would call her later. She had smiled at me, a real Tally smile, like she had done at MPF, and that, at least, had eased my worry.

I figured out something today. Something that will help build her confidence in me. I've got to pay attention to the little things; it's the little things with Tally. The small touches, the smiles, the winks, the whispers in her ear, and the kisses on her neck or cheek. She needs reassurance that everything is okay, that we are okay. She might never admit to that, because she would see it as a weakness, but I see it as a need that I can meet. I decided another thing that I need to do is to show her that I listen to her.

Remembering things she says are important to her and will go a long way in building that confidence. So, I asked Mr. Taggert tonight if he would mind if I brought my girlfriend to see his horses. He was completely okay with it and even told me we could take them out for a ride.

Now, as I sit on my bed, holding the phone in my hands, I wonder if I should tell her about it now or wait until tomorrow when we are face to face. I glance at the clock to make sure it isn't too late, nine o'clock. Surely, she is still up. Finding her name in my contacts, I press call and wait.

"Hello?" I hear her voice, three rings later. She sounds unsure and I imagine it's because she doesn't recognize my number.

"Hey," I say.

"Trey, hi."

"Can you talk?" I ask.

"Yeah, we just finished our homework. Nat just left."

I can't help but wonder if they talked about me, and then I remembered I was dealing with high school girls; of course they talked about me. I hear some shuffling on the other end of the phone and imagine she is sitting on her bed, getting comfortable and hopefully ready to share.

"How was your evening?" she asks.

"Good, I stopped in to check on my mom, then had to work, then homework, time with my grandmother, and now here I am." I tell her, listing off my night, attempting to portray a light heartedness.

"How is your mom doing?"

"It's been a rough few days. The medicine combination doesn't seem to be working for her."

I hear her let out a quivering breath, "I'm sorry to hear that."

I hear worry and apprehension in her voice and for the millionth time I wish I knew why.

"Are you ready to talk?" I ask, gently.

"Yes and no," she sighs, "I'd really rather do this in person."

Her statement surprises me. I would think talking about something painful would be easier over the phone. "Really?" I ask.

"I like to see facial expressions. I can't see what you're thinking if we talk over the phone." she explains.

I don't want to be frustrated, but I am. I don't know when we will have the next time to be alone to talk and I feel like I need to understand her.

"Can you come over?" Her question catches me off guard. I glance at the clock and it reads 9:07. I guess that's not too late but still I wouldn't think her parents would be okay with a guy coming over at this time, especially on a week night.

"Are you sure?"

"Yeah, my parents are at some function thing and won't be home until after midnight."

She gives me directions to her house, which I scrawl on a piece of paper to put in my phone GPS, and I tell her I will see her in a few minutes.

I don't have any problems finding her house, nor am I surprised to see the monstrosity especially knowing that she drives a BMW, but it's still intimidating. The slamming of my truck door reverberates like a gong in the quiet night. As I walk towards the front door, it opens and I see a small silhouette as light illuminates from behind. She looks unsure and nervous. I am neither of those things.

"Hey," I say as I take her in my arms. She immediately wraps her arms around me and I pull her tighter against me, pleased that she feels comfortable enough to allow me to hug her, and then hug me in return.

"Hi," she says softly as I let her go. She steps back to let me in and I try not to look astonished at the inside of her house. But honestly, it's hard not to be. It's huge. The foyer ceiling looms from the height of a small cliff and the staircase, on the right, winds up in an over exaggerated curve. There is a beautiful chandelier that hangs over the entry way, and from what I can tell, is the only light turned on at least downstairs.

"Do you want anything to drink?" she asks.

I shake my head, "I'm good, thanks."

"Follow me," she motions and begins up the stairs. I don't think it would have seemed like such a long trek if the stairs just went straight up, but because they curved out so wide, it seemed to take forever to reach the top. Once there, Tally turns right and walks down a hallway and then left down another hallway. At the very end of the second hallway is a door on the right. I see light peeking out from under the door and I assume this must be her room. She opens the door and steps inside I follow without hesitation.

Her room is simple, or at least simple for what you might think it would be in a house like this. The walls are painted pale green and a long flowing curtain drapes over the single, large window directly across from the door. There is a queen size bed against the far right wall, an armoire across on the opposite wall from the bed, and a desk with bookshelves on either side on the far left of the wall. All the furniture is oak and definitely of high quality. There is a door just beside the farthest bookshelf that I presume is her closet.

I see her watching me as I scan her room, her eyes are wide, and she tugs at her sleeves nervously.

"Nice room," I tell her with a smile.

"It's plain," she says, sounding slightly embarrassed.

"I told you what I had on my walls and you were surprised," I remind her.

She nods, "But you're a guy, I figured you would have some chick pictures up."

"Sorry to disappoint."

"Okay," she says, with an exaggerated sigh, "we might as well stop stalling. Have a seat." She motions to the desk chair. I pull it over closer to her bed where she climbs up and sits down cross–legged. I stare at her and I know that it unsettles her, but I want to see her facial expressions. I guess I actually did understand what she meant on the phone—sometimes body language and facial expressions say much more than words ever can.

She pulls both of her sleeves up quickly and lays her arms on her legs, out stretched as if she were going to give blood, and by the looks of the scars she had given blood many, many times. I feel my heartbeat move up into my throat and feel chills roll down my spine as I stare at her fair, delicate arms. Her arms have dozens of raised lines all over them in no particular pattern. I look closer though and then I see it, the lines are definitely in a pattern; they are letters, which are in turn words. Tally had cut the words *damaged goods* on her arms. The word *damaged* is on her left arm and the word *goods* is on her right. Some of the cuts appear to have been deeper than others, but they were all precise. I look up at her face and as soon as our eyes meet, she turns away from me. I could see the shame wash over her as her shoulders slump and her breathing increases. I stand up and slowly walk towards her. She looks up briefly and her eyes widen, but she ducks her head. I kneel down in front of her and run my fingers over the scars. My insides tighten as if being wrung out by invisible hands and I try not to picture her cutting herself.

"Tell me," I say as gently as I can, but my voice is low as I try to hide the pain I hold for her.

I hear her sniffle and reach up to tilt her chin so that I can look at her face. Silent tears stream down as she wages war with whatever it is that holds her hostage. I stand up, sit down next to her, and wrap an arm around her pulling her close and wait. I will wait for as long as she needs; I will hold her for as long as she needs, but I will not let her bear this alone.

Fifteen minutes pass and I feel her start to move. She wipes her eyes dry and then starts to pull her sleeves down. I stop her, "Are you more comfortable with them down, or do you think it will make me more comfortable?"

She shrugs, "I don't know really."

"Leave them," I tell her as I run a finger over them. She looks up at me, and her mouth drops open.

"Aren't you disgusted by them? They're ugly and their existence makes the words so true."

"Nothing about you could ever disgust me, and you will never be damaged goods, not to me, not to anyone." I tell her.

She leaves her sleeves up and settles her hands in her lap.

"I went into the hospital because they found me in

the school bathroom cutting myself. I had been depressed for months and it was getting worse. I didn't want to tell anyone because I didn't want anything to be wrong with me, but I got to a point where hiding it wasn't an option any more, not by choice, my body took the choice out of my hands. I don't think I really wanted to die. I just wanted the pain to stop. The physical pain from the blade was a relief from the emotional pain that I didn't understand," she pauses and looks up at me. I try to keep my face blank. I don't want her altering her story based on what she thinks she sees on my face. "I was diagnosed with bipolar disorder. I didn't understand how they could diagnose me with that. But then I went through several therapy sessions and long conversations with Dr. Stacey. She discovered that I had actually been in what they call a hypomanic state before the depression began. That's what was so frustrating. Before I began getting depressed, I was happy, even euphoric at times. I didn't sleep much. I would stay up really late reading, playing games on my phone, and even working ahead in some of my classes just because I felt like I could. I was a completely different person, a person I liked, and other people did too. A week before I, what Dr. Stacey calls *crashed*, I talked Natalie into going bungee jumping."

My eyes widen slightly, but only for a second. I saw glimpses of the girl she is describing in the hospital though not to that extreme.

"Dr. Stacey says that most people who suffer from bipolar disorder never seek help when they are manic and that's why it can be difficult to diagnose. Natalie noticed the change pretty quickly but I just kept blowing her concern off, telling her I was just tired and not sleeping well. She didn't catch on to the long sleeves until about two weeks before I was admitted. She was livid, scared, and threatened to tell my parents. I was hysterical and I begged her not to. I think she was scared because she had never seen me that way. I promised that I would stop and that I would talk to the school counselor. Obviously I didn't." She's quiet for a bit and I simply sit, holding her. I won't say anything until I know she has finished and I'm giving myself time to formulate what I want to say. "So that's it, that's why I was in Mercy, that's why the people at school treat me like a freak."

"You are not a freak," I whisper close to her ear. I clear my throat and then pull back so that I can look at her. I can tell she thinks that I'm pulling away because of what she's told me. "Look at me Tally," I wait. Her head tilts slowly until our eyes meet, "I only put this distance between us because I need to look at you. I need to know you are listening to me. Okay?"

She nods.

"I know that was hard for you to tell me, and I'm proud of you and respect you for talking about something that is so painful. I need you to hear me when I say to you that I see you, I see Tally. You are a beautiful young woman who has endured much, and although you will probably endure much more, you have been victorious in your battle. You are so courageous and I know you don't see it, but it's true."

The tension in her lips and the wrinkling of her forehead tells me that she doesn't agree with me.

"I can't make you see yourself as I do. You will have to choose to let go of the shame and allow yourself some mercy. What I can do... listen to me Tally," I say, more sternly than I intend. Her eyes widen but they meet mine and stay there, "What I can do is show you that you are precious. You have much in this life to give and you have a purpose, even if you do not know what it is just yet. I hate that you went through that darkness, but I am so very glad that I met you, and I think there is a reason we met under the circumstances that we did. I know it's difficult to trust, I do, but I am asking you to let me prove to you that you can trust me."

I stare at her as I try to keep my breathing even. I want her to see that after everything she has shared with me, she is still the girl I bumped into at Mercy, she is still the girl that I fell head over heels for in a matter of days before I'd ever even had the privilege of holding her. She reaches up tentatively and I try to hold my breath not wanting to scare her. She rarely initiates touch with anyone, and when she does, it is a gift. She gently brushes my hair back, tucking it behind my ear. After my shower that night I hadn't bothered to braid it so it hung loosely around me.

"I love your hair," she whispers.

I chuckle, "Thank you."

"I'm scared," she admits, as she strokes the long strands of my dark hair. It's difficult not to beg her to run both her hands through my hair.

"I know," I say. "That's okay, but don't run, just don't run, not from me."

She nods and then lets her hand fall back to her lap. I glance at my watch and see that it's been an hour, and although her parents aren't supposed to be back until after midnight, I don't feel that it's right for me to stay. But, I also hate to leave her in such a vulnerable state.

"What are you thinking?" She asks.

"You will laugh."

"Try me," she challenges, and I see some of her spark return.

"I'm trying to decide if I should be a gentleman and not stay here alone with you this late at night, or if I should stay, because I don't want you to be alone after opening, still-healing wounds."

She makes an 'ahh' motion with her mouth and grins.

"You're really thinking about being all chivalrous? Does it really bother you to be here alone with me?"

My eyes narrow slightly, and I reach up and run a finger slowly across her parted lips.

"You mistake my words, beautiful. I didn't say it bothers me to be alone with you. Having you all to myself is my preference. You will find that it is something I will have to control. What bothers me is you ever thinking that I would attempt to take advantage of you in such a vulnerable state, in obviously perfect circumstances."

I feel her breath catch against my finger and watch as heat floods her cheeks. I want to kiss her again, but I've decided to wait until I'm sure it's what she wants, the kiss in English had been like I was sealing the deal *and* it shocked her, which I love doing.

"Oh," she finally says.

"Did I scare you?" I ask and purposely lower my gaze to her lips.

She bites her bottom lip as I stare and shakes her head.

"You're a terrible liar."

She laughs and it's a little breathless. "Yes well, you're too sexy for your own good." As soon as the words are out of her mouth her eyes jump up to mine and her mouth falls open. A tiny screech comes out as she stares at me, "I, oh, I mean," she groans, "I can't believe I said that."

I'm attempting to keep my laugh to a small chuckle, but the expression on her face doesn't help me.

"Sexy huh?" I ask, as I rub my chin.

"Oh shut up, don't even act like you don't know you're hot." she snaps, her embarrassment now turning to annoyance.

I hold my hands up attempting to surrender, but the laughter just keeps coming. She glares at me, but I see the glint of humor and know she isn't really mad. Embarrassed? Yes, but not mad.

I stand after finally composing myself and she half jumps as she tries to hurry and stand as well.

"You're leaving?" She asks and her lips are tense.

I step closer to her and place both hands on either side of her face. She is so small, so fragile, and yet so very strong.

"I'm a phone call away, any time day or night, I will come to you." I stare at her, waiting, giving her the chance to choose. She nods her head slightly as she licks her bottom lip slowly. I follow the trail of her tongue like a predator after its prey. I lean down slowly, giving her time to stop me if she wants, but her eyes close even before my lips touch hers. Her lips are soft and warm. She parts them slightly and I feel the heat of her breath slipping past my own. I step closer, drop one of my hands, and wrap my arm around her, pressing her against me. She is soft in all the places I am not. Her body molds itself to me, and I feel the kiss change, gentle and sweet becomes passionate and firm. She wraps her arms around my neck. I realize she is rising up on her toes because I do not have to bend as far. I have thought of kissing her many times, but never did I imagine that it would feel like this. I can hear my blood rushing through my veins and my heart pounding in my chest. I wonder briefly if it's pounding hard enough that she feels it. I feel her run her hands through my hair and I moan. Her tongue brushes against the roof of my mouth and I feel her shudder against me.

I force myself to pull back, but I don't let her go. My thumb runs along her wet, glistening lips and she darts her tongue out and licks it. I suck in air sharply through my teeth. She grins.

"Vixen," I whisper.

Her face is flushed and warm; her breathing rapid and unsteady.

"I really need to go," I tell her.

She nods, but doesn't step away from me.

"I don't like to be touched." Her words surprise me and I nearly drop my arms, but she stops me. "No, don't let go. I mean I usually don't like to be touched, but with you, it's different."

I brush her hair back and smile as the pink strands glide through my fingers. Her skin is still flushed from our kiss, and I realize that the level of my desire and need for her would probably scare the crap out of her if she knew.

"I really need to go," I say again.

"You said that," she points out.

I smile, "I mean it this time." I lean down, kiss her lips softly, and pull back before I can allow myself more. I release her hair and step back from her. She looks amazing, sultry and much too tempting for her own good.

"Thank you Tally, you are so very brave."

She's biting her bottom lip again and I growl in

frustration.

"What?" she asks innocently, and I know it isn't an act.

"You're sexy as hell and I need to go." I turn and head for her door. I hear her following behind me, but I don't dare turn around, sometimes a guy just knows when it's time to call a game because of rain. As I'm pulling the front door open, I hear my name.

"Trey," her voice is not loud, but it isn't meek either.

I turn and look at her. Thankfully, she has stayed on the steps, a safe distance away.

"I'll see you tomorrow?" she asks, and I see the vulnerability in her eyes.

Reassurance Trey, I growl to myself, she needs reassurance. "Will your parents mind if I pick you up?" I ask.

Her face brightens and I can nearly feel the warmth flowing off of her. She shakes her head, "No, they will most likely be gone by then, but even if they aren't they won't mind."

"I'll see you at 7:45."

She nods and blushes as I wink at her. I close the door quickly behind me trying not to slam it. My good intentions and chivalry only run so deep, and like I had told her, the circumstances were way too perfect.

I get in my truck and grip the steering wheel so tightly that my knuckles turn white. I let out a slow breath and when I'm finally calm enough to drive, I start it up. As I'm driving home flashes of that kiss, of her lips and the way she felt, keep popping up in my mind and I resign myself to the fact that I'm going to have to take another shower before I go to bed. Cold would be good, frigid would be better.

Chapter 18

> **"I've decided that an excellent way to burn calories is smiling. My decision is not based on the fact that I can't seem to get this ridiculous grin off my face. The fact that I think smiling burns calories and I can't stop smiling is simply a happy coincidence." ~Tally**

I swear I am nearly doing a victory dance right there on the freaking lawn, no joke. As soon as I walk out of my house and see Trey's truck sitting in my drive way, I have to fight my hips from wiggling and my arms from rising into the air.

He climbs out of his truck and I'm mesmerized as he walks around the front and opens the passenger door. He is wearing his usual faded jeans, work boots, and this time a red polo style shirt. The red is arresting on him. It brings out the gold in his tan skin and makes his black hair appear even darker. I feel so plain in my shorts and long sleeve tee. It is a fitted tee so at least it shows what little curves I have. Even with the pink streaks in my hair, next to exotic looking Trey, I feel like I could simply blend in with my surroundings.

"Morning beautiful," he smiles at me. My heart stutters in my chest and I bite my lip to keep from giggling. Bloody hell, what is wrong with you, I shout at myself.

"Morning," I say simply. I walk up to the open door, but before I can get in Trey wraps an arm around me and kisses me on the forehead. I lean into him and hate that I have to get in the truck, because it means his arms won't be around me. I climb in anyway, the door is shut, and Trey is in the driver seat before I even get my seatbelt on.

"Can I be frank?" I ask.

"I guess if you want, but it might be a little weird telling people that my girlfriend's name is Frank." he shrugs at me as if he is really serious, and I am really talking about wanting to be called Frank.

"Ha, ha, Swift," I say as I smack his arm lightly, "seriously though, I'm going to be blunt so I hope that you aren't easily offended."

He nods his head as if to say, 'go on.'

"Is this really the way you are?"

He frowns, "What do you mean?"

"You know, so sweet and attentive. We're not going to get six months into this relationship and suddenly you become an asshat right?" I know I must sound like a paranoid ninny, but I need him to be upfront and straight with me.

"This is the only way I know to be Tally," he tells me gently. "I watched my father and how he adored my mother. He treated her like a precious gem. Their marriage wasn't perfect, but there wasn't a day that I ever doubted his love for her." he pauses, "Do I need to back off?" He glances at me quickly before returning his eyes back to the road, and in that quick glance I see worry in his beautiful face.

"No," I tell him quickly. I clear my throat slightly embarrassed that I just word vomited on him. "I mean, I'm not saying I don't like it. I love it," I duck my head not wanting him to see my humiliation at such a needy declaration.

"Hey," he says softly. I glance up at him. He reaches for my hand though his eyes stay looking forward. I place my hand in his and feel the strength and warmth as he wraps his large fingers around my much smaller ones. "Don't ever be afraid or ashamed to tell me how you feel or what you need. I know this is new, but how else will we learn if we aren't open with each other?"

"Are you sure you're only 18?" I ask, only half teasing.

A sly smile forms on his lips. "My grandmother tells me I have an old soul."

"Add a *very* in front of old, and I will agree with her."

We ride in silence the rest of the way to school. It isn't an awkward silence and I don't feel the need to force conversation that just isn't there right now. I keep stealing glances at Trey as he drives. I notice the tight muscles in his forearms as he grips the steering wheel and can't help but remember the few times he has wrapped me in those arms. The strong line of his jaw is relaxed, but his eyes are alert. I see his lips twitch slightly as if he's trying not to smile, and I know I've been caught.

~

Natalie sees me climbing out of Trey's truck and a smile the size of Texas spreads across her face. I groan inwardly knowing I'm never going to hear the end of this. She comes sauntering up, her hips swaying with a slight bounce in her step.

"Good morning, Tally," she says sweetly, too sweetly.

"Nat," I say, with a slight warning I hope she hears.

She ignores me, figures.

"Trey, my main man." Her voice imitates the little girl on 'Wreck it Ralph,' and I have to stop myself from grabbing Trey's arm and running.

"Good morning Natalie," Trey says smoothly as he takes my hand. Her eyes latch onto our clasped hands and if I thought her smile couldn't get any bigger, I was smoking something good.

"How was the rest of your night after I left?" she asks me as we all start walking towards the front doors.

I shrug, "Nothing exciting."

Trey chuckles, and I nudge him with my shoulder.

Nat raises a brow at me as her eyes narrow. "Uh-huh, right."

"How was your night?" I ask innocently totally ignoring her evil eye.

As soon as the words are out of my mouth, she is once again beaming.

"Bobby texted me," she says in sheer delight.

"Aren't you two dating?" Trey asks, as he looks around me to Nat.

Natalie frowns, "Does it seem like we're dating?"

Trey shrugs, "He seems pretty into you, so I just thought you must be together."

Her eyes dart from Trey to me. "Do you think it seems like we're together?"

"Not from your end, but Bobby has been pretty blatant about how he feels. You're just oblivious Nat."

"Really?" She asks.

"Hey guys," Bobby says as he catches up with us in the hall.

"Hey Bobby," Nat and I say in unison. Trey does

the whole guy, head nod thing.

"Bobby, are you into Natalie?" Trey asks, bluntly.

My jaw drops open and Nat's about hits the floor. I look up at Trey and then over to Natalie whose face is in more shades of red than Sherwin Williams offers. I look at Bobby, thinking that he's going to be just as embarrassed, but no, he's grinning like a damn fool.

"You've been here all of two days Swift, and you caught on that quick?"

"That's why they call me Swift," he jokes.

Natalie's head whips around to look at Bobby. He grins at her and then wraps an arm around her shoulders tugging her to him. I hear him whisper, "Morning Angel." They walk off together and I stand stunned, looking from them to Trey.

"What?" he asks me.

"What was that?"

"I just figured they might as well get it out there. Natalie obviously doesn't always have all her French fries in her happy meal, so I thought I'd help Bobby out."

I laugh, "All her French fries?"

He smiles at me and I feel my stomach drop, yeah it's one of those smiles.

"Come on, we don't want to be late." he tells me as he lets go of my hand and wraps his arm around my waist.

My day is much like the day before, other than me fighting Trey the whole time of course. No one bothers me. We walk down the halls together hand in hand talking, laughing and no one says a thing. People always just seem to get out of Trey's way when he's walking so we never have to walk around anyone. There is just something about him that screams *move or die*, and yet I know just how gentle he can be.

~

"How is your one class without Trey?" Nat asks me as we stand at her locker waiting on the guys.

"Everyone just ignores me and I want to keep it that way. So," I say as I flash a smile, "what's with you and Bobby?"

Her face, once again, flushes as she looks down and fiddles with the zipper on her purse. "He asked me out on a date."

"That's great Nat," I pause, "right?"

She nods with a shy smile, "I can't believe I didn't realize he likes me. How long have you known," she snaps suddenly.

My eyes widen at her and I cringe as I say, "Like a year or so."

"WHAT?" she nearly yells, catches herself, and then begins whispering frantically. "You've known for a year that a guy, a freaking hot guy, has liked, me and you didn't bother to tell me? Isn't that against some code in the handbook or something?"

"What handbook?" I ask with a frown.

"The girlfriend handbook, you know, hoes before bros, toys before boys, or, crap I don't know, but there's a handbook." she snaps.

"I plead insanity," I smirk at her.

"You can only milk that crazy crap for so long Baker." her words are sharp, but I see the humor in her eyes and know she isn't really mad at me.

"So, where are you going on your date?"

"Paradise," Bobby says with a wicked grin as he walks up behind Nat. She turns her head slightly to look up at him and he winks. I feel arms come around me from behind and instinctively lean back against the firm chest.

"How did you know I wasn't some strange guy getting grabby with you?" I hear Trey's voice in my ear and his warm breath against my skin gives me goose bumps.

"There is no one in this school, save Bobby, who comes close to having arms as big as you. I was pretty certain it had to be my," the words hang in my throat. I was about to call him my boyfriend, I mean, that is what he is right, I ask myself. But what if I'm being presumptuous? What if he doesn't think of us in those terms, maybe he just wants to say we're dating.

"Your what, Tally?" he says, loud enough for Nat and Bobby to hear.

I feel my face heat up and I try to duck my head but Trey deftly turns me in his arms and raises my chin to look at him. "Your what?"

"My, um, well you know," I'm stumbling around like an idiot searching his eyes for the words he wants to hear, but he gives nothing away. "Grr," I growl in frustration, "My boyfriend." I finally snap out.

A huge grin spreads across his face and I start to smile back, but then I realize he baited me into admitting it. I slap him across the chest. "You butt head, I was all worried that you might not want me to call you that. Why didn't you just say it?"

"Because, I wanted to hear it from you," he says, matter of fact, not bothered in the least by my frustration or that I'm taking it out on him.

I hear Natalie clear her throat behind me. "So you

guys are together?" she asks and I hear the smugness in her voice.

Trey looks down at me and the smoldering heat that seems to always lie just below the surface rises in his eyes, "We are definitely together." he murmurs and then leans down and kisses me softly.

~

"I have something to tell you," Trey says as he pulls into my driveway. I look over at him and the worry I feel must show on my face, because he smiles and says, "It's a good something."

"Okay." I tell him, and feel my shoulders relax.

"I talked with Mr. Taggert and he said I can bring you out to see the horses any time."

"Really?" I ask and fight not to clap my hands like an over-excited child.

"Yes really," he smiles. "When would you like to go?"

I start flipping through my schedule in my mind, like I'm so busy. I have therapy on Thursday and that's about it.

"How about Friday?" I ask.

He nods, "Friday it is." he frowns briefly and I can tell that he is thinking about something.

"What's up?"

"Shouldn't I meet your parents before I take you on a date?"

I had honestly never thought about introducing Trey to my parents, but I suppose I will have to eventually. Part of me doesn't want to. I want to keep him to myself as if he were my own secret paradise untouched and un-scrutinized by my parents.

"I guess so. I'll have to see if they will be home. Their schedules are pretty crazy."

"Alright, I'll just plan to meet them, unless you tell me otherwise."

"Sounds good." I sit there a moment, wonder if I should invite him in or do I just say have a nice evening, and climb out? I look over at him and as usual, I can't tell what he is thinking.

"Okay, have a good evening." I decide to go with the least embarrassing. I start to open my door, but Trey reaches out and grabs my left hand.

"I had a good day Tally," he tells me and the look in his eyes turns my insides to warm liquid. "Come here." He tugs me towards him across the bench seat and brings one hand up to cup my face. As his soft, full lips press to mine, I fight the need to get closer to him, to climb into his lap and beg him to let me stay there.

When he ends the kiss, I take a deep, shaky breath and open my eyes.

"You're really good at that," I tell him honestly.

"Kissing?" he grins

"Yes." I feel a rush of blood bloom on my cheeks, and they warm under his scrutiny.

"It's easy to be good at something that you so thoroughly enjoy."

I let out a nervous laugh, because really what do you say to that?

"K, I'm going to go now," I tell him as I scoot back over to the passenger side and push the door open.

"I'm going to visit my mom, and then I have work. I'll text you later," he tells me. I'm glad for it, glad that he gives me something to look forward to and doesn't leave me wondering what his next move is going to be.

"Tell your mom I said hi."

"I will."

I walk towards my front door and try not to turn around as I hear him backing out of my driveway. I've already made such a fool of myself, drooling over him, and looking at him in awe and wonder. It's freaking ridiculous.

~

I take a seat in Dr. Stacey's office and glance around at my surroundings. They are surroundings that I have become so familiar with over time. It's a place that has grown to be more comfortable to me than my own home and I wonder, not for the first time, if I will ever feel at ease in my house, ever again.

I spent the night before writing in the journal Dr. Stacey had told me to keep. She said that sometimes writing out my feelings might help me see a change in my emotions before they get too far out of control. I asked her what I should write about. I'd never kept a journal before and writing about my day just seemed so redundant. I mean I had just lived it. Why do I need to catalogue it?

So, she said instead of writing about my day she wanted me to attempt to write poems about how I was feeling. She didn't care if they were simple, complex, or rhymed or not. She just wanted me to pay attention to my emotions.

"Hi Tally," she says as she sits down across from

me. She hasn't changed a bit, although why I thought she should have in the past nearly three weeks that I had been gone was a mystery to me.

"Hey doc," I smile, and it's genuine.

"I see you brought your journal." she motions to the notebook lying next to me on the couch.

I hand it to her and as she opens it she begins to read it—out loud. Great, now I get to listen to her read just how bad my poetry is.

"I am broken, but my pieces have been placed back where they belong,

I am a jumbled mess of notes, but they are slowly becoming a song.

I am a torn quilt, but the needle has been threaded to mend the frayed seam.

I am a dull piece of pottery, but the glaze is being added to create the gleam.

I am in this tired and worn body, though I thought that I was lost,

To finally begin to be repaired is good, but it wasn't worth the cost.

I don't want to dance too much, smile too wide, or laugh too hard,

I've been dealt a new hand and I'm waiting on that one bad card."

The silence in the room was suffocating as I watched Dr. Stacey's face as she read it again only silently this time. When she finally looked up at me, I saw a mixture of emotions on her face.

"You are hopeful, but you don't want to be," she finally says.

"I guess that I just feel like that living with this disease is going to be a constant waiting game of when the next shoe will drop."

She shook her head at me. "It doesn't have to be that way Tally. Take your meds, come to your therapy, and work on having a support system. If you do these things, you will be able to catch the swing before it gets too far in the opposite direction. Over time you will begin to gage your moods and pick up on when you need your meds adjusted or therapy to increase."

I glance out the window as if I will find a sign that says Dr. Stacey is right. Listen to her. And, I want to believe her, but when you have been where I have, the only thing you can think is that you know you can't go back. I don't know that I would survive falling that far again.

"I'm dating Trey," I blurt out suddenly. Don't ask me where that came from. It was just one of those things that had been bubbling up and though I tried to swallow it down it refused to go.

Dr. Stacey smiles at me, a gentle smile that said she thought it was a good thing.

"How is it going?" she asks.

"Sometimes he seems too good to be true," I finally admit, out loud. I didn't want to say it to Trey. I didn't want to hurt him.

She nodded, "He's very mature for his age, but then he has been through a lot in his young age. His father died and that tragedy seemed to trigger the schizophrenia in his mom and he has been caring for her. It can be a very tragic mental illness."

I couldn't begin to imagine what Trey had been through, what he was still going through.

"I didn't want to date him."

"Why?"

"For the reasons I told you before. I don't want to

be just one more tragic tale in his story."

She tilts her head at me and looks thoughtful. "In order for you to date Trey, it requires you to trust him to be able to cope with your bipolar disorder."

I nod.

"And you don't think he will be able to?"

"He hasn't seen me at my worst doc. You told me that stress can cause chemicals to get depleted more quickly and that the meds sometimes don't keep up with that, which means I might crash. How is he going to handle that? And then how am I going to handle how he is handling it?"

"You are worrying about something that may or may not happen. You can't live your life like that Tally. If you do your life will pass, and before you know it you will be grown and very lonely."

"You're so cheery doc, thanks." I tell her as I roll my eyes. I know that my worrying will do nothing. I know that it's pointless and maybe that's why I decided to go ahead and date Trey.

"How is school going?" she completely ignores my sarcasm as she often does.

"The first day was hell." I tell her about my locker and as I sit there talking about it, reliving the emotions of seeing those blades on my locker something inside me crumbles. I sit there with tears sliding down my cheeks, and I wonder when I will ever sit in her office and not cry. I'm convinced she pumps something into the air that makes a person feel emotionally naked.

"I guess I was hoping that people would just let it go," I tell her as I wipe my eyes.

"People often deal with things they don't understand in one of several ways," she leans back in her chair and lays her hands in her lap, "they get angry, they get scared or they become defensive. Teenagers are especially difficult because you all are dealing with all the hormones swirling about inside of you as you try and figure out who you are. Your classmates don't understand what they saw last year. They are scared of it, and they are dealing with that fear by being defensive. If they make you out to be insignificant, then they don't have to be afraid of you or what you have done or might do."

"No offense doc, but that's just ridiculous. What they did was cruel."

She nods, "You are correct. It was cruel. I'm not defending them; I'm just trying to help you understand their motivation even if they don't know why they are doing it."

I told her then about Trey and how he had threatened Carter and she didn't seem surprised by it.

"He is a natural protector. In the Native American culture, the men are the hunters, protectors, and leaders of their tribes. It is literally bred into Trey to be that way. My advice would be to be open and honest with him about your feelings and be patient with him. Try not to see your relationship in black and white because life is not black and white. It is full of grayish hues."

"I'll try," I tell her simply. She looks at her watch and I know our session is over. I stand and take my notebook when she hands it back to me.

"Keep writing. You are very good at it."

I smile at her though I don't really know how to take the compliment. "Thanks," is my brilliant response.

As I'm walking out of her door, she calls my name. I look back at her. "Tally, you're doing well. Practice being still this week and make sure you are getting plenty of sleep."

"I'm on it doc," I tell her as I close the door behind me.

~

"Finally!" Candy groans as I step into the hall. I smile at her. "I thought you were never coming out, I mean seriously were you guys trying to come up with a solution for world peace or something?"

"Candy, some of us actually go to therapy and stay for the entire session."

"Bah, who has time for therapy when there are rules to break, patients to scare, and staff to annoy?"

I laugh as she grabs my hand and starts tugging me towards the rec room.

"What do you have up your sleeve now?"

"Have you ever seen nut jobs do karaoke?" she asks me with a twinkle flashing in her eyes.

"No."

"You might want to go pee first, I don't want you having an accident when you're rolling on the floor laughing. Actually we can just get you one of those adult diapers."

"I'm not wearing a diaper Candy," I growl.

"Don't say I didn't warn you when you're walking out of here with pee running down your leg."

Chapter 19

"I'm going to give you a little test. If you are a patient at a mental hospital and one of the paranoids asks you if all the government spies have been detained, do you: A) Calmly tell the patient that, yes, the spies are all gone and they are safe; B) Tell the patient to leave you the hell alone; or C) Whisper in the patient's ear to be very still because he is being watched, and then tell him that in order to escape the spies he has to convincingly pretend to be a chicken. If you answered anything but C, stay away from me because I just might take you out at the knees you pansy." ~Candy

~ Trey ~

As I climb out of my truck, I glance back at Tally. She's nearly bouncing in her seat she's so excited. I smile to myself as I walk around to the passenger door and open it.

"Ready?" I ask as I take her hand in mine.

"Yep," she grins.

Her eyes widen as we enter the stable and she sees just how nice it is. From the outside, it looks like a simple barn, but on the inside, it's beautiful with shaved wooden posts and cedar stalls all of which have been lacquered to a lustrous sheen. Mr. Taggert has spared no expense for his horses, but then he has made good money off of them.

"It's so big," she says as she turns in a slow circle, her eyes scanning over her surroundings. A gentle huff catches her attention as she turns and sees Rosa, a beautiful bay mare, sticking her head out of her stall.

"Who's that?" she asks me as she walks slowly towards the horse.

"That's Rosa, she's my personal favorite."

Tally reaches her hand out slowly and holds it just about the height of Rosa's nose, like she is asking for permission to touch the beautiful animal. Rosa blows air out of her mouth making the same huffing sound that had caught Tally's attention, and then raises her head so that Tally's hand is pressed against her face just above her nose. Tally laughs and turns back to look at me. Her smile is so big. It's contagious, and I can't help but return it. I watch as she steps closer to Rosa and lays her cheek against the side of the mare's face. Her shoulders relax and her breathing almost matches that of the horse.

This is one of the reason's Rosa is my favorite. They say that horses have an ability to connect with broken people and are often used for therapy purposes. Rosa could be a therapy horse. She seemed to sense a person's mood and responds accordingly. In this moment, I know that I am witnessing exactly what a therapy horse does. Rosa nuzzles Tally's shoulder and lowers her head so that Tally can wrap her arms around the horse's neck. Tally didn't hesitate. She buried her face in the black mane and seems to block out the world around her.

I walk over to Lucky's stall and click my tongue at the horse. He comes sauntering over and sticks out his huge brown head.

"Hey Lucky, you want to go for a ride?" I ask him as I clip a lead to his halter and open his stall. I lead him over to the tack room and tie him to the hitching post. I gathered the saddle blanket, saddle, and bridle and get him ready. Once he is ready to go I look back over at Tally and see that she is now brushing Rosa's mane with one of the brushes hanging on the horse's stall and talking to her.

"You want to go for a ride?" I call over.

Tally's head snaps up and she looks at me.

"Really?"

I nod. "Grab that lead that's hanging there on the hook and clip it to her halter. Then bring her over here."

I gather up Rosa's tack, and once Tally has her standing next to Lucky, proceed to saddle her up.

"Who's this handsome boy?" she asks, pointing to Lucky.

"This is Lucky. He's one of the studs, meaning they use him for breeding."

"I can see why they call him Lucky then." She looks at me and winks with a slight blush to her skin that almost causes me to blush in return—almost.

"Okay, instructions," I walk her around to Rosa's side, "to mount the horse you grab the horn of the saddle, that's this." I grab the horn demonstrating how to grasp it. "And, with the other hand you grab the cantle. That's this part that rises up on the back of the seat. Then put your left foot in the stirrup and at the same time you push with your leg, you're going to pull with your arms." I demonstrate for her and then climb back down. "Now, you try."

She places her hands where I had directed and lifts her foot up into the stirrup. As she begins to push and pull, I place my hands on her hips and lift. She swings her right leg up and over and sits in the seat.

She looks down at me with a knowing smile. "You didn't have to help me, I could have done it myself."

"I have no doubt that you could have, but then I wouldn't have gotten to put my hands on your waist now would I?"

Lucky shifts his hooves restlessly as I unhook the leads. I climb up on his back and then look over at Tally. "Okay, riding is pretty easy. A gentle squeeze of your legs will get Rosa going. And, if you squeeze a little harder, she'll pick up her speed. She will turn in whichever direction you steer her with the reins. If you lay them over her neck to the right she will turn right and vice versa. Make sense?"

She gives me a determined nod, "Got it."

"Alright, follow me."

I lead her out of the back of the stable onto the land Mr. Taggert owns. There are trails all over that he has made specifically for his horses, but I don't take one of the trails. I lead her out to an open field.

"So, you ready to test her out?" I ask her.

Tally gives me a flirty smile that makes my pulse speed up. "Didn't you know Swift, I was born ready." To my surprise, she gives a click of her tongue and as if Rosa understands what Tally wants, she takes off. I am too stunned to follow, so I just watch.

Rosa is beautiful when she runs, but the woman sitting astride her only improves the view. I watch as Tally leans forward, her face close to Rosa's mane. The wind blows through her hair, and her body seems to move as one with the mare. As Rosa makes a wide circle Tally sits up straight, stretches her arms out wide and throws her head back. Her eyes are closed and her lips are turned up in a joyfully beautiful smile. She rides with total abandonment of herself. She seems to soar like a bird over the field rising and dipping with the mare's progression across the terrain. Rosa picks up the pace just a tad, but her stride is so smooth that it doesn't even jostle Tally. I can't remember seeing a more beautiful sight. She rides that way until Rosa brings her back to my side.

She smiles at me, her hair wild and her skin red from the winds kiss.

"Did you enjoy that?" I ask.

"You have no idea," she laughs and Rosa seems to hold her head a little higher as if to say *I'm the one who brought her that joy.*

I reach over and pat Rosa's head, "You're a good girl Rosa, love."

"Love?" Tally asks, with a smirk.

"Jealous?"

"Maybe."

I laugh and squeeze Lucky, clicking my tongue. I call over my shoulder as Lucky takes off, "You have nothing to be jealous of baby."

The sun is beginning to set by the time I pull into Tally's drive way. I get out and walk around to help her out of my truck. I take her hand, but make no move to walk her to the door. Instead, I pull her to me and wrap my arms around her, pushing her back gently until she is pressed against the side of the truck.

"Well, hello to you too," she grins at me.

I look down at her face and my eyes roam over her beautiful features. Her perky nose and cute chin, her big eyes and full lips, lips I want to taste.

"Did you have fun today?" I ask before I give in to

my desires.

She nods and bites her bottom lip. "I had the best time I've ever had. It was amazing Trey, really, thank you." To my surprise, she leans up and pulls me down at the same time until our lips are firmly pressed together. Her mouth is soft and warm, and I know I should be gentle, but my restraint can only last for long. I nip at her bottom lip and she gasps. I take advantage and deepen the kiss. She moans and presses closer to me. Her body is lithe and small and feels so good to my hands. I squeeze her hips and then gradually slip my hands up her back. Tally arches back into my grasp and my lips leave hers and wander to her cheek, across her jaw, down her neck to the hollow of her throat. Her head falls back, just as it had when she had been riding Rosa, only now the look on her face is one of desire and longing. I kiss her neck again and listen to the sound of her breathing increase.

"Trey," my name is a plea from her lips, and I pull her closer as if she could possibly get any closer. "Trey I," her words catch in her throat when my hands slip under her shirt and graze across the soft skin of her back. "Oh," she says, breathlessly.

I grin at her, "Like that?"

She nods.

"Your skin is the softest thing I have ever felt," I whisper in her ear. "Tally," I blow gently on her ear and then kiss her just below it. I feel her teeth nip the skin on my neck and I nearly beg her not to stop. I pull back and my breathing is erratic at best. "We've got to stop baby," I tell her gently. She nods and smiles up at me. Her lips glisten in the moonlight moist from our kiss and her chest rises and falls with each rapid breath.

"You're beautiful."

"Thank you, you're not too bad yourself," she teases.

I chuckle and take a step back, my hands on her hips once again making sure she's steady. She lets out a deep breath blowing through puffed cheeks. "Sorry you didn't get to meet my parents, maybe next time though. Okay, guess I better go in." She takes a step towards her house.

I nod and step away from her. "I'll text you tomorrow."

She gives me one last smile as she walks across her lawn to the front door. I see her step into the lighted house, and then she's gone behind the closed door and I want nothing more than to rip the door off its hinges and bring her back to my side.

~

"How is she doing tonight Zeke?" I ask the orderly, as I walk towards my mother's room.

"She's had a rough day. I don't know if she's still awake."

"Okay, thank you for keeping an eye on her for me." The last time that I had been in to visit my mother I had asked Zeke to let me know if my mom began to get worse. He had been more than happy to keep an eye on her, and I truly did appreciate it.

I knock on her door and wait, but there is no answer, so I gently push it open. My mother lies in the small bed on her side. Her eyes are open, but she doesn't appear to be seeing her surroundings.

"Mom," I say, gently, as I walk into the dark room.

The only light is from the moon that shines in through the only window. "I heard you had a rough day again." I kneel down in front of her and brush her hair back from her face. She looks as if she has aged ten years in the past two weeks. Her skin is pale and seems to sag on her bones. She's lost weight and it's causing her eyes to sink into their sockets. I reach out and take her hand in mine. I'm as careful as possible, because she feels like the slightest squeeze would crush her bones.

She doesn't respond to my voice or my touch. She simply lies, staring at nothing. The anger that I keep under tight control pulls against the bonds in my chest. The medicines aren't working, the therapy isn't working, and she is just getting worse. Day by day, she slips further away from me. I can't even begin to imagine what it must be like for my grandmother, even though she is my father's mother, she still feels as though my mom is her daughter. How horrible would it be to watch a disease destroy your child's mind, and in turn, her life?

"I love you mom," I whisper, not knowing if she is listening or if she can even hear me above the other voices. "I love you."

I sit with her long into the night. She never once moves or says anything, and finally, at nearly one in the morning she closes her eyes and sleeps.

As I step out of her room sometime later, closing the door quietly behind me, I nearly jump when I come face to face with Candy.

"Boo," she whispers an inch from my face.

"Candy," I say in a calm voice that belies the pounding heart in my chest. Candy's face is not one that you want to have sneak up on you, nor is Candy herself one that you want coming up behind you without your knowledge.

"You're here awfully late or early," she says as she takes a step back, allowing me some room.

"I sat with my mom," I tell her and she nods, but I can tell her mind is somewhere else.

"How's my girl?" She asks me with eager eyes.

"She's good. She told me about karaoke."

"Bah," she waves her hand at me, "that was tame compared to some of my adventures."

"You've had something worse happen than the patients mooning the staff?"

She grins, "I'll never tell."

"So, has Tally finally given in to her feelings for you or is she still being a stubborn twit?" Candy asks me.

"She's come around, but I didn't give her much of a choice."

"Good for you," she looks away from me briefly, and I notice a strained look on her face.

"Candy are you alright?" I take a step closer and reach out to touch her shoulder. Just before my hand touches her, she begins to crumble. I move quickly, catching her before she can hit the cold tile floor.

"Zeke!" I yell the first name I can think of. I pick Candy up in my arms, and I can't believe how light she is. She weighs nothing at all, and it surprises me that a strong wind hasn't already blown her over. I hear footsteps running towards me and as soon as they come into view, I start heading towards Candy's room.

"She just collapsed," I holler back at the three people following quickly behind me.

An arm reaches around me and opens Candy's door and I walk in and lay her on her bed. One of the nurses and Zeke step around me and begin looking

Candy over. I watch as they check for a pulse and to see if she's breathing. The nurse puts a blood pressure cuff on her, Zeke pulls a phone out, dials a number, and when he begins talking, I presume he's calling a doctor. They work efficiently as if they have done this a thousand times before.

"Yes," Zeke's deep voice rumbles. "She's collapsed again."

Again, I think. I didn't know that Candy was sick. Tally hasn't mentioned it and neither has Candy.

"Her vitals are all over the place." He pauses and nods his head at whatever he is being told. "Alright, see you in a few." He ends the call.

"Is she going to be alright?" I ask the big man.

The look in Zeke's eyes tells me something much different than his words. "She's tough, she'll get through it. But it would probably be best for you to go ahead and go."

I nod and start towards the door, but before I can open it, I hear her voice.

"Do not tell her Tonto. Please, do not tell her."

I look back at Candy, usually so full of life and mischief. Now her eyes are glassy, her mouth slack and her skin pale and dry.

"Okay Candy, but you need to tell her, soon."

She gives me a small nod and then closes her eyes. It was as if it had taken every ounce of strength left in her body to give that one small motion.

~

It isn't until I'm driving home that I realize what I

have promised. If Candy dies before Tally has a chance to find out what is going on, she will be livid with me. I'd told Candy I wouldn't say anything to Tally, but Tally's feelings come before all others, and I refuse to lie to her. I could handle Candy being hurt by my actions, but not Tally.

As I walk into the house I check my phone and see that I can catch a couple hours sleep before I have to be up to go to work. But, when my head hits the pillow, sleep doesn't come. My mind can only think of how hard it is going to be to tell Tally that something is wrong with Candy and I can't help but worry about how this will affect her. She has been through so much all ready and I want her to get to have some peace, some happiness that will help replace the pain from the past months. If it was in my power, I would make sure that Tally would never endure such pain again. But then, as my grandmother would say, *to protect a person from anything bad that might happen to them would actually be crippling to them. For it is by learning to overcome the pain and the hurt of that difficult time, that a person grows and become stronger.*

Tally is strong, no doubt, but everyone has their breaking point.

Chapter 20

"I'm learning something, and it's a lesson that I don't think most people learn until later on in life, way past their teenage years. Happiness is fleeting. It hits like a bolt of lightning, and then it is gone again in the blink of an eye. More life is lived in the valley with the rain than on the mountain top with the bolts of lightning. That may seem insightful for a seventeen year old, but what is truly profound is this: if you want to have a full life, then you will figure out a way to find joy in the rain soaked valley." ~Tally

"How are things with Bobby?" I ask Nat as I lay on the floor of my room staring up at the ceiling. She is on my bed painting her toe nails and humming a Dixie Chicks' song about some loser named Earl.

"Good, but almost too good, you know?"

I snort as a huff of laughter escapes me, "Yeah, I totally know. Trey is...," I pause trying to find the right words, ones that are not insulting, yet truthful, "he's just intense and I keep thinking what if this is just an act, or if this is how he thinks he has to act, in order for me to date him."

"I don't think it is," she says. "I mean, think about it, Tal. He comes from a totally different culture and, based on how he dresses and sometimes the way he talks, it's not like he's Native American and that's just his heritage, it's a part of who he is and part of what has made him who he is. Add to that the fact that his mother is sick and he has had to take care of her. You end up with a guy who never really has been able to be young. He's a grown man with grown man responsibilities. He's a keeper Tally."

I roll over on my side, bending my arm up, so I can prop my hand on my head. I look up at Nat and smile, "I think so too and I'm trying to keep from worrying about the *what ifs*."

"Good. Now back to your original question. Bobby has been great. He took me out last night and we just sat at the restaurant and talked. It's so weird to realize how much stuff we didn't know about one another."

I feel my heart swell as I listen to the happiness saturate Nat's words. Her face lights up every time she says his name and it makes me think about how I feel when I say Trey's name or when I think of Trey. This is what seventeen is supposed to be like I realize: boys, my best friend, painting toe nails, and just living. I try to soak it in like a dry sponge seeking out any tiny drop of water. I want to hold on to this feeling for as long as possible to treasure it for the gift that it is.

"Why aren't you with Trey today?" Nat asks me.

"I actually haven't seen him since Friday. He's had to work and help his grandmother with some stuff. I don't want him to think that I need to spend every waking moment with him. He's been texting me and that's been nice."

"So, what do you want to do today besides listen to me ramble on about my emerging love life?" she flutters her eyelashes at me dramatically.

"I want to visit Candy; I haven't seen her since Thursday. You want to come?"

"Sure, but then afterward we are going shopping."

I narrow my eyes at her, "Shopping for what?"

She lets out an exasperated sigh, "Tally please tell me you haven't totally forgotten about the upcoming Fall Ball?"

"Oh yeah, the dance," I say attempting to seem totally oblivious to it. "Are you sure I should just assume that Trey and I are going?"

"Oh please, even if he doesn't ask you, you're still going." Nat raises an eyebrow, giving me her *just try me* look.

"Why would I go without him?" I ask her.

"Because, it's your senior year and you will be going to every dance we have. You have to make memories Tal, memories that you can smile about."

I can see that she means well. She just wants me to be happy, like Candy. She wants me to experience life.

"Don't argue with me Tally," she continues, "just accept that as long as I am here you will be doing things that you might not want to, but that are for your own good."

"Yes mother," I say, dryly.

"Yeah, well someone needs to be." she snaps.

"You done?"

"For now."

I roll my eyes at her as I stand up. "Good, let's go."

~

As we're walking into Mercy, I feel my back pocket vibrate. I pull my phone out and look down to see a text alert.

Trey: How r u?

Will I try and pretend my face didn't just break into some stupid grin? Absolutely, but the proof is in the pudding.

Me: Good, about to visit Candy.

It's several minutes before he responds and just before we reach Candy's room, he finally does.

Trey: Call me if u need me.

Oookay, I think to myself, that wasn't really the response I was expecting. I just shrug it off.

Me: K

I tuck it back in my pocket and then knock on Candy's closed door.

"What?" I hear her snap from behind the door.

Nat looks at me and I shake my head. "She's always like that."

"Candy, it's Tally and Natalie, can we come in?"

I hear rustling and then the door opens.

She looks so very tired. Her eyes are sunken in and her lips drawn tight across her face. Her usually quick movements are now sluggish, and seem to require an enormous amount of effort.

"Candy are you alright? Don't tell me no, because it's obvious something is wrong."

"If it's obvious, then why bother to ask?" she asks flatly.

"Because, it's not like you are going to offer the information up willingly." I point out.

"I've had a little cold. It's nothing to get your panties in a wad about."

I watch her as she sits on her bed and I honestly wonder how she is going to push herself back against the headboard. She seems so weak, but she manages it, although, she is short of breath afterwards. Natalie glances at me and I see the same worry in her eyes that

I know is in my own.

"It's good to see you Candy," Nat tells her and I believe she genuinely means it. I think that Nat's fondness of Candy stems from the fact that Candy was there for me all summer.

Candy nods at Natalie but doesn't respond. We stand there in front of her bed simply looking at her and it's the first time I can ever remember feeling awkward in front of her.

"Brat," she looks up at me. "Go get us some cards or something. You two just standing there staring at me is making me feel like a cockroach you've stepped on and are waiting for its legs to stop kicking so you can grab it and throw it out."

"Feeling descriptive today I see," I say, as I head for the door.

"I didn't ask for a running commentary on my behavior. Go get the damn cards." she growls at me.

This I can take. Candy growling and snapping means that she's all right. Subdued, quiet Candy scares me.

Natalie stays while I head towards the rec room to grab a deck of cards. As I enter the room, I see Trey's mom sitting over in her usual spot. She, like Candy, seems to be withering away. The bright eyes that had glimmered at me with anger, weeks ago, were now foggy and lost.

I grab one of the decks from the table, and then walk over to where she is sitting. I take the seat right next to her and sit silently for a moment waiting to see if she will acknowledge me.

When she doesn't, I finally speak. "Hi Mrs. Swift," I say softly.

She continues to stare straight ahead, totally

oblivious to my presence.

I try again, "Trey tells me you're having a rough time."

It has to be the sound of his name that makes her respond. She slowly turns her head to look at me and there is a flash of recognition.

"Trey," she whispers and her voice is dry and scratchy as if it had been a long time since her last drink of water.

"I'm Tally, do you remember me?"

She stares and I think she is trying to place me.

"You came back to him," she murmurs. "I told him you would."

Her words surprise me.

"Yes, he can be quite persuasive when he wants to be." I smile warmly.

"He deserves to be happy," she tells me and then suddenly growls. "NO, I will not say such a thing."

I realize that she isn't speaking to me, but to someone that I cannot see, and based on how her body begins to shake, whoever that someone is terrifies her.

"Are you alright Mrs. Swift? Do I need to get the nurse?" I ask her as I lean forward and place my hand on the one she has resting on her lap. It is fisted and she is squeezing it so tight that her knuckles have turned white.

"There is no help for me child. No one can help me." Her eyes meet mine and I steel myself against the sickness I see there. "They are determined to have me, and I'm tired of fighting."

I feel a ripple of fear slide down my spine. "Lolotea, please keep trying. Trey needs you here with him."

I wait for her to respond but her eyes have once

again fogged over and she has retreated back inside. I sit there a moment longer and gently squeeze her hand. As I stand and begin to walk away, I hear a soft voice, "It's you he needs now."

I glance back at her, but she doesn't appear to have moved.

"Did you have to go to the manufacturer to get the freaking cards?" Candy gripes as I walk back into her room.

"I saw Trey's mom and sat to talk with her a moment." I tell her as I grab the only chair in the room and scoot it closer to the bed. I motion for Nat to take the chair and I climb up on the bed next to Candy.

"Her clock is ticking," Candy mutters.

"What do you mean?" I ask.

"There are some who just can't be helped Tally. I've seen it. Some with schizophrenia just don't respond to any treatment and they just get worse over time."

"Are you saying she is going to die?" Nat's eyes are wide.

"Yes, but not from natural causes. They have her on suicide watch especially at night."

"What does that mean?" Natalie asks.

"It means that she has to have someone with her at all times." I explain.

"Trey never mentioned it."

"It just started."

Candy deals out the cards to us and we play rummy, the only card game I know besides slap jack.

"No cheating Candy," I warn.

"Psht, are you kidding? Like I would ever cheat."

"Liars go to hell. You know that right?" Natalie teases.

"I'm going to hell Natalie, but not because of lying."

I can't tell if she meant it to be funny, just one of her off handed statements, but something in the tone of her voice suggests it was more than that.

I spend the rest of our time trying to goad Candy into our usual easy banter, but no matter how many times she responds to me, it's never quite as light as it used to be.

Seven hands of rummy, four arguments, and two cussing fits by Candy later, Nat and I decide we need to be going if we are going to get some shopping in.

"We're going to look at dresses for the Fall Ball," Nat tells her.

"Well, make sure you buy a dress that's just south of *my garage is open*, but just north of *the lights are on*."

"What does that even mean?" Natalie asks.

"Don't ask," I tell her.

I tell Candy bye, no hugs. Candy doesn't do hugs, and we leave.

"She looks anything but alright," Natalie says what I've been thinking.

"Agreed, but she's not about to admit there is something wrong."

~

"Would you say this dress fits Candy's description?" Nat asks me as she turns in the mirror, looking this way and that. The dress is hot pink and looks great against her tan skin. It comes to the middle of her thighs and the top is a halter with a back that opens to just below the shoulder blades. The dress bunches in strategically placed intervals from the bust all the way to the hem. It does awesome things for her figure.

"At this point Nat I don't care if the dress screams *take me now right here on this floor*. We've been at this for hours and you've tried on every dress in five different stores. Buy one already." I groan as I sit on the chairs provided outside the dressing room. My own dress lay next to me on the adjoining chair. I had decided on a black sheath dress that hit about three inches above my knees. It is off the shoulders with a shear peace of floral lace wrapping around the top. The lace continues down covering the nude satin material underneath, and of course I added a pair of long black gloves to cover my self-decorated arms.

"I want it to be perfect," she pouts.

"Bobby thinks you're beautiful already, a dress isn't going to affect that."

"Maybe not, but it will make him drool." she winks at me, and after looking at herself one, more time in the mirror, she nods, "This is the one."

"Finally," I mouth, silently.

~

"What are you guys doing home?" I ask my parents as I walk in the door, dress in hand, from my day of shopping with Natalie.

"We decided not to go to the dinner," my mom tells me.

"Oh," I don't really know what else to say. I stand

there staring at her, unsure if I should keep going on up to my room or say something more.

"What did you buy?" she asks me.

I motion towards the dress, "A dress for the Fall Ball, Nat made me." I find myself smiling and my mom smiles back at me.

"Can I see it?" I see the hopefulness in her eyes, and decide if she's going to try, then I should as well.

"Sure." She follows me up to my room and I hang the dress on my closet door and unzip the bag that it is enclosed in.

Her mouth opens and then closes. She stares at it silently for several minutes and then finally speaks. "It's beautiful, very classy."

I find that I'm happy about her approval, and I feel a tightening in my chest. "Thank you."

"Is Trey taking you?"

"Well, he hasn't exactly asked yet," I say somewhat sheepishly.

She nods and smiles, "He will."

"He wants to meet you and Dad," I tell her impulsively. I had never intended to really push the issue, but for some reason I just blurt it out.

"We would like to meet him as well. I'm pretty sure your father and I have Wednesday night free. Would you like to see if he can come for dinner that evening?"

"Sure, that would be good."

She smiles again before leaving.

It's nearly ten o'clock when I finally hear from Trey.

"Hey," I say as I answer the phone.

"Hi," his deep voice rumbles through the phone and I realize that I have missed hearing it. We haven't talked since Friday, and I am almost thirsty for the sound of him.

"How was your day?" He asks me, and he seems almost cautious as if he's afraid of what I might say.

"It was good. Nat and I went and saw Candy and then went shopping."

"What did you go shopping for?" I notice that he doesn't ask me how Candy is, but then I'm distracted by what I should tell him. If I tell him I bought a dress for the dance then he will think that I assume he is taking me, which I guess I am. If I don't tell him, then I am essentially lying to him and I really don't want to start that up again. So the truth, no matter how embarrassing is what it will be.

"Dresses," I say vaguely. Hey, it's the truth, he didn't ask for details so until then, we will go with only need–to–know information.

"Is it for a special occasion or did you just fancy yourself a new dress?" I hear humor in his voice and for some reason I have a feeling he knows exactly why I went dress shopping.

"Did you just say fancy?" I laugh.

"You're dodging the question baby. What is the dress for?" he asks again.

I inwardly groan as I launch into my tale. "Nat was insistent that we go buy dresses for the upcoming Fall Ball. I told her that I didn't even know if I am going, but she wasn't taking no for an answer, so I just gave in."

"Why wouldn't we go?" he asks

I pause. He said *we*, as in, *he and I*. I do my inner victory dance and fight a smile.

"You hadn't mentioned it and I didn't want to just assume that you were taking me," I tell him even though I obviously had assumed. Proof of said assumption currently hung on my closet door.

"Give a man time Baker," the low hum of his voice sends my insides into a flutter and my stomach tightens.

"I wasn't planning on going dress shopping Swift, it was Natalie's idea and once she gets an idea in her head, as sure as the sun rises every day, she is going to get her way."

He laughs and damn if that laugh doesn't make me want to crawl through the phone and plant a deep kiss on his luscious mouth.

"Tally, are you still there?" Now, his voice sounds slightly worried.

"Yeah, sorry I got side tracked."

"By what?"

My face turns red and I'm so glad that he isn't sitting right in front of me.

"Just a thought, it's gone now." *Liar* that little voice in the back of my mind sings.

"It's late; I better let you get some sleep."

I don't want to get off the phone with him, but I know he's right.

"Alright, thanks for calling."

"You don't have to thank me for that beautiful. It's my privilege. I should be thanking you for answering."

Well crap, what does a girl say to that?

Thankfully, I remember I needed to ask him a question. "Oh, Trey I forgot to ask you, my parents want to know if you can come over Wednesday for dinner."

"Do you know what time?" he asks.

Want to know something sad? I have no idea what time my parents eat dinner. That's how long it has been since we have eaten together. So, I'm just going to make up a time and hope that it works for my parents.

"Five o'clock," I tell him.

He's quiet for a moment and all I can hear is his soft, slow breathing. I assume that he is thinking so I don't interrupt.

"I think that will work," he tells me finally and I let out the breath I had been holding.

"Great, okay so I'll see you in the morning." I try and sound normal even though on the inside I'm begging for the night to go quickly, like a child on Christmas Eve wanting to blink and wake up to find it's morning.

"Sleep well baby," he says and then ends the call.

I want to ask him how? How can I sleep well when I'm worried about Candy and thinking about how much I want to be with him? How can I ever sleep good again when there is never a moment when my mind isn't worried about something? My throat feels like it is closing up and I can't get air in my lungs. *Not again, please not now*, I tell myself, as I try to calm down. I have to be okay. There is no other option. I cannot lose it, not now. I close my eyes and squeeze them shut, fighting tears. Dr. Stacey told me many times that stress causes the brain to use chemicals more quickly than the medicine can help the brain produce them and that, in turn, can cause depression to rear its ugly head. *Panic attacks often accompany the depression Tally*, I hear her voice in my mind. *You will feel like you can't breathe, your heart will race, and you might even think you are having a heart attack. Just keep breathing, think of something that brings you peace, and keep breathing.*

I lie back on my bed and reach for him. His smile, his voice, and his gentle touch. Breathe. I think of the understanding I see in his eyes. Breathe. I latch on to every memory I have of him and drink them in as though I may never have another drink again. Breathe. I feel air saturating my body and relax slightly. It's enough and I keep breathing. A small victory has been made on this night, and I will take it. I don't feel joy for the victory, but I'm alive and for tonight that is enough. It has to be.

Chapter 21

"Life is so fleeting and so unpredictable. We don't know what tomorrow will bring and there is no guarantee that tomorrow will even come. And when the cycle of life hits so close to home, that uncertainty becomes a constant ache in the back of my mind. For one person I love, death creeps in and I wonder how much time I have left with her. And for another person I love, life begins to fill her eyes and I wonder how much time I will be given with her. It is in times such as these that I long for certainty, for something set in stone." ~Trey

I watch her as she walks towards me through the crowded halls. I hadn't wanted her to go off by herself but she insisted that I wait for her at her locker because she just had to run something to Natalie and she would be right back. But, the truth is I still do not trust these vultures not to hurt her. They may have backed off for now, but they are circling, waiting for the moment when she is unprotected. I know I can't shelter her from everything, but I will do my damndest to shelter her from what I can.

Her eyes meet mine and never waver as she continues forward. She doesn't look left or right because she has no one to talk to, no one to wave at or exchange pleasantries with, and for that I am sorry. I feel my lips turn up into a smile without even thinking about it. That is what she brings me, and when she returns my smile with her own, I feel a rightness settle in my bones.

"Ready?" I ask as she reaches me. I reach out for her hand and she gives it to me without hesitation.

"Yep," she answers.

She seems a little subdued today and has for the past two days. I decide to attribute it to nerves over me meeting her parents tonight. I want to ask her if she is all right, but I don't want to make her feel as though I'm waiting for her to crumble.

We ride in relative silence on the way to her house, but she holds my hand in both of hers, drawing circles across the top of it with one of her fingers. Her grip is not tight, yet I feel as if she is reaching for my hand like a lifeline, so I don't let go.

"Does it seem like time tends to speed up every day?" she asks as I turn onto her street.

"Yes," I answer with full understanding of what she means.

"I mean two days passed in the blink of an eye."

"Are you nervous about me meeting your parents Tally?" I finally dare to ask.

Her mouth twitches and her eyes narrow as she thinks about her answer.

"Maybe a little," she admits.

"Are you worried about what they will think of me?"

"I don't care what they think of you." The honesty in her voice relaxes a part of me that I hadn't realized had been tense over her answer.

"I just have no idea how they will act. I've never brought a guy home and they are so rarely home that I don't really feel like I know them."

I pull into her driveway and cut the engine. We sit, staring at the monstrosity that is her house, and though

I am not worried about meeting her parents, I feel the tension radiating off of her and have to force myself to keep from starting the engine and driving away from the source of her stress. I never claimed to be rational when it comes to Tally, but even I surprise myself sometimes by my reactions to things regarding her.

"You got this Baker," I tell her with a gentle squeeze of her hand. I pull away and get out of my truck. When I open the passenger door, I take a step towards her to keep her from climbing out. I take her face in my hands and kiss her gently. I run my fingers across her jaw and pull back to look at her. "We got this."

She nods at me and takes a deep, steadying breath. When I see the tension leave her shoulders, I move back so that she has room to get out. I take her hand and walk with her up to the front door. It opens before she can reach for the handle.

"Hello." A thin woman of average height with chin length blonde hair smiles at us. Her eyes are a startling green, but her smile is warm and genuine. I can see the resemblance between her and Tally though Tally isn't as tall and her eyes are blue.

"Hi mom," Tally answers with her own smile. "This is Trey," she motions towards me, "Trey this is my mom, Paige Baker."

I take her outstretched hand and note how much smaller it is than mine. I'm mindful of how hard I squeeze. I shake it gently and smile, "It's very nice to meet you Mrs. Baker."

"And, you as well, Trey. Please call me Paige."

"Thank you," I say and follow Tally in as Paige steps aside for us to enter.

I try to appear as if I haven't been inside their

home since I am not sure if Tally has told them that I came over. So, I smile and nod when her mom points out the rooms that are downstairs and the ones upstairs. We follow her down a hall and into a large dining room. A man, I presume is Tally's dad, is standing with his back to us looking out a large window. He is sipping from a glass of amber liquid and seems to be lost in thought.

"Dear," Paige says warmly, "Tally and Trey are here."

Mr. Baker turns and smiles at Tally, it's genuine, but strained. He is shorter than me by at least four or five inches, putting him around 5'11". He strides confidently towards us and holds out his hand to me.

"I'm Frank Baker, Tally's father."

"Trey Swift sir," I respond as I shake his hand, with considerably more strength than with Paige. His eyes are the same gray blue as Tally's and his features are what most, I assume, would consider classically handsome. His hair, though salt and pepper in color is still full and thick on his head and his face is chiseled, with a strong jaw, though lined with some wrinkles, they only add to his good looks. As her parents stand side by side in front of us, I see that Tally is a perfect blend of both of them, as if she was given all the best features from the two.

"It's nice to meet you Trey, thank you for accepting out invitation to dinner," he says, as he lets go of my hand. I decide, at this point that since neither of them has made comment on my hair or jewelry that Tally must have explained to them of my heritage.

"Have a seat everyone, everything is already on the table and ready to eat." Paige tells us, as she points to the long table that is loaded with more food than the four of us could eat in a day, let alone one sitting.

Tally grabs my hand and leads me over to the table. I pull out her chair and she gives me a look that says *suck up*. I shrug and wink at her.

When we are all seated, Paige points out what each tray or bowl contains. I make sure to take a little of everything and can't help but notice how little of nothing Tally puts on her plate. I glance at her and when I catch her eye, I frown and nod towards her plate. She shrugs and goes back to moving what little food there is around with her fork.

"So, are you a senior this year as well Trey?" Mr. Baker asks.

"Yes sir, that's correct."

"Isn't it hard starting your last year of high school at a new school?" Paige asks.

I nod as I swallow down a bite of steak. "A little I suppose, but I have a lot going on, so school is just one more thing I have to cross off my list in my day."

"Oh?" Mr. Baker says, looking interested, "What do you have going on that's more important than school?"

"Dad," Tally jumps in. I lay my hand on her leg, a silent message that all is well.

"I live with my grandmother and so I take care of anything she needs, I have a job, and I take care of my mother." I explain.

"Are they sick?" he asks.

"My mother is," I take a sip of my water and swallow before continuing, "that is how I met Tally actually." I feel her foot come down hard on mine, but I was prepared for it. I figure she hasn't informed her parents that we met while she was in the hospital. I decide that I need to see for myself exactly what their reaction was to her being in the mental hospital.

"My mother is a patient at Mercy. In fact, that's where I met Tally, one day when I was visiting my mom." The table is silent when I finish. My knife grates against the plate sounding abnormally loud as I cut another piece of steak. I stick my fork into the piece of meat and pluck it into my mouth. I finally look up as I chew and glance from Tally's guarded eyes, to Paige's wide eyes, and finally to Mr. Baker's narrowed eyes.

"Tally didn't mention that Mercy is where she met you," Mr. Baker grates out.

"Well, you guys didn't really ask me about my time at Mercy, so it's not like it came up," Tally glares at her father. Mr. Baker glances at me and then looks at Tally.

"That isn't the point Tally. You made us think that you met Trey at school."

"I did meet him at school, just not for the first time."

I watch as his jaw tenses and can tell that Mr. Baker is about to lose the calm control that he has been holding onto for quite some time.

"I imagine it must be a tough thing having your daughter be in a psychiatric hospital," I interject. "I know that it has been tough for me with my mom being there."

"It is one thing for a grown woman to be in need of help. It is an entirely different matter for a perfectly happy seventeen year old girl to need help," Mr. Baker tells me, eyes flashing with irritation and what I would guess is fear.

"How would you know if I'm perfectly happy?" Tally nearly yells as her fork falls clashing against her plate. "You are never around to know if I'm happy or not. You can't possibly tell me that you think that you know me or know what I feel when you don't even bother to ask."

Tally slides her chair back and the scraping of the feet against the floor causes Paige to flinch.

"Mom, thank you for dinner, but I seem to have lost my appetite." Without looking at me, she leaves the table and a moment later, I hear the front door slam closed.

Mr. Baker is staring in the direction Tally has gone and Paige is staring at her plate. I see the slight tremble in her lips and know that she is on the verge of tears.

"I should go check on her," I say as I stand. "Paige, thank you for the meal. It was lovely. Mr. Baker, it was nice to meet you."

"I don't think you are the best thing for Tally," Mr. Baker suddenly says as I am turning to go.

I have to clench my jaw shut before I say something that will only get me thrown out of their house. I turn back slowly and pull myself up to my full height.

"May I ask why?" I ask as calmly as I can.

"Because, she doesn't need to be around people with your kind of problems. She needs to be moving forward, moving on with her life, and you will simply be a reminder of what she went through."

"Frank," Paige whispers fervently.

He ignores her.

"I can understand your worry for your daughter," I tell him honestly, "but I think it is the wrong kind of worry. What you should be worried about is whether or not she has the support she needs in order to cope with her emotions. Just because you don't want her to have bipolar disorder isn't going to make it go away. Tally needs anyone who can understand what she is going through and is willing to stick with her even when things are hard. I would think that as her parent you would want that for her." I know I've probably crossed a boundary somewhere in that statement, but I don't care. I don't care if he's her father. He hurt her, and that isn't acceptable to me.

"I think that you need to stay away from Tally and worry about your own problems. You seem to have enough of your own without adding Tally's to them."

"Tally is not a problem!" I snap. "She's a woman who needs her parents to love her through this crap, not in spite of it." I turn once again to go and just as I enter the hall I turn back one more time, "And, with all due respect Mr. Baker, I will not stop seeing your daughter."

I find her sitting in my truck. Tears are streaming down her flushed cheeks as she silently stares up at her house. I climb in and start the engine, and without saying anything, I back out of her driveway.

It's nearly ten minutes before she finally speaks.

"Where are we going?"

"I want you to meet my grandmother," I tell her.

She groans and frantically begins to wipe her cheeks.

"Don't you think we've had enough introductions for one night?"

"You will like her, and she will adore you."

Tally looks out her window and then looks back at me. I can feel her eyes on me, searching for something.

"Your dad doesn't want me to see you anymore." I half expect her to start ranting, but then half of the time she does the opposite of what I expect, so I just wait.

"What did you say in response?" she asks me cautiously.

It's in moments like these that I see just how vulnerable Tally is. She's looking for acceptance and for approval and the two people she needs it most from have not given it to her.

"I told him I would not stop seeing you."

I pull into the driveway of my small house, only now realizing just how small it is after leaving the McMansion that Tally lives in. But it doesn't bother me, and for some reason I know it's not going to bother her either.

"Thank you," she says softly.

I put the truck in park and turn the engine off. When I turn to look at her, I expect to see her looking down at her hands or out the window, anywhere but at me. But she is, she's looking straight at me and her eyes are earnest, desperate for any small sign of possible rejection.

I slide over and cup her cheek. "I'm not going anywhere," I whisper, so close that my lips brush hers. I feel the heat of her breath on my face and can't stand the separation any longer. I lean towards her and press my lips to hers. What starts out as a sweet kiss quickly turns into something more. Both of my hands are in her hair, my fingers running through the strands and pulling her tighter to me. I release her hair and my hands slide down to her waist. I lift her and pull her into my lap until she's straddling me. I feel her chest rise and fall against mine and find satisfaction in knowing that she is breathing just as rapidly as I am.

Our tongues dance and I tug on her lip with my teeth when I feel her hands slip up my shirt. The warmth of her skin seeps into my chest.

"Trey," she whispers pleadingly against my neck. I pull her closer, kiss her neck, and down to her collar bone. Her head falls back, and her body goes limp with desire. I can't take my eyes off of her. I watch as her eyes flutter open, and the longing I see in the blue gray swirl of her irises is like a punch to my gut.

"Tally, I love you." The words leave my lips before I know what I'm doing, and then I'm pulling her mouth to mine again. I'm lost, lost in her scent, her taste, and the feel of her body in my hands. Her shirt inches up as she wraps her arms around my neck and I let my hands slip under, wrapping them around her rib cage. She feels so small, so incredibly fragile. My thumbs rub gently against her soft flesh, and when I feel one of them brush the bottom of her bra, I know it's time to stop. I slowly pull my hands from her shirt and tug her shirt back down. I pull back from her incredible mouth and we're both breathless.

"I'm calling the game baby," I tell her, with a small smile.

"Too much?" She grins.

I give her backside a gentle slap, "Wicked woman." She slides off my lap and adjusts her clothes.

I let out a deep breath and climb out of the truck to open her door. As she takes my hand she smiles up at me, "I love you too by the way."

I feel my heart swell and take up every inch of space in my chest. Words are stuck in my throat, and all I can do is squeeze her hand. We walk hand in hand up to my front door, which I open, stepping back so that she can enter before me.

"Shichu," I call out, as we enter the living room. "I've brought someone to meet you."

I hear her clattering around in the kitchen and tug Tally to follow me. My grandmother is leaned over, her head buried in a cabinet as she searches for something. Finally, she stands up and looks over her shoulder at us. Her eyes land on Tally and brighten as a smile stretches across her wrinkled face.

"Ahh," she says, coming over in front of Tally and taking her hands. "You are the beautiful soul that has stolen Trey's heart."

"Grandmother," I chide as I watch the blush creep up Tally's neck and cheeks.

"I think it would be more correct to say that he has stolen my heart," Tally smiles. "I'm Tally Baker."

"It's very nice to meet you finally Tally Baker, I am Bly." My grandmother holds her hands a minute more before releasing them. "Now, I just finished making a blackberry pie. Would you two like to join me?"

I glance down at Tally as she smiles, "That sounds great."

"So you and Trey are in school together," my grandmother says as she sits down after dishing us all a plate of her blackberry pie.

"Yes ma'am," Tally answers, and then takes a bite, "Hmm, wow this is incredible," she says around the mouth full.

"It's an old family recipe. I'm glad that you like it." There's silence for a few minutes as we all eat our pie. My grandmother sets her fork down looking thoroughly satisfied, and then looks at Tally.

"You have met Trey's mother?" she asks her.

Tally nods, "Yes ma'am. She was very," Tally pauses and glances at me, and then back to my grandmother, "straight forward."

My grandmother and I both chuckle.

"That sounds like my daughter," Bly tells her. "She must have been having a good day."

I glance down at my plate, my jaw tenses, as I think about how long it has been since my mother has had a good day. It's been too long.

"How do you like Broken Arrow?" Tally asks.

"It's not home, but I think it is where we are supposed to be." She pauses, as if contemplating her next words. "How do you feel about Broken Arrow? Do you feel you are where you are supposed to be?"

Tally lets out a slow breath and then looks up at me. Her eyes seem to be looking into me and I wonder what she sees.

"Yes, I'm where I'm supposed to be, although that doesn't mean I always feel safe there. Does that make sense?" she asks my grandmother.

Bly nods, "Faith is believing in things unseen, and that is the hardest kind of belief to have." She stands then and glances out of the window. "I better get to bed; I need all the beauty sleep I can get these days." She leans over and kisses Tally gently on the head, "You are going to be just fine child. The path you walk will not always be an easy one, but you will be able to help so many along the way."

"Good night grandma," I tell her as I stand and hug her. She pats my back and whispers, "She's strong. She just doesn't know it yet, and it will get worse before it gets better."

I want to ask her what she means, but now is not the time, not with Tally sitting right here.

"I had better get you home before your dad calls

the police," I tell Tally, as I grab her hand and pull her to her feet.

"Your grandmother is amazing."

"I think so. She always has little bits of wisdom to spew whether you want it or not." I think back to the many things my grandmother has whispered to me and then to tonight's comment about Tally. So many times my grandmother is right about things, and I really want her to be wrong about this one. I don't want Tally to hurt any more. But, after seeing how her father reacted to her tonight, I can only agree that a storm is brewing, and we just happen to be in the calm of it right now. Pretty soon, the lightning will strike, the thunder will roll, and the downpour of Tally's disease will come flooding in.

~

"Tally, before you go I need to tell you something. I've been meaning to tell you, but I was trying to find the right time." I look over at her as we sit in my truck in her driveway. I had been dreading telling her about Candy because I know just how much she means to Tally.

"When I went to visit my mother the other day I saw Candy. She didn't look very good and while I was talking to her, she collapsed. I had to carry her to her room, and then the nurses came in and they called the doctor, but I don't know what is going on with her. She asked me not to tell you, but I feel like you need to know."

"I knew something was wrong with her, but she

refuses to tell me what it is," Tally admits. "Thank you for telling me Trey, I'm glad you did."

"Are you going to be alright?" I ask her as I brush her bangs from her face.

She smiles at me, though it doesn't reach her eyes. "I'll be okay."

"I'll call you tomorrow," I tell her as I lean over and kiss her gently on the lips.

She nods and then climbs out of my truck. I'd offered to walk her to the door, but she declined, saying that she didn't want to give her dad an opportunity to yell at me.

I wait until she is safely in her house before finally leaving. Something inside me feels heavy as I drive home, and the more I try to pinpoint exactly what is bothering me, the more elusive it becomes. Something is coming. I don't know how else to describe it. I just know that something is coming, and it isn't going to be good.

Chapter 22

"Today I'm up, I'm dressed and I'm leaving my house, that means today is a good day. I'm breathing, in and out, and with every breath I remind myself that even though I feel as though the world is gradually crumbling around me, it is not reality— or is it?" ~Tally

    Days seem to be flying by now that school has started. Trey picks me up every day; he walks me to my classes, sits with me at lunch, and takes me home. The little touches that are as consistent as the beating of my heart are becoming something I crave, though I still don't want to be touched by anyone else. Every night he calls me and we talk about anything and everything. He tells me about his mom and how she is doing and I ask about the horses. His answers always seem to bring a smile to my face.
    I know that my meds aren't working as well as they had been, and I feel myself beginning to slip a little lower every day. I fight the agitation that wants to rear its ugly head at the most inopportune times. I fight tears, even when I'm simply brushing my teeth. I mean, seriously, who cries when they're brushing their teeth? Trey keeps asking me if I'm alright and I don't know how much longer before I scream *no I'm not alright, I can't stand to be in my own skin, and I just want to feel good*. I find myself longing for a manic phase, for the rush and the feeling of complete confidence, but the swings don't happen on command. And I know that the manic

phase is really no healthier than the depression, but damn, anything sounds better than this feeling of utter helplessness.

 My mother keeps trying to talk to me and I appreciate her willingness to move forward, but I just don't have the energy to put forth much effort. My dad hardly speaks to me, and it's probably better that way. I have a very bad feeling that if he gives me one of his snide comments, I just might stab him with the first object I can get my hands on. This is my life right now; this is where I'm at. Is it a good place to be? No, but I don't know what to do about it at this point. Candy is getting worse, and she refuses to tell me what is going on. The last two times I have visited her she nearly fell apart in tears and begged me to stop asking her. I'm at a loss of what to do with her, of how to help her. Candy was my rock. She's crazy, no doubt, but she made me feel like no matter how bad it got I would be okay. Now, I don't know if she's going to be okay.

 "How has this week been?" Dr. Stacey asks me as I take my usual spot on her couch.
 "I don't know doc," I tell her honestly. "I just don't know how I feel, one minute I'm somewhat okay, and then the next I want to scream."
 "I had a feeling that as you began to get back into the daily things of life, school, and your parents that you might begin to slip. Your medicine can only keep up with so much and the stress you are under is causing the chemicals to be used up more quickly. The quick mood swings are a result of the mood stabilizer not being enough. Sometimes in the depressive episode, the emotions are just all over the place right before a major crash."

I feel a surge of anger at her words. My head snaps up from where it had been laying on the back of the couch. "You knew that this would happen? You didn't think that maybe you should tell me?"

"I did tell you Tally. I told you to be paying close attention to how you were feeling, that circumstances can cause episodes. People with mental illness do not handle stress well, they don't handle exhaustion well, and often times will become physically ill because their bodies just can't deal with the mental exhaustion. We've discussed all of this. Now it's a matter of remembering and applying."

I stand up and begin to pace her office, not able to sit still any longer. I feel as though there are ants dancing the jig on my nerves and every part of me is buzzing. I clench my fists open and closed and have to rub my sweaty palms on my pants. I'm so frustrated and I don't want to be. I don't want to feel this way.

"I'm sorry; I didn't mean to yell at you. I'm just," I stop and turn to look at her and I know what she sees. I'm empty. I was like a glass, beginning to be filled up, and then suddenly, as if a hole in the side of the cup magically appeared, the liquid began to drain slowly, until barely a drop remained. "I'm only two months into school, our first dance is this weekend, and I'd rather be buried alive than go, but I don't want to feel that way. I can't do this again."

"I'm going to increase the Lamictal, which is the mood stabilizer and it may take a week before you start to feel better, sometimes it can take two. Be patient." She stands and then walks over to me. She wraps her arms around me and hugs me. I don't know what to do. I feel like it's been forever since someone, an adult hugged me like they cared. I'm stiff and I know I should hug her back, but I can't. My arms stay frozen at my side and I bite my lip to keep the flood gates from opening.

When she finally releases me, she steps back and I see that her eyes are shiny as if she were tearing up. She straightens her suit jacket and clears her throat.

"You are going to be fine Tally, I know it doesn't feel like it, but you are going to be fine."

"Don't start," Candy warns me as I step outside to where she is sitting on a bench. "I know I look like crap. I don't need someone pointing it out. I never understood why people feel the need to tell someone they don't look good, like them not feeling well has somehow made them blind and unable to see their shitty appearance in a freaking mirror."

I sit down next to her and she looks at me. "You look like crap," she tells me.

"I thought you just said you didn't understand why people feel the need to tell someone when they look like crap?" I raise a brow at her.

"Correct, I don't understand why other people do it, but I know why I do it. It gives me the opportunity to tell someone they look like crap. Why would I pass that up?" Candy shakes her head at me as if I had just asked the most ludicrous question.

"Why indeed," I grumble.

"So what's going on? Why do you look so crappy? Did Running Bull break up with you? Do I need to kill him?"

I pat her arm, "Calm down, and put away your weapons, Trey didn't break up with me. I'm just not feeling well."

"No shit Sherlock, I sort of gathered that by the dark circles and pale skin." she points out so helpfully—not.

"You're one to talk. You look like you've been run through the washer twenty times too many and then left soaking wet to dry so you are all wrinkly and sour." I purse my lips at her as I narrow my eyes in challenge.

She grins wickedly, "Really? Well you look like the favorite chew toy of a St. Bernard that he happens to like to hump all the time as well."

I can't help the small huff of laughter that has my shoulders shaking. Only Candy could come up with something so crude, yet so hilarious. "Fine, you win. A worn out, over–humped chew toy is probably as bad as it gets."

"You know better than to get into a putdown war with me, I will shut you down every time." Candy glances back over the field that leads to the pond. The sparkle in her eyes that was there moments ago is now gone and I wonder if she will ever tell me what is going on.

"It's getting late Pinky; you should probably be heading home."

I don't say anything until she finally turns and looks at me. "Tell me you're going to be alright."

She smiles, but it's not her normal smile. "Do you believe in God, Tally?"

I'm thrown off by her question. We've never discussed religion and she's never even hinted at being religious.

"I guess so," I answer.

"I do. I believe that something greater than all of us had to have created us. I was raised in church you know." I watch as she pulls a battered old Bible from behind her where it had been sitting on the bench. She holds it reverently in her hands and stares down at it. "This was the Bible my daddy gave me. At one time, I read it every day."

"What happened?" I ask, drawn in by the vulnerable look in her eyes.

"Crazy happened," instead of the anger I expect to come with the words, I hear sadness. "I was angry with God, have been angry with God for a very long time. Who wants to be crazy? Who wants to lose everything in their life because they aren't in their right mind? So, I put my Bible on the shelf and stepped away from the very thing that could have brought me comfort." She pauses and I watch as she flips through the worn pages. I see red writing scrawled on many of the pages along with pieces of paper stuck intermittently throughout.

"I was lying in bed last night and I just felt so lonely. And, so, for the first time in forty years, I talked to God, to my creator. I told him all the things that I have held inside for so long. I yelled at him, cussed at him, and then held my breath waiting to be struck down by lightning, but instead I felt a peace flow over me like I have never felt before. I've had this Bible stuck under my mattress since I arrived here at Mercy and I pulled it out last night and flipped it open to a random page." Her voice catches and she stops to take a ragged breath.

I don't know what to do. I've never seen this side of Candy. She seems so fragile, so small. I wish I could say that I understand, but the truth is I've never even opened a Bible. My parents aren't religious and I've never thought about it. I guess I figured that someone had to have created the world, but my thoughts never went beyond that.

"I closed my eyes and pointed randomly to the page I had opened, and then opened them to see what scripture my finger had landed on—the book of Luke: Chapter 15, the parable of the prodigal son. My finger was sitting on verse twenty, *"But while he was still a long way off, his father saw him and was filled with compassion for him; he ran to his son, threw his arms around him and kissed him."* When she looks back up at me, her eyes are filled with tears. "I remember the sermon my pastor did on this very passage when I was in high school. He said the prodigal son is us, God's children, and the father is God, and when we come back to God, when we repent and turn to him, He runs to us, before we are anywhere close to Him. He runs to us and wraps us in His arms."

I'm quiet as I stare at her. Tears streak down her worn face, and her lips pinch together.

"Candy, I don't know what to say to that. I don't really know what I believe." I admit.

She shakes her head. "That's okay child. I'm not telling you this because I'm trying to convince you of God's love for you. I'm just sharing this with you because I need to tell someone. Last night God ran to me, even in my anger, fear, and pain, He ran to me, crazy Candy, and wrapped me in His arms and I knew in that moment that everything was going to be okay. It's not the outcome I want, it's not the life I thought I would have, but it's okay."

I feel tears gather in my eyes and I don't really know why I'm crying other than I'm happy that Candy found her peace. I'm happy that this God she obviously loves has bestowed His love on her.

She reaches for my hand and squeezes it. "Now that a crazy old lady has poured her heart out, you need to get on home."

"Candy," I hold on to her hand before she can pull it away. "I'm glad you are crazy, otherwise I don't know that I would have ever met you and that would have been a tragedy."

She smiles at me and for a moment, it reaches her eyes. "I love ya kid," she tells me quickly. I stand to go as I see how uncomfortable she is, Candy's never been one for sentiment.

"I'll see you in a week when I come for my next session," I tell her as I head for the side of the building to walk around to the parking lot.

"Okay, yeah, see you then," she tells me with a final wave.

As I round the corner, I look back over my shoulder and see Candy looking off into the distance, the old Bible still resting in her hands. Her face is peaceful, but she looks so very tired. I watch as she bows her head and closes her eyes. In the stillness of the night, I hear her words clearly.

"I'm ready."

~

"You have to do something different with your hair Tal," Nat whines to me as she slips into her dress.

The night of the dance has snuck up on me and no amount of me complaining to Natalie that I didn't want to go has drawn any sympathy. She had argued that I had to go for Trey's sake, because he might never have been to a school dance. I countered with, 'he's from a different state not a third world country.' She argued that it was our senior year and we had to make the best of it. I told her that others might want to make the best of their senior year as well, and that could quite possibly include me not being at their school dances.

"My hair is short Natalie, what exactly do you want it to do?" I growl at her as I tease the strands to give it a fuller look. I've sprayed enough hair spray on it that even a hurricane probably won't damage it.

"Here, spray some of this glitter stuff in it." she hands me a bottle of liquid glitter.

I raise a brow at her, "Yes, this glitter will make all the difference."

"Quit being a negative Nancy," she snaps at me.

I let out an exasperated breath. I know I need to pull it together, for Natalie if for nothing else. I know she is beyond excited to be going to this dance with Bobby and I don't want to ruin it for her.

"Okay fine, I'll play nice, but I will not be held responsible for my actions if one of those jerks throws a comment at me," I inform her.

"Trey is going to be attached to your hip; they would have to be eighteen bricks shy of a load to even look at you wrong."

I shrug, "I'm just throwing that out there. I reserve the right to go kung fu on anyone dumb enough to mess with the crazy chick."

"Duly noted," she smiles at me and hands me my dress, "Now, go get all beautymified."

I roll my eyes as I snatch the dress from her and stomp to the bathroom.

"Put on your happy face Tally," she calls after me.

"Bite me Nat."

"You look amazing," I feel Trey's breath against my neck as he helps me out of his truck.

"You clean up pretty good yourself," I tell him. He winks at me and in spite of feeling so gloomy, my stomach still does a little flip.

"Ready for this?" he asks as he slips my hand around his arm.

"Do you really want me to answer that?" I ask, dryly.

"We don't have to stay long. Just give me a couple of dances so I can discretely grope you. It's like a rite of passage in high school to grope your girl at a school dance."

I laugh, mostly because Trey is too much of a gentleman to do something like that, but also because I imagine there will be lots of couples crossing through that particular rite of passage tonight.

"Let's get this over with Swift," I grumble as I tug him forward.

"Eager for the dancing or the groping?" he murmurs.

I laugh again and it feels good. I'm not better, but with Trey, in this moment I feel a brief reprieve from the inner turmoil that's been a steady storm inside of me.

I hear Natalie calling my name as we cross the parking lot to the school gym. I see Bobby next to her looking very sharp in a suit with a collarless shirt and vest.

Trey was wearing a suit, but instead of a tie he was wearing a bolo that had a turquoise and silver piece in the middle. He had left his hair unbraided and it shone brilliantly under the moon light.

"Let's go get our dance on," Natalie sings as we meet them at the door.

Trey pulls me onto the dance floor as a slow song begins to play. Not many people are dancing, but he doesn't seem to care. I wrap my arms around his neck and he pulls me close. As I look up at him, I can't help but relax slightly as the safety I feel in his arms washes over me.

"What are you thinking about?" he asks me.

I feel heat rush to my face just as I always do when he catches me in a moment of utter adoration.

"How safe I feel with you." I admit.

His lips curl up in a crooked smile, and he leans down and kisses me on the forehead.

"Good, I want you to feel safe with me."

We dance like that, just looking at each other, stealing kisses every now and then for several songs until they finally put on something a little faster. We take that as our cue to step off the dance floor.

We find Natalie and Bobby sitting at one of the decorated tables. Natalie has her feet propped up in Bobby's lap while he rubs them.

"Ugh," she groans, "those freaking shoes are killing my feet."

"I told you not to put them on so early," I remind her.

"Didn't ask you, just let me complain," she frowns at me.

We hear a commotion coming from the front doors and turn to see Carter Evans, Amber, and their followers come staggering in. It's extremely obvious that they've been hitting the drinks already. When they catch us looking at them, Carter gives me a smirk. It's one of those looks that you know means something is up, and it's not going to be good.

I grab Trey's hand and pull his attention from the group.

"Hey, so have you had enough dancing?"

He glances back over at Carter and then back to me, "Yeah, I'm ready if you are."

"Where you guys headed?" Bobby asks as he slips Natalie's shoes back on to her feet, much to her chagrin based on the frown on her face.

"We were just going to hang out at my house. You guys want to come?" Trey asks.

Bobby looks at Natalie, "You good with that?"

She nods, "I just want to be out of these shoes for like, ever."

Bobby laughs as he stands up and swings her up into his arms. "I guess I'll just have to carry you."

Natalie squeals and I smile at them. She is so happy and I'm glad to see that, to know that she has someone who isn't a constant mess in her life.

As we're walking out of the gym, I pull on Trey's hand, "Hey, I need to step into the ladies room."

He nods, "I'll wait for you."

As I'm walking out of the restroom, Natalie and Bobby come rushing back in from the parking lot.

"They have a death wish," Natalie growls.

My heart plummets, because I know who *they* are. Trey takes my hand and calmly walks out of the gym. His long strides are difficult for me to keep up with and I find myself nearly skipping. I can hear Natalie cussing a blue streak behind me, and when my eyes land on Trey's truck, I understand why.

"Oh my," I can't even finish—I'm speechless. Trey's truck has been totaled. The windows have been smashed in, the tires slashed, and obscenities spray painted all over it. I feel Trey's grip tighten around my hand. I remember back to the glimpse of his anger I saw when I was still at Mercy, and I know that things are about to get ugly.

"Bobby," Trey says through gritted teeth, "Please, take the ladies home."

"Why don't I let them take my car and I'll stay with you?" Bobby suggests.

I clear my throat and pull my hand from Trey's. "If you think that I'm leaving you here, then you have another thing coming."

Trey's eyes flash with anger and his lips tighten, "You are not going to witness what I'm about to do."

"I know you're angry about your truck Trey, but it's not worth getting into trouble."

Trey lets out a humorless laugh, "You think I'm angry about my truck? No Tally, it's not the truck that has Carter Evans life in danger. It's what's written on the truck."

I turn my head back towards the truck and look more closely at the words sprayed across it in black paint. My eyes widen as I see the words *damaged goods* on the hood. My breath catches in my throat as I glance down at my glove covered arms. Someone knew. Someone knew what I had on my arms and I don't know how. But then my mind flashes back to the girl who had found me in the bathroom with a blade in my hand—Amber.

Chapter 23

"My father once told me that a man who cannot control his anger is one of two things: either he's flippant and uncaring of the feelings and safety of others, or he has been pushed beyond reason because someone he loves has been hurt. As I stare at the words on my truck, words that the girl I love has carved into her arms because of pain most of us can't imagine, I am a man who has been pushed beyond reason. I am a man about to lose control." ~Trey

"Tally," I attempt to keep my voice as calm as possible because she is not who I am angry with, "please take Bobby's car and go home." Her body is rigid with frustration and determination.

"I will say it one more time, just so we're clear," she takes a step closer to me causing her to have to tilt her head back a little further, "I am not leaving you."

I'm seriously considering picking her up and putting her in the car. And, just as I'm taking a step forward to do just that, I hear my name.

"Trey!" I turn slowly, and as I do, I push Tally back behind me.

Carter Evans and his devout followers are making their way towards us. I nearly laugh when he stops a good twenty five feet away. Smart man, but still beyond stupid, if he thinks staying that far away is going to keep him safe.

"So good of you to save me the trouble of having to drag you out of the gym Carter," I tell him calmly, "I do thank you for that."

There's something to be said for the type of rage that brings about calm behavior. It seems to terrify others more than a raging fit. I watch as the blood drains from Carter's face. I begin to take slow measured steps towards him and silently thank the group around him who are holding him hostage. Carter is a coward, but he's also proud, which means that he won't run while his friends are all standing here watching him.

"I've come to the conclusion that you are unhappy in your life," I continue as I walk closer, "because you seem to have a death wish."

"You must have me confused with your girlfriend," he spews the words at me as if they are acid in his mouth.

"You see, there you go again, opening your mouth and proving me right." I'm standing less than a foot away from him now, and his eyes are beginning to betray the fear that is prancing just beneath the surface. "You want to die." I say slowly with punctuation after each word, and then I grab his throat before he even realizes what is happening. I drag him forward so that our faces are less than an inch apart and stare into his eyes. I want him to see death, to know what it looks like to stare into the face of someone who could kill him if it was what needed to be done. I wasn't really going to kill him, not yet anyway. He had yet to physically harm Tally, though the emotional harm he and his cohorts had done, might actually be worse. But it would be easier to justify murder if it was in defense of a victim. As it is, I cannot justify killing him, so I will settle for humiliating him as well as give him a physical reminder of why it would be unwise to continue to pick on my girlfriend.

"You are going to apologize to Tally," I look back over his shoulder at the faces that watch in rapt attention and sick delight. Vultures, all of them, they look on as one of their own is being dealt with. Instead of jumping to his aide, they salivate at the mouth for the blood they hope is going to flow. I meet Amber's eyes as I say my next words, "And, since I can't hit a girl you will take Amber's punishment for her part in this."

I release his throat. He takes a quick swing at me, but I quickly grab his arm and pull him forward and around wrenching his arm behind him. I pull up so that the arm is straining the shoulder and causes Carter to have to walk on his tip toes to relieve the pain. The fight is abruptly gone out of him aside from cussing under his breath and informing me that I would be sorry.

"You can't prove I did anything," he growls at me.

"I'm not trying to prove anything to anyone. I already know who did it." I push him to his knees in front of Tally, and when he starts to struggle, I grab his hair in my hand and pull until he is looking up at her.

"Apologize to her." My voice is calm despite the boiling fury building inside of me.

"You want me to apologize to her for trashing your truck?" he asks me through clenched teeth.

"No, I want you to apologize for what you spray painted across the hood of my truck."

Carter's eyes flick towards the truck and then back to Tally, who is staring at me like I've grown a third head.

"I told you to go," I remind her.

"And I told you I wasn't leaving." she crosses her arms across her chest, and then looks down at Carter.

"I didn't paint those words. Amber did." Carter's voice is beginning to shake.

"And, I told you that you would be taking Amber's punishment for her part in this because I don't hit girls." I turn to look at Bobby, "Could you grab the pair of pliers out of the glove box in my truck please?" Bobby doesn't even flinch, just goes and gets the pliers and brings them to me without a word. He's watching the group behind me, making sure that no one decides to stick up for their leader.

"Now, you are going to apologize to Tally," I tell Carter. "Or, I'm going to break your fingers one by one. Bobby could you please come hold his arm out for me?"

When Carter makes no move to apologize, I wrap the pliers around the knuckle of his ring finger on his right hand and begin to squeeze. I see the moment the pain registers on his face as sweat breaks out across his brow.

"Wait! Stop, okay I'll apologize."

I let up on the pressure, but I don't remove the pliers from around his finger.

"I'm sorry Tally," he tells her, and there is a slight smirk on his face. "I'm sorry that you're in desperate need of attention, and so you tried to off, AHH!" The sick crunching sound of Carter's knuckle buckling under the pliers is drowned out by his scream. I hear the gasps behind me and the murmuring that follows but tune it out as I stare down at the now broken Carter Evans.

"That was a dumb thing to say."

He tries to jerk his arm back, but Bobby is holding it firm.

"You broke my damn finger, you jack ass," he

screams, and his voice is strained with pain.

"I told you that I would break your fingers one by one. Did you honestly believe that I was bluffing?" I look up at Tally and feel my face soften at the sight of her. "Baby, please go home. Let me deal with this, and then I will come see how you are."

I don't think she is going to agree, but when she glances down at Carter's crushed finger something in her eyes changes.

She nods slowly and her shoulders slump forward as exhaustion seems to wrap around her like a blanket. "Okay, but you had better come see me tonight."

I watch as Nat takes her hand and they head to Bobby's car. Apparently, Nat and Tally leaving is a cue to the group behind me, and they begin to head back to the gym, either because it's not as interesting as they hoped, or they can't stand the sickening crunch of bones. Whatever the reason, it's fine with me. The fewer witnesses, the better.

Within a matter of minutes Bobby, myself, and Carter are the only three left in the parking lot, not even Amber had stuck around to back up her man.

"I told you once already that if you didn't leave Tally alone that I would make sure you would never forget your high school years, that they would forever be branded on your skin. Had all you done was vandalize my truck I would have let it go, after all what other behavior can I expect from a child, but you had to bring my girl into it. That was your mistake." I take the pliers from the broken finger and move onto the next and with a squeeze. I break that finger as well.

Carter slumps forward as he bites back a scream. His body is shaking with rage and pain and I imagine that if he had a gun he would probably shoot me.

"I'm tempted to break all of your fingers because then you wouldn't be able to hold any form of utensil, writing or otherwise, but I'm hoping two will get my point across. It's your senior year Carter. Try and use what little brain cells you have left, and heed my warning, stay away from me and Tally. Leave her alone, completely. I won't tell you again." I release his finger and glance at Bobby. He releases Carter's arm.

Carter climbs to his feet and takes a few steps back. His eyes meet mine briefly and then drop to the ground.

"It's not like I've physically harmed her man, you take things way too serious."

"Are we clear Carter?" I ask without acknowledging his ignorant statement.

"Yeah, we're clear. Just stay the hell away from me." He snarls, as he begins backing away.

Bobby and I stand, silently watching as he backs all the way to his car and then climbs in.

"You think he'll tell someone?" Bobby asks me.

I shake my head, "No, he's not about to admit that he got dealt with. Even if he did, I won't deny that I did it. There are many things that I will turn the other cheek about, but not when it comes to hurting Tally. She's hurt enough for one life time."

I look back at my truck and realize that I have no way to get to Tally's house.

"I texted Nat. She's coming back to pick us up. She said she just dropped Tally off." Bobby must have read the look on my face when I glanced at my trashed vehicle.

~

"How are you?" I ask Tally, as we stand on her porch. By the time Natalie dropped me off at her house Tally was changed into a pair of jeans and a t-shirt and was patiently waiting for me outside.

"Worried about you," she admits and the look on her face confirms her answer.

I pull her into my arms and close to my chest. "I'm fine. I'm sorry you had to see that, and I hope you know I would never hurt you."

She pulls back and looks up at me, her brow furrowed and mouth tight. "I know you would never hurt anyone you didn't think deserved it. Trey I know your character and I know you were just defending me."

"I know, but I can't deny that I have a temper and sometimes it's hard for me to get a hold of it. I just don't want you to ever be afraid of me." I watch her face carefully looking for any contradiction in her body language or expression from her words. I don't see any.

"I love you," I tell her as I lean down and kiss her lips gently. "You need to get some rest and I need to go cool off."

She lays her head on my chest and wraps her arms around me tightly. "Thank you Trey."

This time it's my turn to pull back and look down at her, "For what?"

"For thinking I'm worth it."

Chapter 24

"I live in this constant state of confusion. I'm grateful for Natalie and Trey, but at the same time, I hate that they must endure the crap that comes with all *my* crap. Not only do they have to deal with my emotions, but now they are dealing with the prejudice and utter asshole-ness of those who just don't know how to handle someone who is different. I'm so torn over wanting them, needing them in my life and yet I feel as though I am condemning them to a life they don't deserve."
~Tally

It's Sunday; it's been two days since Carter and his cronies destroyed Trey's truck and humiliated me with my own words. I haven't seen Trey. He's been working, but he's called and checked on me several times and each time he called, I had to bite my tongue to keep from crying or begging him to never leave me. Yes, I am just one big ball of warm fuzzies. In all honesty, I'm beginning to get on my own damn nerves.

I've debated going and visiting Candy, but I just don't know if I can handle seeing her so weak and weary. So instead, I sit at my window and watch the wind blowing the trees and the world going on even as I am crumbling on the inside. My mom has checked in on me and keeps asking about the dance, and I keep side stepping around the topic. My dad, well, he's still being an ass, so I just pretend he isn't here.

It's just one of those days where I find myself with too much time to think, when I really don't need to be thinking.

My phone rings and I answer it without bothering to check who it is.

"Hello," I say.

"Tally?" Candy's voice comes through the ear piece. She sounds off, as if she's been stretched too thin, and I immediately know that something is wrong.

"Candy, what's wrong? Are you alright?"

"Where is Trey?"

She uses his given name, and that's when my stomach hits the ground.

"He's working, why?"

"The hospital has been trying to get a hold of him. His," her voice cracks and I hear her breath catch in her throat. This is so unlike Candy, and it's beginning to really scare me.

"Candy, please, what is going on?"

"Trey's mother is gone." She finally says.

"Gone? You mean she's left?" I ask, nervously.

"No, Tally, I'm sorry to have to tell you, but we need you to get Trey. His mother committed suicide."

The last word is like a hammer blow to my head, and I have to tighten my grip around the phone to keep from dropping it. I grab the window sill and lower myself slowly to the floor. I'm trying to take in breaths, but like many times before, I can't get anything in. Suicide, Lolotea had taken her own life. I feel myself begin to shake, and I can barely hear Candy speaking over the sound of blood pulsing through my ears. I can't decipher what she's saying. The world around me suddenly seems dark and I know that at any moment I'm going to suffocate, I'm going to die right here on my bedroom floor.

"Tally please get a hold of Trey, and tell him to

come to Mercy. Tally!" Her sharp tone breaks through the utter shock.

"Okay," I murmur, and hit the end button.

The phone falls from my hand and I jump up to run for the bathroom. I feel the bile rising quickly in my throat, and my eyes begin to water. I barely see my mom out of the corner of my eye and hear her ask me something, but I have to get to the toilet before I puke all over the carpet.

I feel a cool cloth on the back of my neck, and then my mom is helping me sit down on the edge of the tub.

"Tally what's going on?" She asks me calmly.

"I need you to take me to Trey, please." I tell her with shaky breath. My hands feel clammy and I begin to nervously rub them against my jeans.

"Okay, can you tell me why?"

I look up at her and feel my eyes fill with tears again. I can't imagine losing my mother, and especially not by her own hand. I know it's going to devastate Trey, and I wish there was something I could do to spare him the pain, that is bound to bring him to his knees.

"His mother has committed suicide, and the hospital can't get a hold of him." My mother's mouth drops open, and her hand comes up to cover it. Her eyes are wide and immediately fill with tears. I know why, I know it's more because she is imaging that it's me, that I am the one who has given up on life and chosen to end it.

"Please mom we must hurry," I stand up on shaky legs and grab the hand towel to wipe my mouth. I quickly turn on the faucet and get a handful of water to wash out the vomit taste. Then I grab my mom's hand

and pull her behind me.

    I'm having a hard time remembering the way to the Taggert's house. My brain is such a mess and my chest is tight with anguish. I have to keep wiping my eyes so I can see to direct my mother to turn in the right places. I keep trying to go over the words to say, how to say them, and what to do once they are said. I've never had to tell anyone that a family member is dead, let alone that they took their own life. When we finally turn down the road that leads us to the Taggert's ranch, I realize that I'm not ready. I'm not ready to bring Trey's world to a cold, soul–stealing halt, but then I don't have a choice. I see Trey's battered truck, tires replaced, but the windshield is still shattered and it's in need of a new paint job. It seems so trivial now, so irrelevant compared to the coming news.

    My mom puts the car in park, and I ask her to wait for me. As I climb out of the car, I have to reach out and grab for the roof to keep my legs steady. I walk slowly, almost in a haze towards the horse stalls, and the burden I carry feels as though it will push me into the earth at any moment.

    I step around the corner and into the entryway of the stable. I see him across the way in front of the tack room. He's sweaty, shirtless, and magnificent, and I'm about to crush him.

    His head turns and when his eyes land on me, they light up and a smile stretches across his face. It lasts only a second, and then he registers the look on my face, which I imagine is terribly pale and tear streaked.

    He walks quickly to me covering the distance in a matter of seconds.

    "Tally, baby, what's wrong?" His hands come up

to cup my face and I choke back a sob. How am I going to do this? I groan inwardly.

"Trey," my voice is hoarse and I have to clear it before I can go on. "Trey, Candy called me. The hospital has been trying to get in touch with you."

I watch his face, see a shadow fall across it, and his eyes glaze over with fear.

"Your mom, she," my hand shakes as I bring it up to lay it on his chest, "she's gone. She, oh god, I don't know how to say this," I know I need to pull myself together, but the more I try, the more I feel my resolve crashing to the ground, "she killed herself." The words fall from my lips with the weight of a thousand pounds.

Trey's hands fall to his sides, and he seems frozen. His eyes are narrowed, and his face is still as stone.

"I need to get to Mercy," he says, finally. I nod and take his hand.

"My mom can drive you."

He clings tightly to my hand, and when we get to the car, he tugs me to the back seat with him. Once settled he wraps his arms around me and pulls me as close as the seat belt will allow him to. He doesn't speak. He just holds me and stares straight ahead.

I call Dr. Stacey on our way to the hospital, so as soon as we walk into the building she is there waiting for us.

"Trey," she says his name with such compassion that tears fill my eyes again. "Come with me."

Trey begins to follow her and, to my surprise, he

glances back and grabs my hand.

"I need you," he tells me bluntly.

I squeeze his hand reassuring him that I'm here.

Dr. Stacey leads us to a door on the same hall as the quiet rooms. She stops and turns back to look at Trey.

"I'm so sorry that this has happened Trey, and I honestly can't tell you how it happened. We had your mother on suicide watch, but she slipped out at some point. She went to the pond."

I look up at Trey when I feel his hand tighten around mine.

"She can't," he pauses and seems to gather himself, "she couldn't swim."

Dr. Stacey nods, "It was too late by the time we got to her. We tried to do CPR." She looks down at the ground before finally turning the door knob and pushing the door open. I feel bile rising again as I remember the night I saved Candy from the pond and an image of Trey's mother, flailing, eyes wide as her head bobs up and down in an attempt to stay above the water. I grit my teeth and push the image away. Trey needs me now. I can't fall apart, not here.

As we step into the room, I see Lolotea lying, still on the bed. It feels as though the temperature in the room drops several degrees. I shiver as I stare down at her still form. Her eyes are closed and except for the pale pallor of her skin, she appears to be sleeping.

Her face is peaceful and all the fretting and fear that had once marred her beauty is now gone. How wonderful it must be to be free of the pain, of the guilt, and humiliation of a disease that was incurable, and in her case, untreatable.

I watch as Trey steps up next to the bed and kneels

down next to it. His large frame seems to dwarf the bed and her body. He reaches up and gently strokes her cheek. I know he sees the same peace that I do, but that does not make the pain any less severe.

He leans forward and lays his head against her arm and his shoulders begin to shake as he lets reality set in. He makes no noise, but I can almost feel the grief pulsing off of him in waves as it drenches me. I feel as though I'm imposing, standing there watching him grieve for his mother, but I can't move.

My body tenses as I see her move. I take a step back and my breathing becomes erratic. Her head, it's turning and then she's looking at me. Her eyes are wide, but devoid of emotion. Her mouth opens and my steps freeze.

"He should not have to endure this a second time," her voice is as dry and lifeless as her decaying body and sounds nothing like it once did. "He needs peace, he needs hope. Can you give him either?" I know it's not real. It can't be real, and yet I'm shaking as if I have just seen a dead person talk. I blink several times, and when I look again, she is lying as still as when I first entered, no sign that she had ever moved or spoken.

Her words reverberate through my mind and I know she is right, whether it was real or not I know what it is. It's my conscious speaking, and I know that I can't give him peace I can't give him hope. How can I, when on my own I have neither of those things? I wanted Trey and I to work so badly, I wanted to believe that we could be together, but this is a wakeup call. The reality is: I will live with this disease for the rest of my life. I will have times when I want to die because the grief inside of me will be too much, and if I stay with

Trey, every time I get that low it will be a reminder of what his mother did. He will live in fear of the possibility that he will come home to find my body, lifeless, and limp.

In that moment I want to turn and run. I want to run as fast and as far as I can from the room. As I watch the man I love weep over his mother, I know that I can't walk away just yet. He's been through so much and though breaking up with him now might seem cruel, in the long run he will thank me. It may take a while, but he will see that he needs so much more than I will ever be able to give him.

When Trey is ready to leave Dr. Stacey tells him to just let her know when the funeral arrangements have been made and when the funeral home will be coming to get her.

"Will you step out for a moment?" Trey asks me as my mom pulls into his driveway. I nod and scoot out after him. He pulls me into a hug and I hold him tight knowing that I only have a limited number of these moments left.

"Are you going to be alright?" I ask gently.

He pulls back and looks down at me. How someone can still look so beautiful after crying is beyond me, but he does.

"Can you stay with me?" he asks me quietly as he brushes his thumb across my lips.

I feel the battle inside me as I consider what I should do. Part of me doesn't want to make this any harder than it's going to be, but the other part of me is selfish and wants to be with him as much as possible. As I stare up into his dark eyes, I see the pain and the devastation, and I know I can't leave him like this.

I nod and then walk around to the driver's side of the car. My mom rolls down her window, and is nodding before I ask. "Stay with him."

"Thank you," I tell her. She reaches for my hand and her lips pinch together as she holds back tears.

"I love you Tally."

"I know mom," I hold tight to her hand and meet her eyes, "I love you too." I step away quickly because I don't have the energy to deal with her emotions, mine, and Trey's.

Trey takes my hand and leads me to his front door. He hadn't called his grandmother. He had wanted to wait to tell her face to face. My gut tightens as I imagine sweet Bly having to hear that her daughter is gone, dead before her.

"Grandmother," Trey calls out as soon as we step over the threshold.

She comes around the corner into the living room and looks at both of us. Her shoulders slump forward and a single tear drops from her eye.

"She's gone," the old woman says before Trey can even speak.

He releases my hand and walks over to her, gathering her into his strong arms. When they finally part, Bly walks over to me and hugs me tight. When she releases me she looks into my eyes, and I fear she will see my plans, see my determination to let Trey go.

"You are not her," she whispers to me. I feel tears rush to my eyes and I bite my cheek to keep them from falling. I wish it was enough to change my mind, but when I look up at Trey and see his pain, I know that I can't stay.

~

We spend the rest of the evening just talking. Bly tells me stories about Lolotea and her son and how they met and the joy on her face testifies to the love she felt for her daughter-in law.

"She's at peace," Trey tells me as he holds me on his couch.

"Yes," I agree.

"Part of me is angry at her, but another part of me is relieved that she is no longer suffering." he admits to me.

I look up at him and hope that my smile is reassuring, "It's okay to be angry, and it's okay to be relieved. You love her and both of those emotions convey that love."

He leans his head forward and presses it to mine. I feel the warmth of his breath against my face and my heart feels as though it's going to beat out of my chest and jump into his in an effort to stay with him forever.

"Tally," he whispers my name and the reverence in his voice takes my breath away. "Thank you for staying with me, for being here. I know this has to be difficult for you. I don't think I could get through this without you."

I squeeze my eyes close and try to hold back the shutter of agony that rushes through my body as I realize that my heart will not be the only one breaking when I tell Trey it's over.

Chapter 25

"When my father died I was twelve and I thought it was the greatest pain I would ever endure. I was wrong, so, so very wrong." ~Trey

  I can feel her pulling away, and there is nothing I can do about it. The past two days have been hell and I haven't had time to think, let alone talk to Tally about what is going on with her. The funeral is in an hour and though I considered taking my mother back to our people, I decided to bury her here in Broken Arrow because I have no plans of leaving. My life is here now, with Tally, so it just didn't make sense for me to bury my mom far from me.

  My grandmother is holding up much better than I thought, and I think like me, she has found some comfort in knowing that my mom is no longer enduring the fear and pain of what she lived with. I'm angry for the way that she left this world, but at the same time, I can't judge because I was not in her shoes. I have no idea what it was like to live in a world that no one else could see, one that obviously terrified her. I grieved for her, but I know that she would rather I celebrate the life she had, the one where she was happy and whole rather than wallow in the tragedy of her death. So today as I watch my mother's body be laid to rest, I will be sad at losing her, but I will remember the life she lived. I will honor her as my mother and remember her before her mind was taken by schizophrenia.

As I help my grandmother out of my truck, I see Tally walking towards us. I had wanted her to ride with me, but she had insisted on driving herself. She wore a simple black dress and black gloves, and as she walks towards us, slowly, regally, she is the picture of grace.

"She's a beauty," my grandmother murmurs to me.

"I agree," I smile down at her, and then look up to see Tally standing next to my grandmother.

"Hi," she says with a small, apprehensive smile. She always seems to greet me this way, and I always find it necessary to remind her that she is mine, and that she doesn't have to wonder if it has somehow changed since the last time I saw her.

I step towards her and cup the side of her face as I lean down and kiss her. She feels tense and it reminds me of when I first dared to touch her. Gradually she has come to welcome my touch and kisses, but this feels different and it angers me. I pull back and look down at her. I search her face, hoping that she will give something away, but I can't tell if she is being so distant because of my mother's death, or if there is something else. I do know that I've had enough of her holding herself back from me, and that it would end today.

The only people at the graveside are me, my grandmother, and Tally. Among my people, the burial process is very private and usually only relatives and very close friends would attend. My grandmother, being very traditional, has gone through a purification process for the past twenty–four hours. She is the one presiding over the funeral since my mother was not a Christian and we are not doing a Christian burial. It is a short ceremony in which my grandmother praises the joys and sacrifices of my mother's life. She then asks the spirits of those who have gone before her to guide her to the place of our ancestors so that she may be at peace. It is a healing process for me, to lay my mother to rest and to know that she is united with my father now.

"You will be missed Lolotea, and though we are thankful that your suffering is over, we will never forget you just as we remember those who have gone on before you. I will see you soon daughter. Save a place for me at the feast."

As my grandmother closes with a final prayer to our ancestors, I take Tally's hand in mine, and lift it to my lips, giving it a gentle kiss. Her scent is comforting to me, and I long to pull her into my arms and hold her. She brings me a measure of peace. It is a balm to my heart, and I want to have her all to myself for a little while.

"Thank you grandmother," I tell her as she turns from my mother's grave. She will not look back. It is forbidden to look back at the grave for worry that the spirit will not move on. So I turn as well, and force myself not to watch as they begin to lower her into the ground.

"Her spirit is at peace. That always makes a ceremony much easier," she tells me.

After I help my grandmother up into my truck, I turn to see Tally standing a few steps away.

"Will you follow me home?" I ask her.

"Yeah, okay," she says, but there is no smile on her face now, and her eyes are guarded. She turns to walk towards her car, I take two quick strides, and catch her around the waist. I pull her back to my chest and lean my mouth down next to her ear.

"You would walk away from your man without so

much as a kiss?" I feel her body shiver and I want to scream in victory at finally getting a reaction from her.

She turns slowly and looks up at me. Her hand slips around the back of my head and pulls me down until our lips touch. Her lips are hesitant at first, but then quickly become more confident in their assault on my mouth. I pull her tight against me and attempt to drown in her taste. Having her in my arms, her mouth against mine is right, she is where she belongs, and I am where I belong as well. And even as right as it is, as fervently as she kisses me, there is still a part of herself that she is holding back from me. It's unacceptable. I want all of her. I have given her every bit of myself, and I will have every bit of her as well.

My grandmother hugs Tally before she goes into the house and I wait leaning my back against my truck. I watch as she slowly walks towards me, her movements stiff and hesitant.

"Are you ready to tell me what's going on with you?" I ask, and barely hide the anger that has been festering at her constant distance. She stands nearly five feet from me and makes no move to close the distance.

"I am," she says simply.

I wait. She stares at me, then looks down at her arms, and begins fidgeting with her sleeves. When she finally looks back up at me, I see wetness gathering in her eyes.

"I only came over here to tell you that it's over."

I tilt my head slightly as my eyes narrow on her. I

don't say anything; I want to see if she will give me her ridiculous reasons for thinking that she is right in breaking things off between us.

"I'm breaking up with you Trey," she reiterates.

"I am completely capable of understanding your words, Tally. You do not have to repeat them in a different way," I growl. She takes a step back, and I know that she feels the rage she has provoked in me.

"I am so sorry for your loss, truly I am, but it has made me realize that this can never work. You don't deserve to be with someone who has the potential to end up at the same end as your mother."

I can't stop the flinch that comes from her words, as if she had slapped me hard in the face.

"I am never going to be completely okay. I will always be a wild card and you shouldn't have to live with that. Please hear what I'm saying and know that this is the hardest thing I've ever done in my life, but it's the right thing to do."

I can feel my blood beginning to boil and wonder if she sees steam coming off of my skin.

"I am so very sick of you telling me what you think I deserve or need. I love you Tally and you own my heart and soul, but you do not own my free will. I choose who I want to be with; I know what I deserve and what I need. You can't determine that for me and it's beginning to piss me off that you seem to think you are entitled to make my decisions for me." My voice is shaking with anger and I know part of it is from fear. Fear of losing her, fear that she will choose someone else.

"Fine," she snaps back, "you are correct; I can't make your decisions for you. I, however, can make them for me, and I'm telling you that I can't be with you."

"And, who can you be with Tally?" I take a step closer to her. "Who do you think you need? Who is better for you than me? Who can make you breathe?" I know my words are cruel, but I can't stop them. She needs to see the ignorance of her choice and I will say whatever I have to in order for that to happen.

"WHO?" I yell.

"NO ONE!" Her hands are fisted at her side, and the tears that she had held in her eyes are caressing her cheeks. "No one, is that what you want to hear? Do you need to humiliate me in order to make yourself feel better?"

"I'm not trying to humiliate you baby, I'm trying to make you see reason. You are mine Tally. You need me, you want me, and you complete every part of me that has been missing. I won't give you up, no matter how badly you think you want that."

Her eyes narrow and pierce me like daggers. She pulls her shoulders back and her chin rises defiantly. "It's over Swift. Stay away from me."

She turns and walks quickly away and gets into her car. I watch as she backs out, and then speeds away, her tires squealing as she goes.

"You are mistaken Tally Baker," I mutter to her retreating tail lights, "it is never going to be over between us, and nothing will ever keep me away from you."

Chapter 26

"I've heard it said that trials come in threes. I hope it isn't true because I don't think I can handle one more thing, not now, not without him." ~Tally

Some believe that it's possible to die from a broken heart. At one time I would have said that that was a ridiculous statement, but that was before my own heart had been ripped from my chest leaving a gaping hole. It's my own fault, I get that, and I think that quite possibly makes it even more painful.

I haven't been back to school since before Trey's mother's death. Dr. Stacey wrote me a note to take a couple weeks off and I don't think I have ever been more grateful. It's been a week since I've spoken to Trey, though it hasn't been a week since I've seen him. He comes to my house every day after school, knocks on the door, and asks to speak with me. My mother tells him I don't want to see him, and if she isn't there to answer it, he pounds on the door and yells through it. Today will be one of those days.

I walk down the stairs and place my back against the door, waiting for him. I need the closeness, knowing that all that is separating me from him is the couple of inches of thickness that is my front door. I've been drowning again; breathing gets more difficult every day, and the nights are nearly unbearable.

I hear his truck and feel the ache that has been ever present begin to grow even stronger. My chest constricts, and when I hear the first knock, I turn and press my face to the door.

"Tally, open the damn door." His voice isn't as patient as it has been, and I wonder if he is finally growing tired of this. Will today be the last time he comes? Have I finally succeeded in pushing him away for good? The thought is enough to drive me to my knees, and I hit the floor as a sob escapes my throat. He pauses and I know he heard me.

"OPEN THE DOOR!" His knocking increases in speed and intensity, I'm confident that he could break the door down if he wanted to, and I almost hope that he does. I honestly don't know how much more of this I can take. How many more days until I cave, rip the door open, and throw myself into his strong arms.

"I know you're there baby, I can feel you through this door. I feel your pain, and if it's half as bad as mine, then I know you are dying. I can't...," I hear a thud against the door and this is different than his fist. I imagine his forehead hitting the door in frustration and hurt and it breaks my heart all over again. "I can't breathe; how can you think this is the right thing for us when I can't function without you?"

My hand reaches up and caresses the door, imagining that it is his face and that he's staring back at me soaking in every detail. He's quiet and I know he's getting ready to leave. I don't want him to leave. I need him more than I've needed anything in my life. "I need you Trey," I whisper against the cold door. "I can't breathe either." He can't hear me, but he knows. He knows I'm dying right along with him.

I hear his engine start up and then fade away as he drives away. I slip further down the door until my face is pressed against the floor. I can't swallow as the anger and pain swell up into a scream that rushes from my lungs.

"I CAN'T DO THIS!" I yell as my hand beats against the floor, the sting against my palm I welcome like an old friend, grasping for that tiny relief. I know that I need to get up. I need to get to my room before my parents get home and somehow I force myself to crawl up the stairs, though with every step the sobs continue to wrack my tired body.

I collapse on my bed and press my face into the pillow attempting to muffle the screams of rage. The heat of my tears burns my skin, and I wonder, not for the first time, if it is possible to run out of tears.

~

"Tally you have to get up."

I hear Natalie's voice, and for a moment, I want to jump up and wrap my arms around her, but I don't want to leave the safety of my bed.

"TALLY, GET UP!" Her voice is sharp, and I cringe at the fury and anxiety that lace her words.

I roll over and peak out from the covers. The sunlight streaming through the now open curtains causes me to squint. I look up at her. She's standing a few feet from my bed, her arms are folded across her chest, and her forehead is wrinkled in worry.

"You've been hiding in here for nearly two weeks; it's time to start living again. I know you're hurting, I know you miss him, but life goes on and you have to go on with it."

"No, I don't." I inform her bluntly.

"Do you want to go back to Mercy? Because if you keep this up, your parents are going to make you go back."

"Frankly Nat I don't give a damn where I go. I just want to be left alone. I know you're worried about me and I love you for it, but please, this time, just let me be." I plead with her and need her to hear me, because I just can't do it, I can't go to school and see him every day.

"Okay, you brought this on yourself; don't say I didn't warn you."

My door swings open, and in walks Dr. Stacey. I slowly sit up as I watch her walk into my room. She smiles warmly at Natalie, "Thank you, I'll take it from here."

Natalie shoots me one more worried look before leaving.

Dr. Stacey looks around my room, and I know she must think a tornado has been wreaking havoc because the floor is covered in clothes, papers, and books.

"It seems that not only have the chemicals gotten out of whack, but so have your circumstances." She takes a seat on the chair at my desk and leans back crossing her legs. She seems so out of place in my mess, and yet she doesn't appear bothered in the least.

"Life happened, and I don't know how to deal with it. I don't know if I can deal with it." I tell her.

"I understand that, but this is not healthy and will only lead you further down a road that you don't belong on. I know it sucks to have to hear this again, but Tally your disease will always be a part of your life and you can either let it rule you or you can be the master of it. We have gone over all the things you need to cope in situations that feel completely overwhelming, but it is up to you to implement them. You cannot alienate yourself from your support system."

"I know. I know everything you are telling me to

be true, but I don't care!" I turn towards her so I can see her more clearly. "This is where I am right now, and I don't know how to move forward."

She stares at me for a few silent moments and then looks over at my desk. She grabs a piece of paper and a pen and turns so that she can lay her arm on the desk to write.

"We're going to make a plan and you are going to live the plan out minute by minute, hour by hour, small victory by small victory." she looks down at the paper and begins to write. I sit watching her, knowing that whatever she is writing is pointless, but I will let her give her little speech, and then crawl back in my hole once she is gone.

"Okay," she finally says. "Number one: you will get up and take a shower. Number two: you will put on clean clothes. Number three: you will eat something. Number four: you will make your bed." she looks over at me, "Those are the things you will do for the next three days. I will be back on the fourth day and we will set more goals. If you cannot meet these goals, then I will recommend that you be readmitted to Mercy, and I will put you on suicide watch."

My eyes widen at her announcement and for a brief moment, I think that she is bluffing, but then I look in her eyes and I know that she will do exactly what she says she will.

I give a slight nod to tell her I relent. She stands, leaving the paper on my desk. As she pulls the door open, she looks back at me, "You can do this Tally, and when you figure out that it's okay for people to love you, that you deserve love, you will find that life is much more bearable. I'll see you in three days." She shuts the door behind her, and I'm left sitting in my empty disaster of a room. I'm left alone, desperately wanting to do what doc is telling me to, but feeling utterly powerless to follow through.

~

It's day two and I'm up, showered, dressed, and I'm exhausted. I'm still in too much anguish to feel any victories. It's getting close to time for Trey to be show up, and I'm trying to steel myself for the onslaught of emotions that come when I hear his voice.

The knocking comes, but only once. I hear several voices and know that there is more than just my mom and Trey talking at the front door. The murmuring goes on for a few moments, and I hear the deep timber of Treys voice, but I can't make out his words.

The talking ceases, and I begin to hear footsteps on the stairs. I feel my body growing tense as I begin to hope, and yet, dread at the same time that Trey might open my door.

There is a soft knock, and then Dr. Stacey's voice comes through, "Tally, can I come in?"

I frown at the door. She told me I had three days.

"Yes, you can come in," I tell her. She opens the door just enough to squeeze through and I wonder what or who she is trying to keep from me. Once the door is closed, she walks to the bed, and takes a seat next to me. She seems nervous and ruffled. These are two words that have never described Dr. Stacey, before, until today.

"I have some very difficult news Tally."

My heart sinks, and I feel the color drain from my

face. I can't handle anymore. I just can't handle anymore.

"Candy has passed away."

I feel the world drop out from under me. How can this be happening? What the hell have I done to deserve such horrific tragedies?

"I don't think she ever told you, but she had cancer. It started in a lymph node in her breast and quickly spread. She chose not to have chemotherapy because the doctors weren't very sure it would prolong her life any. She didn't want to spend her last months too sick to live. Zeke found her in her bed this morning."

I don't know what it is about utter despair that makes me need to vomit, but for some reason that seems to be an automatic response. I lunge for the trash can next to my desk knowing I will never make it to the bathroom. The retching of my stomach pushes loud gasps from my chest and tears, that I'm so sick of crying, begin, once again, to make my cheeks their home. I hear my door open, but don't turn to see who it is. I know who it is the minute his hand touches my neck. I don't hesitate as I turn and throw myself into his arms.

I don't know how many times a person can be crushed and ripped to pieces. I fear that I just might die as I gasp for breath between sobs. Trey's arms tighten in an attempt to hold me still. He shifts me, and when he sets me on his lap, I know he must be sitting on my bed. I bury my face in his neck and wrap my arms around him. Over and over, I breathe in his scent, but the comfort I usually find isn't there, not this time. The hole Candy's death has left in me is too deep for any comfort.

"I'm here baby, I've got you." I hear his voice, and his chest vibrates against mine as he speaks. I cling to the sound. I am so desperate for any part of him. The longer I cry, the longer I think of the loss, and the angrier I become. I want to scream and punch something. I need to hurt physically to cope with the emotions, but I know that isn't the right way to deal with it so instead I sink deep into my love's arms and let him rock me and stroke my hair and back. I squeeze my eyes closed tightly and eventually the tears exhaust me, and I feel myself allowing the darkness to swallow me.

Before I'm completely gone, I reach for consciousness and whisper, "I love you."

"I'm not going anywhere love, rest now." He lays us down, me on my side and him behind me. He wraps his body around mine and pulls me back against him. I feel his breath on my neck as I drift off and I try to focus on that feeling instead of the knowledge that I will never see Candy again.

I awake to a strong arm holding my midsection and for a moment I start to panic. Then I remember that Trey is with me, that he came in after Dr. Stacey told me ... I freeze my mind before I let the thought go any further. I'm not ready. I need a moment without the blur of tears and the chest tightening sobs.

I feel Trey stir behind me and lay my arm over the one he has across my midsection.

"How are you?" His voice is gravelly from sleep, and I imagine what it would be like to wake up to that voice every day.

"I'm tired. I'm just so very tired."

"I'm so sorry baby. I know what she meant to

you."

I turn so that I'm lying facing him. He looks exhausted and I know it's my fault. I did that to him and for what? All the tears, pain, and despair that came with the decision to try and push away the best thing that ever happened to me.

"It doesn't feel real. As stupid as it sounds, I just never thought she would die. She always seemed so invincible, so capable. I just can't imagine a world without her." I look at his face and see the expression I've come to know as his listening face, and it's one of the many things I adore about him. He doesn't just listen to me, he hears me.

"She was definitely one of a kind," he smiles a small crooked smile and I imagine he is remembering some of the things she said and did. He was right. There was no one like Candy and I doubt there ever will be.

"My parents know you're up here with me?" I ask, suddenly realizing that I'm lying with a guy in my room with the door closed.

"Yes," his face is suddenly stern. "Your father didn't want to let me in, but your mother insisted that he allow it. Dr. Stacey arrived at the same time I did. She told me what had happened and there was no way in hell I was leaving you."

"I'm glad you were here, that you're here now."

"You're going to be okay Tally." he says it with such conviction, I want to believe him.

"I wish I knew that to be true."

∼

Trey has to leave after being with me for nearly twenty four hours. Candy's funeral is tomorrow and he's promised to pick me up. As I watch him drive away, I know that tomorrow can't come soon enough.

I spend the day alternating from tears and grief to anger and despair, sometimes pacing my room and other times staring up at my ceiling from the floor. Natalie has called several times but I just can't talk. My mom has checked on me several times, and one of those times I actually broke down and cried in her arms.

I'm lying in bed trying to fall asleep when my phone beeps, indicating that I have a text message.

Trey: luv u

I stare at the message and wonder how he can say those words when I was so cruel.

Me: why?

I hold my breath as I wait for his response.

Trey: You were made 4 me, and I 4 u. U r mine.

"Damn tears," I mumble as I wipe the stray drop away.

Me: can't breathe w/o u

Trey: breathe baby, I'm here, not going anywhere, breathe.

And though it hurts, I do.

I begin getting ready for the funeral, the second in 3 weeks. I stare long at the girl in the mirror and almost don't recognize her. My face is pale and I've lost weight, causing my eyes to sink into their sockets. My eyes look empty and I find that I have to look away because seeing the evidence of how far I've sunk is too much.

～

Trey pulls up to the funeral home and I wonder if he's thinking about his mom. I turn to look at him and all I see in this moment is the strong, confident man who handles everything thrown at him. He climbs out, walks around to the passenger side, and helps me get out of his truck. He takes my hand and leads me to the front door. I look around as people I recognize from Mercy file into the funeral home.

"Tally," I hear Dr. Stacey's voice behind me.

I turn to look at her and she motions for me to step aside. I walk over and feel Trey behind me, a pillar of strength ready to catch me.

"We found this on Candy's bedside table," she holds out a folded piece of paper that has my name hastily written on it. "I have not read it and I'm sorry to give it to you now, but I wanted to make sure that you received it."

I reach out with a shaky hand and take the paper from her. I can't take my eyes off of it and don't notice when Dr. Stacey walks away, leaving me with Trey and my note from Candy.

I unfold it slowly and can't seem to force my fingers to stop trembling. Trey's hands come down on my shoulders, steadying me.

I read the words written in her handwriting and

feel as though my heart has been run through with a stake. She asks the impossible, and yet I know that if she were here she would demand even more.

Trey gathers me in his arms and kisses my head. "Bossy to the end." I hear the small smile in his voice. Keeping an arm around me, he guides me into the building and into the viewing room. Her casket is closed and I imagine that since she knew she was dying she went over all of her wants with Dr. Stacey and she would expect them to be followed to the letter. I'm glad that I don't have to see her still and lifeless. I would rather remember her as I had known her, vivacious and so very full of life.

I don't hear most of what the minister says and I tune out the music. I'm broken inside; I don't need music to add to the torment. Once we are at the graveside I feel as though I just might scream that no one knew her as I did or understood her as I did. I want all of these people to go and just let me be miserable next to the grave of one of the best people I've ever known. I don't want to hear one more sappy word about how she was caring and loving. Candy was cantankerous and mischievous. She loved trouble and sought it out as often as possible. She loved to annoy those around her and lived to drive the crazies even crazier. Did none of these people remember all the stunts she pulled, all the yelling and tampering? Can they not remember her as she was?

Finally, people begin to disperse and the area slowly empties. I feel Trey's eyes on me, but I can't look up at him. I stare down at the casket that they are now lowering to the grave. I don't move as the workers begin to cover it with dirt. I find myself not believing that she's in there, hoping it's some elaborate hoax, but

I know it's not.

"I'm going to let you have some time with her," I hear Trey tell me. He leans down and kisses my forehead, and then leaves me there. I'm thankful he understands that I need this time, I need to say goodbye, although I don't know how. Candy never was one for goodbyes. I'm still standing there long after the workers have finished and gone. I remember the peace I felt when Lolotea was buried, knowing that she no longer had to carry the burdens of this life, but I can't find that peace with Candy's death.

My knees hit the ground before I even register that I'm falling. I stare at Candy's grave and my heart begins to crumble. Anger, pain, fear, and regret all dance inside of me, each of them vying for the top spot in my broken heart. I don't understand how she was okay with this. That's what she told me on that bench that night; that she was okay, that she was at peace. How could she be okay with being eaten away with cancer, only to then die alone in the mental hospital? I look up at the cloud-covered sky and narrow my eyes.

"She said you comforted her! That you gave her peace and she knew everything was going to be okay. Did she know you were going to take her!?" I yell to a God that I don't know, a God Candy claims created us and loved us, but in that moment, all I can see is a God who had taken someone I needed desperately. "Did it ever occur to you that I need her!? Did you ever think that maybe she had more living to do?" Tears stream from my eyes and I struggle to take breaths in between sobs. "She wasn't done; I wasn't done." The words grow weaker as my body shakes with overwhelming sorrow.

My shoulders slump forward and I lean down until

my face is pressed to the dirt that has yet to settle over her casket. I cry, heedless of anyone who might see me or hear me. I cry for Lolotea, for the agony she endured, and for how she gave into it, ending her life and unable to see how it would hurt Trey. I cry for Trey, for the pain I saw in his eyes when I told him about his mother, and then for the hurt and anger he must have felt when I broke it off with him. I cry for Candy, I cry for me, and I cry for the lives that will never be. How do I move forward? How do I keep going?

My hand reaches into my pocket, and I pull out the folded note from Candy that Dr. Stacey gave me. There was only one sentence on it: *"Live Tally, live for all of us who can't."*

"HOW!?" I scream into the ground. How am I supposed to live when I have lost so much in a matter of days? How am I supposed to want to live? I close my eyes as I hold the note close to my chest. I feel the crisp October evening air caressing my wet cheeks and the setting sun only adds to the chill. I know I should go. Night is falling, and I know my parents will be worried, but I don't care. My sleeve rides up a little as I shift onto my side to curl up in a ball. I see the words I carved into my skin, and I know now, that they will always be true. I will always be damaged. I've lost so much in my short life, and those losses have done irreparable damage inside of me.

I hear a soft murmur in my ear and I feel my body being jostled. I try to open my eyes, but they feel swollen and sluggish. Where was I? I try to clear my mind, to think back to what I had been doing, where I had been.

"I've got her." I hear a deep rumble against my ear and realize that I'm being carried. I know that voice, it's Trey, and he's carrying me.

"Take her up to her room please." And that was my mom. I feel myself being laid down on a soft surface, and when I finally manage to get my eyes to cooperate, I open them and see that I'm in my room. I look up and see Trey leaning over me. The worry on his face tells me I must look pretty rough. I was in the cemetery for Candy's funeral. I lay down next to her grave and bawled until I was drained; I must have fallen asleep.

I feel him step back and find myself reaching for him. Desperate to know he isn't going, frantic for him to know that I need him.

"Hey," he says to me softly. "Rest baby, I love you, and I'm not going anywhere."

He doesn't give me a chance to respond. He leans down, kisses me gently, turns and leaves, and then closes the door quietly behind him.

I lay there staring up at the ceiling and let out a deep breath. Candy is gone, Lolotea is gone, I am damaged, but Trey loves me and he isn't going anywhere. For now, that's enough. I'm so tired, and I don't want to think, so I close my eyes and shut the world out.

Chapter 27

"Sometimes it takes falling to rock bottom and enduring utter devastation in order for us to realize just what we need, what we can't live without. And the best part about rock bottom is you can only go up from there." ~Trey

She's been asleep for nearly eighteen hours. I've been sitting by her bedside for most of those, only stepping away to use the bathroom and call my grandmother. I can't stop seeing the desperate look on her face and the way she had reached out for me. It gives me hope that she has realized that we belong together, no matter how uncertain the future is. The one thing that is certain is that she belongs with me and I with her.

I watch the slow, steady rise and fall of her chest and hope that she isn't dreaming, but that she is getting the rest she so desperately needs without the disturbance of things better left to deal with in the light of day.

I hear the door open behind me and turn to see Tally's dad come in. He has been treating me with begrudging acceptance since I brought Tally home from the cemetery. He too must have realized that I'm not going anywhere, so he can continue to be an ass, or he can get over it. It seems like he is attempting to work on accepting it.

"She's still sleeping?" He asks.

I nod, "She needs it."

He's quiet as he walks around to the other side of

the bed so that he's facing me.

His gaze meets mine, and his eyes reveal a vulnerability I have yet to see. "I love her very much, and I know I haven't dealt with everything she has been through very well. But, I'm going to do better."

I don't know why he's telling me this, other than maybe he just needs to get off his chest that he knows he has wronged his daughter, a confession of wrongdoing, and the desire to let someone know that he wants to right the wrong.

"Tally needs to hear that," I tell him and try to make sure I don't sound disrespectful. I only want him to see that in order for her to begin to heal she needs to know that he loves her as she is.

"I know, I will tell her."

I watch as he leans down and kisses her gently on the forehead and then quietly leaves. I wonder at the awkwardness of his movements and am curious how long it's been since he has shown her any real affection.

My attention is brought back when she finally begins to stir. I stand and walk over to the bed and sit down next to her. She opens her eyes and they meet mine immediately. I smile at her and reach forward to brush her cheek needing the contact, the connection with her.

"You stayed," she says groggily.

"I told you I wasn't going anywhere," I remind her.

She stares at me intently and I see a war waging in her eyes. "I'm so sorry Trey." The words spill from her lips as they tremble.

"Shh, not right now baby. Let's get some food in you and a shower. Then if you want to talk, we will talk."

~

Two hours later, we're sitting on the tailgate of my truck. She's been fed, showered, doted over by her mother, and hugged by her father. She's holding my hand in both of hers and drawing circles on the palm of it.

"I'm not good right now. I was getting low before everything happened, but now, now I feel empty." She looks up at me and I want to kiss the insecure look off her beautiful face. "You were right, I can't breathe without you, I need you, and I'm hoping that I haven't driven you away. I'm asking for your forgiveness, but I also need you to see where I am right now."

I stand up from the tail gate and turn to stand in front of her. I spread her legs so I can stand in between them and meet her gaze.

"You are stuck with me Tally. I love you, and the only way I know how to do this is all the way. I will take you any way you come to me. And, if right now, that is with sorrow running through your veins and darkness seeping into your bones, driving away the warmth of the light, then I will wrap you in my arms until the darkness is gone and the sorrow is replaced by joy, no matter how long that may take. You are mine to care for and I am yours. There is nothing to forgive baby. You were scared. I get that. The only thing I need to know is that you will trust me, and when you begin to doubt me because of where you are or because you feel you are a mess, tell me so that I can show you that I am not going anywhere."

"How will you show me?"

I grab her face gently and dip my head to her

mouth. I take what is mine and give what is hers, showing her with my love what words don't always convey. She is all that I need, all that I want, and as I kiss the woman I love, the woman I will spend my life with, I pour every ounce of myself into it. It's the only way I know how to love her.

I pull back, but continue to hold her face in my hands. Our breathing is rapid and we both struggle to get it under control. I taste her on my mouth and know that I could get drunk on her taste. "Tally Baker, beloved of mine, I'm going to marry you. When you feel the seeds of doubt slip in, when your reality becomes one that I can't see, you remember those words. You will be my wife and I will spend the rest of our lives reminding you that you may have bipolar disorder, but it does not have you. It cannot have you because I have claimed you and I don't share."

Epilogue

**"My name is Tally Baker. I'm 18 and have been living with bipolar disorder for nearly a year. Today is a good day. I've had lots of good days and know that for now the depression has passed. I know the pendulum of the disease is swinging the other way and that I need to pay attention to how I'm feeling. I know that I am the one in control of this disease. I know that I am not in this alone."
~Journal entry Tally Baker**

"Trey asked me to marry him today. He informed me that since we have both graduated from high school there was no reason for us to just keep putting off the inevitable." I laugh out loud in the empty cemetery as I lean against Candy's tombstone. "I wish you could have been there. You would have loved what he said next. So after he informs me that we should get on with getting married he says, *we need to get married young, so that I will have many, many years of bedding you.*" I look down at her grave as if she can see me and roll my eyes. "He seriously said *bedding you*. I mean who says that? Of course you know I said 'yes.' I mean who could resist such a romantic proposal?"

I lay my head back and let the summer sun warm my face. I've been making weekly visits to Candy's grave and, much to my surprise, have found that my time here talking to a tombstone has become a form of therapy, and although I don't know if she can hear me, I can't help but imagine her sitting here next to me making smartass comments the entire time.

It's been over a year since I met Candy. It's been

over a year since my world fell apart. I look down at my bare arms. The words still stare back at me, a reminder of where I've been, but also a testament to the fact that I survived. I didn't do it alone, and though some might think that it is a weakness, they would be horribly wrong. The battlefield of the mind is not one that can be defeated unaided. When perception becomes altered and falsehoods become reality, the ability to reason and be reasoned with becomes nearly non-existent. Dr. Stacey still reminds me that meds are 10% of the treatment and therapy is 90%. Therapy includes not only your doctor, or your group sessions, but also the support system that you need to build around you. My support system happens to include a dead crazy old lady, and it makes me smile to know that Candy would undoubtedly tease me mercilessly over it.

"All right you crazy old bat, my ride is here," I say as I look up and see Trey walking towards me. He reaches out his hand, and I grab it, letting him pull me to my feet.

"Did you tell her?" he asks me with a mischievous grin.

Yes, my now fiancé, even talks as if she can hear me. How I love him, and his ability to roll with me, crazy and all.

"Yes, I told her."

"What did she say?"

I can't help the bark of laughter at his question. Only Trey could ask what a dead woman's response was to a question and say it with such seriousness that you think he expects an answer.

"She said to let her know when you decide to quit *bedding me* and just go at it like rabbits."

Trey throws his head back laughing and the

sunlight shines on his long black hair. His face is bright with joy, and when he looks at me, as he is doing right now, I can't help but reflect that joy back at him like a mirror.

"Today's a good day," he tells me as he wraps his arm around my waist and leads me back to the truck.

"Yes, it definitely is," I agree.

"Does that mean a victory dance?" he raises his eye brows at me suggestively.

"I think these victory dances have gotten a little out of control."

He shakes his head, "No such thing."

I tap my finger against my lips as I climb into the truck, "Hmm, okay I will give you a victory dance if you go tell my dad we're engaged—while I'm conveniently occupied with Natalie."

He raises a brow at me as a smirk slides across his mouth, "You're telling me that my girl, who has been through hell and back and survived, is scared to tell her daddy she's getting married?"

I nod, not embarrassed in the least.

"Nope, no deal babe. Sorry but we're in this together."

"Always," I tell him as I lean over with a grin on my face and kiss him.

I'm Tally Baker I have bipolar disorder. I am a survivor, but I refuse to let that be my only legacy. I choose to live, not just endure, but to really live.

From the author:

Thank you so much for taking this journey with me. This book has been one of the hardest things for me to write and I hope that maybe just one person will find hope and encouragement through Tally's story. If you have a mental illness, please know you are not alone. I pray you will make the choice to live. I pray you will not let the disease rule you, but that you will take control and know that you can live a full, abundant life. I don't say that flippantly. I say it in all sincerity and I say it from experience. My name is Quinn Loftis. I have bipolar disorder. I have survived, but I refuse to let that be my only legacy. I choose to live, not just endure, but to really live.

God bless you and thank you again for taking your time to read 'Call Me Crazy.'

Sincerely,

Quinn

CPSIA information can be obtained at www.ICGtesting.com
Printed in the USA
LVOW12s1021210615

443285LV00006B/921/P